Praise for
Beverly Brandt

Match Game

"*Match Game* is one of those reads that you don't want to put down. It's so much fun and so easy to read that you just can't help but adore the characters and the situations they find themselves in . . . Ms. Brandt has written a delightful book that is sure to leave you smiling!"
—*The Romance Reader's Connection*

"Hilarious . . . will have readers laughing out loud."
—*Romance Reviews Today*

The Tiara Club

"*Steel Magnolias* meets *The Sweet Potato Queens* in this book about friendship, beauty pageants, Southern living, deep dark secrets, and the sacrifices we make in the name of love. After laughing and crying along with Georgia Elliot and her friends, you'll wish you had a Tiara Club of your own. Don't miss this witty, charming novel!"
—*New York Times* bestselling author Joan Johnston

"A heartwarming tale of Southern love and friendship, which proves that retired beauty queens are more than meets the eye. It's the *Ya-Ya Sisterhood* with sizzle."
—Cara Lockwood, bestselling author of *Dixieland Sushi*

continued . . .

Dream On

"No one in Brandt's tale is who or what they seem to be, and their journey involves one madcap situation after another, a powerful love attraction, and a whole lot of fun."
—Booklist

Room Service

"A fine, funny tale."
—Booklist

"Brandt dishes up another lighthearted office romance touched with humor and suspense . . . this is fun, breezy beach reading."
—Publishers Weekly

Record Time

"A wonderfully entertaining book!"
—Elizabeth Bevarly, author of *You've Got Male*

"A sparkling, fast-paced romp. Witty and entertaining to the satisfying end."
—Stephanie Bond, author of *In Deep Voodoo*

"Brandt maintains a delightful balance between control and confusion, and pads her story with a cast of well-drawn ancillary characters . . . this fun, feel-good romance is the perfect pick-me-up for rainy days."
—Publishers Weekly

True North

"Sassy and sexy with a touch of suspense! Beverly Brandt makes sparks fly."
—Julie Ortolon, bestselling author of *Too Perfect*

Dating Game

Beverly Brandt

BERKLEY SENSATION, NEW YORK

THE BERKLEY PUBLISHING GROUP
Published by the Penguin Group
Penguin Group (USA) Inc.
375 Hudson Street, New York, New York 10014, USA
Penguin Group (Canada), 90 Eglinton Avenue East, Suite 700, Toronto, Ontario M4P 2Y3, Canada
(a division of Pearson Penguin Canada Inc.)
Penguin Books Ltd., 80 Strand, London WC2R 0RL, England
Penguin Group Ireland, 25 St. Stephen's Green, Dublin 2, Ireland (a division of Penguin Books Ltd.)
Penguin Group (Australia), 250 Camberwell Road, Camberwell, Victoria 3124, Australia
(a division of Pearson Australia Group Pty. Ltd.)
Penguin Books India Pvt. Ltd., 11 Community Centre, Panchsheel Park, New Delhi—110 017, India
Penguin Group (NZ), Cnr. Airborne and Rosedale Roads, Albany, Auckland 1310, New Zealand
(a division of Pearson New Zealand Ltd.)
Penguin Books (South Africa) (Pty.) Ltd., 24 Sturdee Avenue, Rosebank, Johannesburg 2196,
South Africa

Penguin Books Ltd., Registered Offices: 80 Strand, London WC2R 0RL, England

This book is an original publication of The Berkley Publishing Group.

Copyright © 2006 by Beverly Brandt.
Cover art by Masaki Ryo/CWC International, Inc.
Cover design by George Long.
Text design by Kristin del Rosario.

First edition: October 2006

Library of Congress Cataloging-in-Publication Data

Brandt, Beverly.
    Dating game / Beverly Brandt.—1st ed.
        p. cm.
    ISBN 0-425-21181-9
    1. Dating (Social customs)—Fiction. 2. Naples (Fla.)—Fiction. 3. Chick lit. I. Title.

PS3602.R3635D37 2006
813'.6—dc22

                                                                         2006020601

PRINTED IN THE UNITED STATES OF AMERICA

10   9   8   7   6   5   4   3   2

*This book is dedicated to all the people out there
who felt like losers in high school.*

I suspect that includes just about everyone . . .

• ACKNOWLEDGMENTS •

My thanks to Cindy Hwang and Leis Pedersen, and everyone else at Berkley who had a hand in getting this story from manuscript to finished book.

I'd also like to acknowledge the amazing writers of the TV show *Moonlighting*, which started my lifelong love of romantic comedies back in the 1980s. I had such fun paying homage to the writers by working some of my favorite jokes from the show into this book. To see some of their most memorable lines, check out *Moonlighting* at www.imdb.com.

{one}

Lainie Ames's return to Naples was supposed to be the sort of local-girl-makes-good story that would make viewers of Oxygen or the Hallmark channel wish they'd bought stock in Kleenex.

She had choreographed her arrival in her mind, watching it over and over again like a favorite episode of an old TV show.

Scene one: The chauffeured black limousine drives slowly from the airport to her dad's crumbling old house in her crumbling old neighborhood. Raggedly dressed children playing in the street stop to gape as her long, slim legs swing out of the car. Four-inch-high red stilettos hit the sidewalk. The driver reaches out and offers his hand to the lone occupant. The camera focuses on her French-manicured nails. Her five-carat sapphire ring glistens in the sunshine. The director refers to this scene as "Lainie's Triumphant Return."

Cut to reality.

Lainie flicked the gas gauge of her seven-year-old convertible with her index finger, but the needle didn't budge off the E. Everything she'd managed to salvage from her life in Seattle was stuffed into the tiny trunk of her car, and the car itself was on borrowed time. She was three months late on her payments. It wouldn't be long before the repo man caught up with her and took even that.

As she slunk past the McDonald's on the corner of Sunshine Parkway and Main Street, she prayed she wouldn't run out of gas. If she could just make it to her dad's house, no one would ever have to know how low she had sunk.

Lainie curled her hands into fists so she wouldn't have to look at the ragged nails. Her last manicure had been a month ago, and she didn't have the money to have the acrylic tips she loved so much professionally removed. Instead, she'd used nail clippers and a pair of tweezers to yank them off herself, exposing the thin, abraded nails beneath.

"It'll get better with time," she muttered to herself, acknowledging on some level that she wasn't just talking about the sad state of her fingernails.

When she decided to come back for her fifteen-year high school reunion, Lainie had not envisioned that she'd be limping home on broken pride and gasoline fumes.

She pulled her hair back with one hand as she turned left— away from the Gulf of Mexico and the multimillion-dollar mansions of west Naples—and headed for her dad's house. Without the setting sun glaring into her eyes, Lainie stopped squinting. She'd forgotten how intense the rays could be down here in southwest Florida; how even sunglasses weren't enough to block the sun.

That had never been much of a problem in Seattle.

She could count on her fingers the number of days a year she'd actually been able to keep the top down on her convertible without also activating the heated seats. The car was impractical. She'd known that from the day she bought it. But she'd signed the contract anyway.

Lainie tapped the gas gauge again as the weathered sign at the entrance of her old neighborhood came into view. Someone had named the housing development with its row after row of identical homes Willow Run. Lainie had no idea why. There wasn't a willow tree within five miles of the place.

But there was the sign. Sitting right where it always sat. A handful of white rocks had been tossed down around it, and scraggly bushes were planted at either side. Lainie couldn't help but roll her eyes at the sight. It was so pitiful. The upscale housing developments in Naples had grand entrances—brick walls with the names of the neighborhoods written out on tile backsplashes and strategically placed accent lighting that brought the surrounding hibiscus and bougainvillea to life. Some even had trickling fountains with brass egrets gracefully drinking from them.

Not Willow Run.

Of course, this development wasn't exactly what anyone would consider *upscale*.

Lainie blew out a disgusted breath and turned onto the neighborhood's main street.

There it was. Third on the left. The one with the peeling seafoam green paint on the front door and the weeds threatening to take over the flowerbeds. It had the unkempt look of a once well-loved pet that no one cared for anymore. Like an old cat left at home when its owner went off to college.

Lainie's grip tightened on the steering wheel, and she squeezed her eyes shut, but she could still see the house, as though its image had been burned onto her retinas.

She opened her eyes and was surprised to find herself silently praying for another gallon of gas. Anything to not be here. Not yet.

In answer, the convertible's engine sputtered a warning.

Figures, Lainie snorted. She had long ago realized that someone up there had it in for her. Why should her luck change now, when her life was at its worst?

She winced and tapped the brake when the curb reached up to scrape the bottom of her car as she pulled into the driveway, then winced again as the door to her father's house was flung open even before she had a chance to put the transmission in park.

Ready or not . . .

"Lainie! You made it!" her older sister Trish exclaimed, as if there had been some doubt in her mind that Lainie could make it across the country by herself. It wasn't exactly brain surgery to get on I-5 South, take I-10 East, and then hook up with 75 outside of Tallahassee all the way to Naples. Two turns. One left. One right. That's all it had taken to get from there to here.

"Yep. Here I am." Lainie tried to fake enthusiasm, but the words sounded as hollow as she felt inside.

She put a hand over the key in the ignition and hesitated. It wasn't too late. She could put the car in reverse and be back on the interstate in ten minutes.

If she didn't run out of gas and end up stranded on the side of the road.

With a sigh, Lainie killed the engine. This was it. The end of the line.

"It's so good to see you," Trish was saying as Lainie came to terms with her fate. Over the years her once-hip older sister—half sister, Lainie corrected—had morphed into the plump, motherly type. When Lainie and her dad had moved down to Naples in the middle of Lainie's junior year of high school, twenty-six-year-old Trish had seemed so cool. She was a teacher at Golden Gulf High, had her own apartment, and drove a vintage Mustang convertible.

The cherry on top was that Trish could buy beer. Even better, she *did* buy beer for Lainie on the infrequent occasions her little sister asked her to, which increased Lainie's stock with the few friends she made before heading off to Seattle after graduation.

Now, fifteen years later, Trish was the mother of a fourteen-year-old son and an eleven-year-old daughter. She lived on the same street as their father, still worked at the high school (where she was now a guidance counselor), and was married to the man she'd started dating the winter before Lainie had left town.

Nice, but definitely not cool anymore.

"Is this all you brought?" Trish asked, frowning into Lainie's backseat.

"The rest of my stuff is in storage back home. I figured I might as well leave it until I decide where I'm moving next," Lainie lied smoothly. No need to let Trish know that she'd had to sell everything she owned to raise the money to get back to Naples. Better to let her believe Lainie's story that coming here was simply a prologue to the next chapter in her little sister's life.

"I'm coming home to figure out what to do with the rest of my life" was the story she'd told her family. They hadn't yet guessed that this was a euphemism for "I lost my job, the bank foreclosed on my house, and my husband left me with a mountain of debt I can't pay."

"Well, that's fine. You can borrow anything you need from me. Plus, that means it won't take you long to unpack. I thought we could go out to dinner at the Ritz tonight. You always loved that. Dad asked me to tell you that he's sorry he had to work tonight. I know he's looking forward to seeing you."

Uh-huh. Dad looked forward to work and that was about it.

It must be nice to live in Trishville, where children were more than just obligations to their parents.

Lainie popped open the minuscule trunk of her car and pushed open the driver's-side door. She swung her feet out of the car and felt the warmth of the pavement through the thin soles of her worn tennis shoes.

She sighed as the last image from her make-believe TV episode disappeared in the face of ugly reality.

There would be no chauffeurs, no red stilettos, no street urchins stopping to gape at the glamorous vision alighting from a long black car. There were no slender legs—Lainie had been too caught up in losing everything she had to even think about an exercise program—no French manicures, and no sapphire ring, since it had been pawned in a desperate attempt to keep Lainie out of bankruptcy court.

Most important, there would be no high school reunion. Not for her.

Lainie slammed the door of her convertible and turned, squinting as the sun's rays got caught in her rearview mirror, blocking out the image of the weary woman she had become.

No, there was no way she'd face her former classmates like this: as big a loser now as she had been fifteen years ago.

{ two }

Dinner at the Ritz.

When Lainie was in high school, the Ritz had been the ultimate in dining experiences. All the popular boys brought their dates here on prom night. To Lainie, "Dinner at the Ritz" conjured up images of tuxedoed men and bejeweled women, though she knew that most of the hotel's guests didn't really dress like that. Still, as she followed Trish into the impressive lobby, she inhaled deeply of the scent of success that oozed from every corner of the place.

During the good years—back before "startup" became a dirty word—Lainie and Ted used to go to dinner at all the nicest hotels in Seattle. They'd even had Sunday brunch at the famed Georgian Room at the Fairmont Olympic on University. But even though she'd had plenty of money to pay for their meals back then, Lainie always felt like an interloper. She kept waiting for the other diners to point at her and whisper that she didn't belong.

Like she needed anyone to tell her that.

Lainie smoothed a hand over her hair. She'd blown it straight half an hour earlier, but it had a tendency to grow exponentially in the humid Florida air. If she didn't keep it down, it would look like one of those Chia pets before the hour was out.

Next, she tugged at the side seam of her white silk-and-linen pants and resisted the urge to pull her thong panties out of her butt crack. A little discomfort was a small price to pay for no visible panty lines. These were her most expensive slacks—she'd paid over two hundred dollars for them at the Nordstrom half-yearly sale—and the last thing she wanted was to ruin the look with underwear that everyone could see. She'd topped the pants off with an orange silk tank and an orange-and-yellow patterned blouse, and her sandals were beaded with matching orange stones. It had taken her months to find just the right sandals for this outfit, and Lainie was glad now that she hadn't let them go for the paltry five bucks that one woman at the Garage Sale from Hell had offered her.

Lainie had been outraged, but almost desperate enough to take it. Instead, she'd snatched the sandals from the woman's hand and—finally cracking under the pressure of having curious neighbors paw through everything from her underwear to her measuring cups—had scooped up all she could carry and screamed at the last few onlookers to go away.

People say you can tell a lot about someone by how they act under pressure.

Lainie did not want to think about the conclusions one might draw about *her* after that day.

She relived that scene in her nightmares occasionally, and, though she didn't like to admit it, she believed she'd actually been foaming at the mouth. Spittle had definitely been involved.

Shaking her head now to clear out the image of that horrible day, Lainie straightened her shoulders and lifted her chin as they came to a stop in front of the maître d'. Could he tell she was broke just by looking at her?

Lainie didn't think so. She had on all the right clothes. Her hair was straight and shiny. And thanks to the decade-old tube of toothpaste she'd found at the back of a drawer in her old bathroom, her breath was minty fresh.

Nothing about her screamed deadbeat.

At least, she hoped not.

She nodded calmly to the man as he gave her the once-over. Checking to make sure she wouldn't offend his regular patrons, Lainie guessed.

Satisfied that the riffraff was at least properly clothed, the maître d' dipped his chin and said, "This way, ladies."

And so it was that Lainie found herself seated at a table for two in the Ritz-Carlton, feeling every bit the same awkward, gangly kid who hadn't belonged here fifteen years ago.

"I'm going to have the lobster," Trish announced without even looking at the menu.

And I'm going to have an entire bottle of Chardonnay, Lainie thought. That is, until she glanced down at her menu and saw that she couldn't even afford a glass of wine, much less a whole bottle.

"The grilled vegetable dish looks good," Lainie mumbled, without bothering to read any of the descriptions. It looked good because it was the cheapest entrée they offered. Plus, since she was having veggies for dinner, she could use that as her excuse for not having a salad. Or dessert. Anyone who ate eggplant and whole-wheat couscous for dinner *had* to be a health nut who wouldn't even dream of ordering—Lainie turned the menu over and nearly swooned at the luscious dessert offerings—key-lime cheesecake with a macadamia nut crust covered with a layer of molten chocolate and topped with lightly whipped cream or bread pudding served warm with amaretto crème anglaise and fresh blueberries.

Lainie swallowed a mouthful of drool and hastily pushed her menu away.

At least the bread would be free. She'd just have to fill up on that.

When the waiter arrived, Trish ordered a glass of wine, a Caesar salad, and the lobster. Lainie wanted a glass of Chardonnay so badly that her hands shook, but she summoned up every ounce of willpower she had and ordered the grilled vegetables and a water. With extra lemon.

Yeah. She was really stickin' it to the man there.

With a self-mocking smile, Lainie settled back in her seat and forced herself to relax. After being on the road for so long, it seemed odd to be among people again. For seven days she'd been alone, with nothing but her own thoughts for company.

Needless to say, she had not been thrilled with her traveling companion.

"So are you excited to be home?" Trish asked, her pretty blue eyes sparkling at Lainie from across the table.

For about the millionth time, Lainie was struck by how different she and her older half sister were. Trish was blond-haired and blue-eyed and all soft around the edges, just like you'd expect a happy, fortyish mother-of-two to be. Lainie was about five inches taller than her sister, with thick dark hair and brown eyes. She wasn't thin by any stretch of the imagination, but she wasn't contentedly plump, either. She was more . . . medium.

Mediocre.

For a few years she'd fooled herself into believing that she was something more than that, but it had only been temporary—like a spun-sugar castle that melted in the first drop of rain.

Lainie tried to muster up a half-smile, but was pretty sure she failed. "Yes, I'm looking forward to having some time to decide what to do with myself after this," she lied.

"It must be nice to have all that money from your stock options to fall back on. You can do anything you want now." Trish sighed and gave her a look that was more I'm-happy-for-you than why-couldn't-it-be-me. Lainie didn't think her older sister was even capable of feeling an ugly emotion like jealousy.

Must have come from her mother's side of the family.

"Yes, it's great." Lainie wondered how long she could maintain this phony smile before her face cracked.

Lie #1: She'd told Trish and her dad that the startup company she'd nearly killed herself working endless hours for back in Seattle had been sold to a private company and they'd all made a fortune on the options.

The truth: The company had gone bankrupt after asking everyone to take 50-percent pay cuts a year ago and then writing payroll checks that bounced for the last two months.

Lie #2: She'd told her family that Ted, her husband of three years, had decided to join the Peace Corps and help starving children in Africa, that they had just "grown apart," and that their divorce had been amicable.

The truth: Ted was a compulsive gambler who had accepted every credit-card offer that had come in the mail over the past two years and had run up nearly a quarter of a million dollars in debt before Lainie discovered what he had done. He was currently wanted in Nevada for check fraud, and their divorce had been granted in absentia. Lainie hadn't seen him in nearly a year.

Lie #3: She was tired of being a computer programmer and was down in Naples trying to "find herself" and figure out what career to pursue next.

The truth: She'd never finished her computer science degree

and had ended up in an admin job that paid well enough but nothing like she could have made as a programmer in Seattle at the end of the 1990s. To make matters worse, work was the only thing she'd ever been able to rely on in her life. When it turned on her, Lainie tumbled into a depression so deep that just getting out of bed every morning was too much to contemplate. By the time she'd finally gotten up enough energy to start showering again, her life had caved in around her like a fallen soufflé.

She wasn't here in Naples because she wanted to be. She was broke and didn't have anywhere else to go.

Lainie felt tears well up in her eyes and blinked them back, reaching for her glass of water with (free) extra lemon.

Ah, self-pity. My old friend.

She was about to take a sip of water when her chair was suddenly jostled from behind. Lainie felt the sweaty glass slip out of her hand and tried to grip it tighter, but knew that it was hopeless. The glass fell to the table with a loud clatter that had the diners around them stopping mid-bite to stare.

"I'm so sorry," a deep male voice said as a heavy, warm hand landed on her shoulder.

Lainie just stared without moving at the puddle of water now dripping onto her white linen pants. As if the thought were coming from a long way away, it occurred to her that she should do something to stop it, but she couldn't figure out what.

Besides, why bother?

This was one small disaster in the string of large disasters that made up her life.

The man reached over to the chair he'd vacated a second ago and grabbed his napkin. Then, as if staunching a wound, he held it to the edge of the table to stop the water from dripping onto her lap.

"Everything will be all right. Give me your name, and I'll get your dry cleaning bill," he said.

Lainie looked at him then, this man who thought that her life could be fixed with one good washing. She might have laughed hysterically, if the breath hadn't left her lungs when her eyes met his.

It was one of those moments you read about in *Cosmo* or in a romance novel. He was . . . amazing. Handsome. With dark brown eyes and thick hair that flopped over his forehead as he leaned down, trying to hold back the flood. He smelled amazing. Like he had just taken a shower and put some spicy cologne on his neck.

And she . . . she just sat there like an idiot. Paralyzed by the sudden realization that she was looking at him the way a woman looks at a man she's attracted to. It had been so long since she'd felt anything but despair that the awareness of him hit her like a punch to the gut.

"Excuse me, Mr. Danforth. I'll take care of this."

Lainie blinked her way out of her shock to find their waiter hovering anxiously behind them with several clean napkins in his hand.

Say something, she urged herself as the silence went on a beat too long.

She opened her mouth and finally managed to croak out that she was fine—it was only water, after all.

The man winked at her and said, "Good. I promise it won't happen again."

Then he stepped back and let the waiter take over, and if Lainie was disappointed that he hadn't insisted on getting her name and number, she refused to admit it. Instead, she tried to enjoy her meal and not eavesdrop on the man and his—quite young and quite lovely, Lainie couldn't help but notice—dinner companion. But mostly, she spent the rest of dinner trying to figure out how to suggest that she and Trish split the bill so that Lainie would only have to pay for what she had ordered. Even then, she was going to have to pray to the bank gods that she could slip another twenty-five bucks past her limit without them sending the credit police in to confiscate her plastic on the spot.

What would another pebble matter on the mountain that was her debt?

By the time Trish had finished the last mouthwatering bite of her key-lime cheesecake—which Lainie refused to sample since she was already feeling awful about not being able to split the check fifty-fifty; no sense making it worse by scarfing down half of her sister's creamy, drool-worthy dessert—Lainie had come up with a little speech about hoping it was okay if she just covered her own expenses tonight since she hadn't had a chance to transfer money from her investment account and wasn't sure how much was left in checking, because everyone *knows* you should have your money out there earning interest for you, so would Trish mind if she just got her own dinner this time if Lainie promised to treat the whole family to a meal out another night?

Whew. And trying to make that sound like anything but the rehearsed speech it was wasn't going to be easy.

Which was why, when the waiter stopped at their table with that little black bill-holder thingy in his hands and said, "Is there anything else I can get for you ladies this evening?", Lainie choked on a lemon seed in her haste to get her spiel out before Trish could suggest they split the check in half.

Not noticing that her sister was gasping for breath, Trish began rummaging around in her giant Mom-purse, her arms swallowed up to the elbows in faux leather as she moved aside packs of gum, writing instruments, extra notebooks, half a dozen half-used Chap Stick tubes, a super-sized bottle of Tums, a tube of Neosporin,

SpongeBob bandages in every size imaginable, assorted feminine hygiene products, a cell phone, a Palm Pilot, enough napkins to sop up the entire Gulf of Mexico, two raspberry-oatmeal breakfast bars, and a peanut butter sandwich that she'd forgotten to throw away last week, all in her search for her wallet, which appeared to have gone missing.

"I can't believe this. The kids must have left my wallet out again after they were done scavenging through it like the little pickpockets they are," Trish said with an indulgent eye-roll and exaggerated sigh. "I was going to treat you to dinner on your first night back, but would you mind getting this one? I promise I'll buy next time."

The blood drained from Lainie's face as she silently calculated the cost of Trish's expensive dinner.

Two glasses of wine: Eighteen dollars.

Caesar salad: Eight-fifty.

Lobster Thermidor: Forty-five bucks.

Dessert: Twelve dollars.

Knowing you're about to be humiliated in front of the sort of people you've spent your entire life trying to impress: Priceless.

Lainie's throat seized up and she found herself looking around desperately for an exit. Maybe they could just quietly slip out without paying? If Trish would excuse herself to go to the restroom, Lainie could meet her sister out in the lobby and tell her she'd paid the bill and they could make their escape before the waiter figured out they'd given him the slip.

Or maybe she could pretend to be a guest at the hotel and charge the meal to some random room number? But what if she picked a number that didn't exist? Or what if the waiter checked the name against the room number before they had a chance to escape?

No, she'd have to go with Plan A.

"Sure, I'll get this one," she said, hoping Trish didn't notice the wobble in her voice. "Do you need to run to the ladies' room before we go?"

"No, I'm fine. I'll just finish up my wine and then we can go."

Lainie had to fight the urge to wail and bash her head on the table. Why, why, why couldn't things go her way, just this once?

There was no way she could slip another hundred bucks onto her already-maxed-out credit cards. Twenty dollars, she might have been able to get away with. But not a hundred.

So now what?

She couldn't just blurt out the truth, not after lying to everyone about the circumstances of her homecoming. There had to be another way.

But after willing her mind to come up with something brilliant and getting nothing in return, she did what anyone in her situation would do—she ran for the bathroom, the back of her chair bumping Mr. Hunk's as she stood to flee.

Lainie mumbled an apology but was too distracted with trying to find a solution to her predicament to hear what he said in return. Her forehead furrowed in thought, she pushed open the door to the ladies' room, her mind registering the opulent facilities as she paced the marble floor.

All right, she told herself, ignoring her reflection in the mirror above the bank of sinks, it was time to attack this problem logically.

She couldn't try paying for the meal with her credit cards. If she attempted to put the entire bill on any one card, the waiter would probably chop the thing in two right in front of her and her sister. She could ask him to split it among all of her cards, but how could she explain that to Trish? There was no plausible excuse that she could come up with for having to do such a thing. Besides, there was no guarantee that that would work. All of her cards were maxed out. If any one of them refused the charge, she'd look like an even bigger loser by having to make the waiter go back and try again.

So, if she couldn't pay the bill, what other choice did she have?

Maybe she could go talk to the manager. Explain her situation. Ask if there was some arrangement they could work out? Like maybe she could wash dishes or something. Wasn't that how it always worked in the movies?

But what if he (or she) said no? Then Lainie would have no other choice but to tell Trish that she didn't have any money.

Aargh.

Maybe she should just come clean. What difference would it make if Trish knew the truth, if they all knew that no matter how hard she had worked or how far she thought she had come, that she was still the same pathetic, unworthy—

No.

Stop.

She wasn't pathetic. She wasn't unworthy.

Up until a few months ago she could have proven that. She'd had the right car, the right house, the right address in the right town. The clothes, the shoes, the haircut. The manicure and pedicure. All those things showed the world that Elaine Ames was *somebody*.

She was going to get that all back.

She just needed a little time to get on her feet again; time without everyone feeling sorry for her and giving her pitying looks like she was some sort of loser or something.

Lainie put her hands on the cool marble countertop and faced herself in the mirror. "You are not a loser," she said, raising her chin a notch.

Which sounded good echoing off the walls of the empty bathroom, but didn't do much to fix her issue with the dinner bill.

Lainie sighed and turned away from the mirror.

Okay. How else did people get out of paying for their meals? She could hardly go back and complain about the quality of the food now. She was embarrassed to admit that she'd—and, yes, she knew this was impolite and even a bit disgusting—waited until Trish wasn't paying attention and had used her finger to lick her plate clean before the waiter had come to take it away. What could she say? She hadn't had anything to eat since Gainesville, and even that was just the few leftover French fries she'd saved from the night before when, in desperation, she'd scrounged up a dollar-fifty from under the driver's seat of her car.

So acting as if she hadn't enjoyed the meal was out.

Which left only one other option: the old waiter-there's-a-bug-in-my-soup routine. Only, in her case, it would have to be a bug in her water.

For the first time in days, Lainie felt a tiny flare of hope welling up inside her. After all, how hard could finding a cockroach in Florida be?

{ three }

Lainie checked all the stalls, but apparently the bathroom at the Ritz-Carlton had been declared a cockroach-free zone. There wasn't even a spider or a trace of a web. Not a beetle, not a crane fly, not so much as a mosquito to be found.

Damn.

Lainie squatted down and stuck her head under the counter to see if there were any insects lurking around there, then hastily straightened up when she heard the bathroom door open. She smoothed a hand over her hair and attempted to look nonchalant as the gorgeous young thing from Mr. Hunk's table sauntered in on red stiletto heels that were a perfect match for the ones in her episode of "Lainie's Triumphant Return."

The girl—she couldn't have been more than twenty—said a cheerful hello as she passed Lainie and went into a stall. Lainie mumbled what she hoped was something polite, but all she could think was that the jig was up. It had been a stupid idea anyway. What would she have done if she'd found a roach? Carry it back to the table by its creepy hairy legs, hoping that nobody would notice?

Okay, so it hadn't been one of her more well-thought-out plans.

She was just going to have to give up and tell Trish the truth. Or some watered-down version of the truth anyway. Like maybe all of her assets were tied up right now (which was partially true— they were tied up in other people's bank accounts), or that her wallet had been stolen (which was not true at all, but maybe she could leave it here in the bathroom and see if someone would take it . . . for all the good it would do them), or . . .

Hey, wait a second. That last idea wasn't bad. She could toss her wallet in the trash and say it had been stolen.

What a great idea.

Lainie hurriedly unzipped her purse and took out the tan wallet containing all her credit cards, frequent flier cards, her Barnes & Noble discount card, her expired AAA card, and her driver's license. She planned to extract her license before tossing the whole thing into the trash, but when she heard the toilet flush, she knew she didn't have time.

With a small pang of doubt, she threw her wallet into a hole that had been cut in the counter which led to a rattan hamper below. Regular trash cans were apparently not good enough for the patrons of the Ritz. Then, convinced that she was doing the right thing, Lainie pulled open the bathroom door and headed back to the restaurant, where her sister was engaged in a conversation with the people at the next table. Since Trish worked at the high school in town, Lainie assumed they must be parents of one of her students.

She pulled out her chair and was about to sit back down when she saw something out of the corner of her eye and froze.

No, it wasn't an elusive cockroach.

But this . . . this might be even better.

Lainie's eyes darted right. Then left. Then right again.

Then, barely thinking about what she was doing, her hand snaked out and, in a movement nearly invisible to the naked eye, she pushed the next table's bill—with its shiny gold card sticking out the top—onto the floor beneath her chair.

Telling herself all the while that what she was doing was wrong, she nonetheless sat down, kicked the bill under the table, and then reached down as though searching for her napkin. She felt the smooth, cool plastic between her thumb and forefinger and gave it a tug, closing her eyes for just a moment to ask the credit card gods' forgiveness for what she was about to do.

As God is my witness, I'll never go hungry again, she silently vowed as she straightened up with the gold card clasped firmly in her grip.

No, no. Wrong movie.

Lainie shook her head and amended her promise. As God was her witness, she'd find a way to pay back this—she glanced at the gold American Express card in her hand—Jackson Danforth III. Yes, she'd find a way to repay him, if it was the last thing she ever did.

Even if that name *did* make it sound like he wouldn't notice an extra hundred bucks on his credit card statement . . .

After slipping the AmEx into their black bill-holder thingy, Lainie caught the waiter's eye and looked meaningfully down at the table. If he could have the card back by the time Mr. Hunky Danforth and his underage date returned from the restrooms, no one would ever have to know what she'd done.

Except her, of course.

Lainie forced a smile at her sister as Trish introduced her to the couple at the next table. They made idle chitchat about the weather in Seattle versus that of South Florida, everyone laughing as they all agreed that, yes, the summers in Florida sure were hot and that, yes, it sure did rain a lot in the Pacific Northwest.

And then—finally—the waiter reappeared.

Lainie watched his approach with one eye on him and the other on the entrance of the restaurant.

She found herself hoping for something she'd never hoped for before. *Please, let him get caught in his zipper*, she prayed, then winced. How low had she sunk? Wasn't it bad enough that she was— temporarily, she made sure to add—stealing from the poor guy? Did she have to wish him bodily harm, too?

Just let him take extra long to dry his hands, then, she amended.

She nearly jumped out of her seat as the waiter ambled to their table. "Hurry up!" she wanted to shout, but she managed to restrain herself.

"Thank you very much, Miss—"

The man yelped when Lainie *did* jump out of her seat and grab the bill from his hands just as he was opening it to read her name off the credit card inside. Damn, that was close.

"You're welcome," Lainie answered smoothly, ignoring the odd looks she was receiving from both the waiter and her sister. She signed the bill with a flourish, generously adding a 20-percent tip and making a note of the total so she could be sure to pay it in full as soon as she got back on her feet.

Then she reached down and slid the credit card back where she had found it. When she straightened up this time, she had Mr. Danforth's bill hidden under her napkin, intending to drop it on his table as she made some excuse to go to the ladies' room again so she could retrieve her wallet. No sense leaving it there now that the whole problem with the bill had been solved.

Who knew that living a life of crime would involve so many trips to the restroom?

"I'm sorry, but I've got to go to the bathroom again. That goat cheese didn't agree with me," she told her sister, clutching her stomach as if she were in an antacid commercial.

"Do you want a Tums?" Trish asked, and reached into her enormous handbag.

"No, thanks. I'll . . . Uh, I'll meet you in the lobby in a minute," Lainie said. She pushed her chair back and stood up, pressing her napkin to her side to hide the other table's bill. She turned around to find Mr. Danforth bearing down on her with his date at his side. She had to get rid of his bill before he spotted her, so she sidestepped awkwardly and dropped it, napkin and all, onto his seat. He might wonder how it had gotten there, but at least he wouldn't catch her standing there holding the evidence.

Lainie inched the strap of her purse over her shoulder and then smoothed her palms down over her wrinkled linen pants.

With her chin held high, she swept out of the dining room without a backward glance. If she could just get her wallet and go, this nightmare of an evening would be over.

The heavy wooden door of the ladies' room didn't dare creak when Lainie pulled it open. Warily she stepped into the room, as if expecting an ambush. When nothing but silence met her ears, she took another step and then another toward the bin where she'd dumped her wallet.

She wrinkled her nose with distaste as she peered into the dark abyss.

Every time she thought she couldn't sink any lower . . . she did.

A year ago nothing could have compelled her to root around in the trash. Even if she'd dropped a hundred-dollar bill in the garbage, she would have just shrugged it off.

This, she supposed, was her punishment for believing—even for a short while—that she deserved the life she had been living.

Well, no sense crying about it now. She had been dealt a blow and now she had to live with the consequences.

Lainie closed her eyes—she couldn't bear to watch herself do what had to be done—and plunged her hand into the trash.

"It's just paper towels," she muttered to herself as she felt around for her wallet. She thought she felt the leather under her fingers, but her roving hand jostled the lightweight trash and it sank farther down, toward the bottom. Lainie gnawed on her bottom lip as she stood on her tiptoes, trying to get her hand deeper into the hamper.

There. She could feel the corner. Just another inch.

She turned and leaned over the counter. Just a little farther now.

Her fingers closed around the square of leather just as she heard the bathroom door open. Lainie pulled back, whacking her hand on the soap dispenser as she tried to move away from the sinks.

But she realized that she hadn't been fast enough when a familiar voice asked from behind her, "What in the world are you doing?"

Something was up with her sister.

Trish Miller sneaked a look at the woman sitting in the passenger seat next to her. Okay, so she didn't know Lainie as well as she should. It wasn't exactly easy to be close to someone who lived on the other side of the continent and only came to visit every few years. And, no, they didn't have some special sisterly bond. They hadn't even grown up in the same household; hadn't met each other face-to-face until Trish was in her mid-twenties. The only thing they had in common was their father, and from what Trish had observed over the years, her younger half sister had some unresolved father-daughter issues that caused both Lainie and their dad to circle each other warily whenever they were in the same room.

Trish felt an embarrassing mixture of guilt coupled with grate-fulness whenever she thought of the difference in how she and Lainie had been raised. Her own mother had gotten pregnant by the handsome sailor stationed in Jacksonville—didn't matter that he had graduated from high school only because he'd been sleeping with his English teacher, who had some influence over his other in-structors and managed to get him enough passing grades to get by, or that he'd enlisted in the Navy as a cook, figuring that if he had to work for his government-issued trip-around-the-world, he might as well do it without having to think too much. He hadn't figured on falling in love with the service, or that he'd actually enjoy being a cook. He also hadn't figured on impregnating the first girl he met after being stationed in Florida

Trish's mom hadn't figured on it, either. But when the symptoms of her pregnancy became too obvious to ignore any longer, Linda Lee Mabry did what she thought best for her baby: She told Carl Ames that she wouldn't marry him.

And unlike all the other good-girl-gets-knocked-up stories that happened during that era, Linda Lee's parents didn't kick her out of the house or try to force her to marry a man she didn't love or even try to pass the baby off as a midlife mistake on Trish's parents' part. Instead, they welcomed their granddaughter into their lives, ignor-ing the few raised eyebrows at their church and local grocery store until their daughter's "shameful" behavior was forgotten.

Five years later Linda Lee married and had two more children—both boys—and Trish's stepfather never once treated her as any-thing but the blessing her own mother and grandparents did. For that, Trish was grateful.

Lainie hadn't had it quite so good, though no one in Trish's family knew the whole story. That, however, didn't stop them from speculating.

What they did know was that Carl Ames stayed in the Navy as long as he could without getting promoted above E-4. From Jacksonville, he moved to Virginia Beach, and then to San Diego, and then to Bremerton, Washington, where he once again got a local girl pregnant. But unlike Linda Lee, this one said yes when Carl offered to "do the right thing" and marry her. Carl was twenty-eight at the time—plenty old enough to be well-versed in the use of a condom—but he apparently hadn't figured out yet that the consequence of having unprotected sex was the appearance of a squalling infant nine months later. How else did one explain how Carl had managed to father *two* unwanted children before the age of thirty?

From what Trish had gathered, Carl Ames wasn't exactly gracious about accepting his own responsibility for the conception of his second daughter, though after Lainie's mom died when she was only six, Carl hadn't tried pawning her off on his parents or anyone else. Still, that seemed like a small consolation for not being wanted—a point that Carl never hesitated to tell his youngest daughter in those early days after her mother's death.

Trish winced as she turned into the housing development where she lived. She had a clear memory—as vivid as if it had just happened last week—of the first Christmas after Carl and Lainie moved to Naples. Trish and her now-husband Alan had started dating early that year, and they'd spent the morning with his family and the afternoon with her mother and grandparents. They'd been lying on the couch, cuddled in a cocoon of young love, full bellies, and too many gifts when Trish's mom called her out to the kitchen and suggested that it might be nice for Trish to go over and visit her dad.

"After all, it is Christmas," Linda Lee had said.

And Trish, who had corresponded on and off with Carl for years, who had faithfully received birthday cards and Christmas gifts for twenty-five years, all mailed from faraway places like Guam and California, agreed.

Trish slid a sideways glance over at her little sister and found herself blinking back tears. Her heart still broke a little every time she remembered that day—walking into Carl's house with a rewrapped tin of Almond Roca under her arm for this sort-of family she didn't know, standing in the two-foot-by-four-foot darkened linoleum entryway while she and Carl awkwardly exchanged Merry Christmases. Trish had been shocked by the difference between their house and hers. Mom's was all light and noise and tinsel strewn everywhere because her little brothers had thought it was funny to throw it on the dog whenever she galloped past in her own frenzied holiday merriment. Their tree was so big that her stepfather had to cut the top off before it came to a point, which made it look like it had grown up into the attic. And the smells! Trish had gone out onto the patio and then come back in again just so she could be hit full-force with the aroma of roasted turkey and apple pie.

She did her best to hide her dismay as she glanced around her dad's house, wondering where her half sister was.

Lainie wasn't in the living room, where their pitiful Charlie Brown tree stood. With their eight-foot ceilings, they could have gotten a bigger tree, but instead, theirs was no more than four feet high, with sparse branches and dry needles that were barely hanging on to life.

Trish set the tin of Almond Roca on the wobbly dining room table.

"It looks like your tree needs some water," she said. "Do you have a pitcher?"

She was caught between wanting to escape this dreary place and needing, at the same time, to fix it up.

"I'll get one. Why don't you sit down?" Carl said.

Trish did, perching on the edge of the fake leather sofa that she could have told her dad was totally impractical for South Florida. In the summer their bare legs would get all sweaty and stick to it.

"Hey, Trish. How are you?"

She looked up from her perch on the couch to find her dark-haired, dark-eyed half sister watching her from the shadowed hall-way leading to her room.

Wary.

The word popped into Trish's mind, and she found herself nod-ding slightly. Yes, that was the perfect word to describe Lainie. *Wary.* Like a turtle sticking its nose out of its shell, poised at any second to retreat once again to safety if it sensed danger.

Trish forced herself to relax. If they were both on edge, they'd never have a chance to become friends.

She patted the seat next to her. "I'm fine. Why don't you come sit down?"

Lainie's gaze flicked to the kitchen, where sounds of their father rummaging through cupboards could clearly be heard, and then back to Trish. "Okay," she said.

Her sister's choice of attire seemed odd to Trish. Her family dressed up for the holiday—not in that too-formal way where your clothes pinched at you and made it impossible to relax after pig-ging out on dinner, but in a way that made you feel pretty on this special day. But Lainie was wearing worn jeans with a hole above the knee that she stuck her finger into as she sat down on the couch next to her sister. Her feet were bare, her toenails ragged and un-polished, and it was impossible to tell if she was fat or thin beneath her oversized T-shirt in a color that Trish could only describe as drab. Her long dark hair was up in a messy ponytail, as if she hadn't bothered to brush her hair before pulling it up. She kept her eyes downcast as the silence lengthened—the only sound coming from the kitchen where there was a loud *thunk* and then the noise of their father cursing.

Trish cleared her throat and licked her dry lips. She wished she'd brought the new strawberry lip gloss that had been in her stocking this morning, then she felt a pang of guilt and revised her wish— she wished she'd brought several of her new treasures to share with Lainie. From the absence of tinsel, shredded wrapping paper, and bows, she guessed her little sister hadn't gotten much in the way of presents today.

"Um, have you guys already opened your gifts?" she asked, silently praying that Lainie had at least received *something.*

Lainie pulled at the hole in her jeans. "Yeah. I got . . . you know. Perfume. A manicure kit." Her sister looked up and into her eyes for just a second before dropping her gaze again. "A new pair of jeans. They're the wrong size, but Dad says I can exchange them."

"I could go with you if you want." Trish perked up. She was always up for shopping.

For some reason Lainie's cheeks reddened. "N-n-no. That's all right," she said quickly, and Trish frowned. Why wouldn't her sister want to go shopping with her?

"Why not? I know all the cool stores," she assured her, wondering if maybe Lainie thought she was too old. She remembered at sixteen thinking how ancient anyone over twenty was, so she could hardly blame Lainie for feeling the same way.

"I like to shop by myself," Lainie insisted, never once letting on that the reason she didn't want Trish's help was because she didn't want her sister to know that her dad bought her clothes at the local Goodwill.

Okay, fine, be that way. Trish shrugged and slid forward on the cheap vinyl couch. She wasn't going to make the effort to be nice if

Lainie didn't appreciate it. She was new in town and Trish could show her all the best places to go and shop and hang out, but if she didn't want Trish's help, then that was fine with her. *She* didn't need the hassle. She had a job and friends and a boyfriend and a great family and plenty of fun things to do.

And Lainie had nothing.

The thought hit Trish like a wrecking ball to the chest. She was *supposed* to be the grown-up here. Maybe there was more to Lainie's defensiveness than just being an antisocial teenager.

Trish took a deep breath and relaxed back into the couch.

"Well, if you ever do want me to show you around, I'd be happy to. You've got my phone number at the apartment, right?"

Lainie nodded.

"Good. So . . . um, have you and Dad already eaten?" she asked.

"No. We're going down to the restaurant later. We're making a special Christmas dinner and employee's families can have the buffet for half price," Carl said, coming out of the kitchen with a broken measuring cup full of water.

Guess he couldn't find a pitcher.

"Do you want to come? Dad's got to work," Lainie added, the hopefulness in her eyes heartbreakingly easy to read.

Trish swallowed her distaste. Did she want to eat at some buffet dinner set out as a "gift" from the restaurant manager in return for making peoples' family members work on Christmas Day or would she rather have a home-cooked meal with her mom and the rest of her family? Tough decision.

"Um, I can't," she said. "I'm supposed to have dinner with my family. Actually, they're all, uh, waiting for me back home. I'd better get going. Mom'll kill me if I stay here too long and her turkey gets dry." She added what she hoped was a lighthearted laugh, but the truth was, she couldn't wait to get out of this depressing place with its nearly dead Christmas tree and awkward silences.

It didn't occur to her until later, when she was mock-seriously threatening one of her brothers with death if he even *thought* about flinging his mashed potatoes at her, that she should have invited Lainie to come have dinner here. Her mother wouldn't have minded an extra person. As usual, there was enough food to feed a small country. But then, Trish thought—and now wondered if she had just come up with the rationalization to alleviate her own guilt—if Lainie had wanted to come, all she'd had to do was ask.

{ four }

Lainie was out of shampoo, but she wasn't about to ask her dad if she could borrow any. The last time she'd visited, she'd been overdue for a cut-and-highlight and had stopped in at one of the salons on Naples's touristy Sunshine Parkway. After paying nearly two hundred dollars to be foiled and fluffed, she'd stocked up on twenty-dollar-a-bottle shampoo, conditioner, and shine treatment, and when she'd inadvertently left the receipt next to her purchases on the kitchen table, Dad had made her feel like an idiot for spending so much money on her hair.

"I could get a dozen bottles of that two-in-one shampoo-and-conditioner down at the Wal-Mart for what you spent there," he'd said, shaking his head as if to say that she didn't even have the sense God gave a chicken.

"I can afford it." Lainie tried to shrug it off, though she felt her shoulders hunching closer up around her ears with every minute she was there.

"But it's silly to waste your money like that. You should be saving it."

It took superhuman strength to unclench her teeth in order to get any words out around them. Her father had no business trying to be the spokesman for fiscal responsibility. She'd be surprised if he had more than a thousand bucks in savings—and this after not pitching in one cent to help either of his daughters go to college.

"Well, I don't like that green stuff you buy. It's not good for my hair," she'd said. And with that, because winning an argument with him was impossible, she grabbed her purchases—and the offending receipt—and shut herself in the small second bathroom, safe in the knowledge that her father would never bother her there.

So, after making such a big deal out of it, there was no way she could ask to borrow "that green stuff" he used. Instead, Lainie thought as she pulled aside the surprisingly bright yellow shower curtain in the guest bath, she'd have to use the sliver of soap that was perched on the edge of the tub.

She locked the bathroom door and turned on the water without having to step from the center of the room. Every time she came back to Dad's house, she was struck by how small it was. True, everyone in her generation expected to raise their families in Mc-Mansions, where anything under three thousand square feet was considered a "charming bungalow" by real estate standards. But no one could argue that a house less than half that size wasn't small. And this bathroom was barely bigger than the guest room closet, leaving Lainie feeling claustrophobic as she pulled the oversized T-shirt she'd slept in last night over her head and dropped it on the back of the hideously flesh-colored toilet.

She showered as quickly as possible, hoping that she wouldn't wake her father up with the sound of water flowing through the pipes. She knew she'd have to see him sometime—probably this afternoon before he went to work—but she couldn't face him this morning.

It had been bad enough dealing with Trish last night, knowing that she at least probably *was* happy to see her. Not that her dad would be unhappy about her stay in Naples. Most likely, he didn't care one way or another. Sure, she could use her old bedroom for a while. Wasn't like it inconvenienced him at all.

Lainie tried not to tangle her hair any more than necessary as she stepped out of the shower and toweled off.

She often wondered how low long it would take Dad to notice if she simply disappeared. Of course, she wasn't much better. It wasn't like she made the effort to call him every day, either.

Lainie wrapped her hair up in the towel, turban-style, and then wiped the steamed-up mirror with a dry washrag. Why did being here make her feel like she was sixteen again? Why couldn't she come to Naples, just once, and act like the confident, successful adult she was?

Or, rather, the confident, successful adult she *used* to be.

She sighed as she pulled a jar of moisturizer out of her makeup bag. She didn't feel quite so confident or successful this trip, but wasn't that why she was out of bed, showered, and getting made-up at eight-thirty this morning rather than hiding under the covers like she'd rather be?

She had to find a job. Any job. Today.

She'd tell Dad and Trish that whatever she found was just a way to keep her from getting too accustomed to sleeping in while she thought about what new career she wanted to pursue. That was a total lie, of course. She needed a job because she needed a paycheck. Now.

Her makeup finished and only half her hair missing after dragging a brush through it, Lainie quietly opened the door to the bathroom and peered out into the hall. She remained still, listening to the sound of the air conditioner wheezing through the metal grates in the ceiling, until she was certain that her dad was still asleep in his bedroom on the other side of the house. Then she tiptoed back into the bedroom she always used when she visited and closed the door behind her.

It was a regular-sized room with a regular-sized closet, furnished with the double bed and five-drawer dresser Lainie had used when she was a kid. She'd stacked the few items she'd brought with her from Seattle into the closet last night and she winced now as one of the louvered doors squeaked loudly as she pulled it open.

"Does WD-40 fix rust?" she wondered aloud. If you believed her father, you could build the Taj Mahal with nothing but duct tape and WD-40.

She pulled two handfuls of on-the-hanger, dry-cleaner-bag-covered clothes out of her suitcase and hung them on the metal bar in the closet. She'd managed to salvage about two dozen of her favorite outfits from the Garage Sale from Hell, and she felt a pang of wistfulness as she looked at them all now. Her clothes used to take up three of the four closets in her and Ted's four-bedroom, three-bath house. She'd had slacks from Ann Taylor, skirts and blouses from Nordstrom, embroidered jeans and cute little T-shirts from J. Jill. They were all gone now, victims of the ruthless purging she'd done to raise money and spare herself the expense of having to ship or store all her extra belongings.

Lainie pulled the dry cleaner bags off her clothes and palmed through each outfit, one by one. After reviewing all her choices, she decided on a pair of slimming black pants and a black-and-white striped, zip-front Lycra shirt that she knew looked good on her. She'd wear her black boots, the ones with the four-inch heels that made her feel like she could kick ass or dance on tables, depending on what she was in the mood for, and finished off her look with the small black Coach handbag with silver stitching that she'd refused to part with.

When she was dressed, Lainie slipped out of the bedroom and walked to the kitchen, holding her boots so she wouldn't make too much noise. If she'd had any money, she would have left right now and headed to the nearest Starbucks for a triple-shot Venti Americano. But since she was broke, she was going to have to settle for whatever Dad had on hand. Another one of the items she'd salvaged from home was an espresso machine that Trish had given her a few years ago for her birthday, but—alas—she didn't have the coffee beans to make herself a fresh cup.

She forced herself not to shudder when she opened a cupboard and realized that all her dad stocked was Maxwell House.

Pre-ground.

Ugh.

It wasn't even whole bean.

She opened the top and took a whiff, and then *did* shudder. No way could she drink this. Not after living so long in a city where there was an espresso stand on every corner, where every cup of coffee was brewed to order, every fresh-roasted bean ground on the spot.

"There's some of that gourmet stuff you like in the freezer. Your sister brought it over when I told her you were coming home."

Lainie froze with the coffee lid halfway back on the can.

Why hadn't she just left two minutes ago?

She took a deep, calming breath, filling her lungs with coffee-scented air and courage. Then she turned to face her father.

"Hey, Dad. How are you?" She tried for a bright smile, hoping it didn't look too much like a grimace.

He looked . . . the way he always looked. Big. Intimidating. Even in her four-inch heels, he was half a foot taller than her. His dark hair was thinning, the bald spot that had started out on the back of his head growing ever larger in its quest to conquer his entire skull. He'd gone through a fleshy period about a decade back where he'd put on quite a bit of weight around his middle, but he'd managed—Lainie didn't know exactly how, or what had motivated him to do it—to lose it all in the last few years.

"I'm fine. You get in all right?" he asked.

Lainie nodded. "Yeah. No problems." Well, except for nearly running out of gas twenty miles back, she amended silently.

Her dad opened the freezer door, pulled out a brown bag, and handed it to her. Lainie spied the label of a local gourmet coffee vendor and wished Trish was here now so she could fall at her feet and thank her. If she were careful, the bag would last her a good two weeks—long enough for her first paycheck to arrive if she got a job in the next couple of days.

She reached for the coffeepot.

"You're up awfully early. Usually when you come home, you sleep till noon."

Lainie's teeth clacked shut. "Usually when I come to Naples, I fly, and my body clock is three hours behind," she reminded him. Just like she always did when he mentioned how late she slept.

Her dad grunted, and Lainie found herself putting the coffeepot back. She didn't want any coffee after all. What she really wanted was to leave. Now.

"Well, I think I'll save this for later," she said brightly, wedging the bag back in the freezer between a pound of butter and a half-empty box of chopped spinach.

"Where you off to?" her father asked, pulling the Maxwell House out of the cupboard for himself.

Lainie blinked once, then again. She hadn't thought she'd run into him this morning, so hadn't thought up a story to tell. "Uh, I'm meeting a friend for breakfast and then thought I'd do a little shopping," she lied.

"Oh. Are you getting back in touch with some of your old high school friends now that your reunion is coming up?"

Now, why in the hell would her dad remember something like that? Lainie couldn't even recall telling him about the reunion in the first place. Why would he find that important enough to save in his memory banks, when she'd bet he didn't even know which college she'd attended or the name of the company she'd worked at for the last six years?

"No," she said. "This is a former colleague who just happens to be in Naples this week. On business." Wow. This lying stuff was getting easier by the minute.

"You wearing those? Better be careful you don't trip. You might break an ankle." He raised his eyebrows at the boots Lainie had left on a chair in the dining room adjacent to the kitchen.

She wondered what he'd do if she let out a bloodcurdling scream and clamped her hands to her cheeks like Edvard Munch's subject in his famous painting *The Scream*.

"I'm sure I'll be fine. I don't know what time I'll be home. I assume you're working tonight?" Lainie tugged her purse on over her shoulder and then put her boots on the floor—absently noticing that her father had had the dingy gray linoleum replaced with now-fashionable terrazzo—all the while thinking that her arrival home tonight would just happen to coincide with the beginning of her father's shift down at the restaurant.

"Yes. I'm still working the five-to-midnight shift," he answered.

Good to know. Lainie wasn't too picky about what job she'd take next, but now it had one absolute, nonnegotiable requirement—that it kept her out of the house from eight to five while her dad was at home and awake.

{ five }

Lainie leaned nonchalantly against a jacaranda tree with its Dr. Seuss-like purple flowers and tried to pretend that a) her feet weren't killing her from the half-mile walk into the touristy area of town on four-inch heels, and b) that she wasn't attempting a Jedi-like mind trick on the man sipping his Grande Chai Soy No-Foam Latte (she was just guessing—he looked like the Grande Chai Soy No-Foam Latte type) to get him to abandon his table and leave his newspaper behind. She didn't want him to leave his half-drunk coffee, however. The smells coming out of the Starbucks on Sunshine Parkway were making her drool. If the guy left his coffee . . . Well, she wasn't sure she'd be able to control herself.

It was true. She was a caffeine addict.

Fifteen years in Seattle would do that to a person.

The man's desire to linger was stronger than her fledgling

powers, though, and he just kept sipping from his cup and rustling the newspaper while Lainie continued to stand there and stare.

After another minute she finally gave up. The guy was not going to budge. And it wasn't any latent psychic tendencies that told her that, but the fact that the guy had just unwrapped a piece of iced lemon pound cake to go with his latte.

With a sigh Lainie sat down heavily on the bench next to the jacaranda tree and dabbed at the perspiration on her upper lip. In late April the highs reached into the mid- to upper-80s. She didn't mind the heat, and she'd always thought it was funny how everyone talked about how hot it was in Florida during the summer, when—in Naples, at least—it never got above the low-90s. Yeah, it was humid from about the middle of May through the end of September, but the same could be said of places like New York and Boston, and most of the Midwest, too. And at least it was never sixty-two degrees and chilly in the middle of August.

As far as she was concerned, the only thing she really didn't like about Southwest Florida was the hurricanes. Nothing anyone could do about those, though.

But for now, the weather was perfect. A light breeze blew in off the Gulf of Mexico, keeping the humidity relatively low. A few cotton-ball clouds rested in the sky, not doing anything but lazing around.

It was one of those mornings that made Lainie wonder if there was anywhere prettier on Earth than right here.

She relaxed against the worn wooden bench, thinking about what a nice picture the mostly two- and three-story, gold-colored office buildings across the street with their wrought-iron balconies and heavy planter boxes filled with bougainvillea and impatiens made. A fountain halfway down the block splashed onto the sidewalk and provided a convenient spot for people out walking their dogs to stop and chat while their pets lapped at the water. The pedestrians filling the sidewalk were a mix of tennis-shoe-clad tourists and snowbirds escaping the harsher temperatures of the Northeast, peppered in with a few size-two local socialites dripping with diamonds and platinum AmExes.

Lainie squinted against the morning sun's rays. She hated job-hunting. The whole interview thing, with the stupid questions that people thought up—especially in Seattle, where the whole Microsoft mentality and its "Why are manhole covers round?" thing had taken hold. Bad enough to be asked to list your greatest strengths and weaknesses (which the smart candidate knew to use to her advantage by giving some bullshit answer like "My greatest weakness is that I get so focused on a task that I sometimes forget to even eat. Why, one time I was working so intensely toward a deadline that my coworkers set up an IV to feed me high-calorie liquids intravenously. I am just *that* dedicated to my work." This said with the most humble smile one could possibly muster.); Lainie had no idea what sort of sick mind had come up with the idea to start asking job-seekers idiotic things that had nothing to do with the work they'd actually be doing. As far as she was concerned, the only people who needed to know why manhole covers were round were a) those in the business of manufacturing the damn things, and b) the guys who worked in the sewers.

But, whether or not she liked the process, she was going to have to do it.

If she'd been back in Seattle, there were people she could call who might be able to get her hired without having to go through the whole applications and interviews thing. Before she'd been evicted from her house, she'd thought about going that route. After she lost the house, though, something snapped inside her. Getting out of bed was too much trouble, lifting the phone a nuisance she couldn't be bothered with, and making sense of her dwindling finances became impossible.

Like always when faced with a crisis, Lainie had retreated into herself.

She hated admitting that she was vulnerable, but she had—in those early days, before she'd lost all hope—reached out to someone she had thought was a friend.

"I'm in that big house all alone. If you ever need help, you can come stay with me," her former boss, Sarah, had said after meeting Lainie for drinks one night and hearing just a portion of what Lainie was facing.

After getting the foreclosure notice from the bank, Lainie had reluctantly called Sarah to take her up on her offer. She didn't like to take advantage of her friends, but she was out of options.

She'd known that something was wrong from the very start. For one, Sarah seemed irritated that Lainie had brought her ailing fifteen-year-old cat with her. Lainie promised her that Kittycat was housebroken and that she was sure they wouldn't be there for more than a week or two at the most, but Sarah seemed put out. Lainie didn't know what Sarah had expected. She knew Lainie had a cat. What was she supposed to do? She'd had her baby since she was a kitten.

The problem, Sarah told her, was that her snooty pedigreed Himalayan with its stuck-up nose and tail-in-the-air walk—had spent the day on top of the fridge because he was annoyed at having to share his five thousand-square-foot palace with another cat. Lainie didn't know what to tell her. The bank had chosen the rare week in Seattle's history where the temperatures were soaring near the hundreds to kick her out, and Sarah's place—like most homes in western Washington—didn't have air conditioning. Lainie couldn't shut her cat up in the second-floor guest room all day. The poor thing would die within an hour.

She begged Sarah to give it one more day to see if the animals would learn to tolerate each other. Sarah reluctantly agreed . . . after closing off the upstairs so her pampered pet could at least have a peaceful night.

Which would have been fine, if only it hadn't been two-hundred-freaking-degrees up there.

Even with all the windows open and two fans blowing directly on her, Lainie thought she was going to roast. But after making sure Kittycat had plenty of water, she fell into a fitful sleep . . . only to wake at two in the morning with the dreadful feeling that something was wrong.

Unfortunately, she was right.

One of the screens on the second-story windows had come loose when Kittycat had gone roaming in the middle of the night and jumped up on the sill to take a gander outside. Both screen and cat had fallen to the rock pathway in the backyard, thirty feet below.

Her cat's brittle, arthritic bones had been crushed in the fall, and when a silently crying Lainie had rushed her to the emergency vet that night, they'd compassionately told her that it would be best for Kittycat if they ended her suffering now.

That was the night Lainie gave up hope.

Losing her husband had been frustrating, the job disappointing, the house devastating, but losing the pet she'd loved since college was more hurt than her heart could bear.

After leaving the vet's office, Lainie had spent the night at a rest area, in the backseat of her car. She'd left the top down, half-hoping that the rapists and serial killers that inhabited rest areas in all the urban legends would swoop down on her in the early-morning hours and put her out of her misery.

But no one had bothered her. Not that night, or the next. Or the next.

Lainie had no idea what had finally made her leave the rest stop. She couldn't even say how long she'd been there when the thought struck her that living in her car—even if it *was* a Mercedes—was not a lifestyle she wanted to continue. Nor could she say what had made her call her dad and tell him she was coming to Naples. All she remembered was waking up one day, watching a tired-looking family of five trudge toward the restrooms, and knowing, with absolute certainty, that she had to leave Seattle. She couldn't stand it there, not one more day.

So she'd driven back to Sarah's house in the middle of the afternoon, hauled herself up onto the garage roof, popped another loose second-story screen, taken what few belongings she had left, and driven away without looking back.

Maybe she should have stayed, asked another friend for help in finding a job or a cheap place to live. But she couldn't stand the thought of having to look into the eyes of one more person who knew what a failure her life had become.

At least here in Naples, she could hide that failure under a false image of success.

Even the job search shouldn't be *that* bad. After all, the crash of the startup company where she'd worked hadn't been her fault. And it wasn't like 50 percent of the workforce these days hadn't experienced something similar. So she might as well get on with it.

Lainie put a hand to her forehead and shaded her eyes as she looked up and down the street. Sunshine Parkway was home to ice-cream shops, cafés, boutiques, shoe stores, art galleries, real estate offices, and insurance agents—none of which had "Help Wanted" signs hanging in their windows.

No. That would be too easy. Nothing like that ever hap—

Lainie blinked.

What was that, stuck in the corner of the window of that business across the street?

Could it be . . . Lainie leaned forward and squinted hard at the black-and-white rectangular sign.

Yes. It was. The letters were faded from being exposed to the sun, but even so, she was able to read the words "Help Wanted" on the sign.

She stood up and looked both ways before crossing the street. The morning traffic was almost nonexistent; most people out this early either lived in the second- and third-stories above the businesses on this street or were staying at one of the hotels on the beach, an easy walk only a few blocks away.

Pausing for a moment outside the door, Lainie peered through the glass with "Rules of Engagement" written on it in black paint.

Hmm. What type of business was this? A dating service, maybe? Well, that was fine. Lainie didn't care, as long as it paid by the hour and didn't require her to take her clothes off.

Even that last item might be negotiable . . .

She pulled open the door and winced as a set of bells tied to the handle on the inside jangled loudly in the quiet reception area. A curly haired brunette looked up from behind the glassed-in office on the left-hand side of the room and smiled.

"Good morning," the brunette said. "Can I help you?"

Lainie took a deep breath and smiled back. "Yes, I'm here about the Help Wanted sign," she said, pointing toward the sign that could be seen through the slats of the half-open blinds.

The brunette's forehead crinkled when she frowned. She stood up and leaned out over the sliding window that separated her office from the reception area outside. "Well, I'll be darned. I never noticed that before."

Lainie swallowed her disappointment. She should have known better than to expect it to be that easy. "So, does that mean there's not a job opening?" she asked, just to be sure.

The brunette shot her an assessing look, but Lainie refused to glance away. There was nothing shameful about needing a job, right? And it wasn't like she'd come crawling in on her hands and knees. Sheesh. She wouldn't have even asked if not for the sign in the window.

Lainie stuck out her chin and clenched her fists as her sides.

"Stay here. I'll be back in a second," the woman said, then disappeared down the hall, leaving Lainie with the urge to race out the door.

But she didn't.

Instead, she focused on removing her fingernails from the palms of her hands, where they'd left small, half-moon shaped indentations in her flesh. If she didn't need the money so badly . . . Well, if she wasn't in this position, she wouldn't be here in Naples, so she might as well just stop her brain from going down that path. She was here, and she needed a job, so she'd stand here and wait for the other woman to return, just like she'd been told.

Soon she heard the murmur of voices from down the hall. Lainie looked up as the voices got louder and saw that the receptionist had returned with a short, stylishly dressed woman of indeterminate age.

"Hello," the woman said warmly, holding out one tanned hand. "I'm Lillian Bryson. Maddie here tells me you're looking for a job."

Lainie introduced herself and took Lillian's hand, then found herself being led down the hallway and into a comfortably furnished office.

"Take a seat. Can I get you something to drink?"

Lainie sat. "No, thank you. I'm fine."

"Are you sure? I just made a fresh pot of coffee."

"Coffee would be nice." Just the thought made Lainie's mouth water.

"Wonderful," Lillian said, sounding as if it were her life's mission to get everyone who entered her office to accept something to drink. She poured coffee into two mugs and asked Lainie if she wanted cream or sugar before handing the steaming cup over.

Lainie sat in the overstuffed red-upholstered chair and inhaled coffee fumes like the addict she was.

"What kind of work do you do?" Lillian asked, taking a seat in the chair next to Lainie and cradling her own cup of hot java.

"I've done a variety of jobs. Worked fast food in high school, manned the computer lab in college, but I've mostly been doing admin work for the past few years."

"Do you have a college degree?"

Lainie smiled to cover how much she hated that question. "No. I went to the University of Washington for several years"—six years to be exact—"and learned a lot about a multitude of subjects, but I never earned my degree."

Please don't ask why, Lainie prayed as she took a sip of still-too-hot coffee. The thing was, she didn't have a good reason. She just couldn't seem to stay focused enough, she supposed, to figure out a major and get her diploma. Instead, she just kept taking undergraduate courses until it became evident to everyone—including herself—that she was never going to finish. At that point she gave up and got a job at an insurance company in Seattle that nearly sucked all the life out of her before she quit. Then she moved on to the startup that finished off the job the previous one had started.

"So what brings you to Naples?" Lillian asked, and Lainie breathed a sigh of relief at being spared her most dreaded question.

"I guess I'm just at the point in my life where I need to shake things up. You know, try something new. And I have family in town, so . . ."

Lillian smiled. "So here you are."

"Yes. Here I am." Lainie couldn't help but notice the wistful tone of her voice, and she could only hope that Lillian hadn't heard it, too.

"Well," the owner of Rules of Engagement said after a pause that was neither too long nor too short. "I'm afraid that I don't have a job for you. I know I should take that Help Wanted sign out of the window—it's been there since I bought this place, and I guess I just thought it was quaint to leave it where it had been for so long. To be honest, you're the first person who's ever seen it and come in asking for a job."

Gee, wasn't she lucky?

Lainie's teeth snapped together—God, she was going to grind her teeth down to stubs if she didn't stop doing that—as she tried to swallow her humiliation. She hated making a fool of herself, hated thinking that this woman and the receptionist out front were laughing at her.

She slid her coffee cup onto a coaster on the table beside her chair and started to get up, but Lillian's next words stopped her.

"But I seem to recall the owner of the business next door mentioning something about hiring on some extra help. Would you like me to give him a call?"

Lainie clasped her hands in her lap. "I would appreciate that."

"Why don't you head on over. I'll give him a call and tell him you're on your way. It's right next door at Intrepid Investigations. Just ask for Jack."

Lainie wasn't going to wait for another invitation. If Lillian Bryson wanted to help her get a job, whatever her reasons might be, that was okay by her. "Great. Thank you," she said.

Hugging her purse to her chest, she hurried out of the office and back out into the sunshine. Next door—right where Lillian had said it would be—was Intrepid Investigations. Lainie knew she should wait out here for a few minutes, to give Lillian time to call this Jack and let him know she was coming, but . . . she couldn't.

She took a deep breath and flung open the door of Suite B.

Then her purse slid from her nerveless grasp when she spied the man sitting at a large desk across the room, holding the phone to his ear.

"Yes," he said. "She's just come in. Name's Lainie Ames, huh?" There was a pause, and then the man from the restaurant last night—Jackson Danforth III—speared Lainie with his dark eyes and said, "Isn't that interesting? I believe Ms. Ames and I have already met."

six

Jack Danforth hadn't actually seen the woman steal his credit card last night at the Ritz, but all his instincts had warned him that something was up when he returned to his table with his half sister, Kim. A quick call to the one-eight-hundred number on the back of his card confirmed Jack's suspicion: He had unwittingly treated the women at the next table to dinner.

Which he could certainly afford, but Jack kinda liked knowing his dates' names before shelling out for a good meal. So, after discovering that he'd paid for four meals instead of the two he'd planned on, Jack had put his superior investigative talents to work by stopping off at the table next to the one where the women had been sitting and asking the occupants—who he'd seen chatting with the freeloaders—if they happened to know either woman's name.

Trish Miller. That was the pretty blonde. She was a counselor at Golden Gulf High School. They didn't remember the brunette's name, but Jack figured it'd be easy enough to find out. She was Trish Miller's sister and had recently moved from Seattle to Naples.

Piece of cake, Jack had thought.

As a matter of fact, he'd been just about to start his investigation into Ms. Miller's sister's whereabouts this morning when the phone rang.

And then, who should walk into his lair but the culprit herself?

He'd like to say that he wished all his cases were that easy, but the truth was . . . they pretty much were. Mostly, he shadowed cheating spouses or ran the occasional background check for one of his few clients. Naples wasn't exactly the most exciting locale, criminally speaking.

Fortunately, he wasn't in the P.I. racket for money.

"So. Lainie Ames." Jack slowly lowered the phone from his ear and laid it on his desk, then leaned back in his chair and laced his fingers together behind his head.

She was busted and she knew it.

Jack could read the guilt in her big brown eyes as easily as if she'd been holding up a flashcard with the words *I'm a crook* written on it in bright red ink.

He was curious to find out how she was going to handle the situation, but before she could do anything but shoot a longing glance at the door behind her, his half brother-slash-receptionist-slash-junior-P.I.-in-training burst forth from the lunchroom and announced, "I've got it!"

Both Jack and Lainie turned to look at him.

"Listen to this!" Duncan said, holding a piece of yellow lined paper with both hands as he read:

Spouse got you down? Marriage in a rut?
Think your wife's cheating?
Feel it in your gut?

Sir, don't despair. Don't get so depressed.
Intrepid can help you,
Find whatever she's repressed.

So give us a call. Do it right now.
Our hidden cameras will catch
That unfaithful cow.

Duncan smiled expectantly, but Jack didn't say anything for a long moment. Finally he cleared his throat and nodded. "That was great."

"Do you think the last line was a little, er, harsh?" Lainie asked.

Now it was Duncan and Jack's turn to stare at Lainie.

"Never been cheated on, huh?" Duncan shook his head sadly, as if that were a bad thing.

Lainie's cheeks grew small patches of red. "Actually, I have," she admitted. "You're right. It's not harsh at all. I don't suppose you could change it to 'unfaithful *bitch*'?"

Duncan frowned down at the piece of paper in his hands, a twin set of lines appearing between his brows. "Well, it wouldn't rhyme," he mumbled, as if deep in contemplation. Then, without another word, he turned and walked back into the lunchroom.

"That should keep him busy for another hour." As he spoke, Jack stood up and walked to the front of the office, where, with a theatrical flourish, he pulled out his keys, locked the front door, turned to Lainie, and added, "Which is good. It'll give us plenty of time to talk."

* * *

Lainie gulped. Not just swallowed, but actually gulped like some cartoon character. The phrase *Nowhere to run to, baby. Nowhere to hide* popped into her head as she took a step backward and bumped into the edge of an empty chair.

She eased herself down into the seat. She didn't know why she felt safer that way, but she did. Maybe because her back was now covered.

The way he was stalking her made her believe that Jack Danforth knew about last night. If so, why didn't he just come out and accuse her of stealing his credit card? Maybe he liked seeing her squirm. Maybe he'd been the type of kid who pulled the wings off of butterflies and fried ants on the sidewalk using a magnifying glass.

She was beginning to understand how those ants felt.

Lainie dabbed at the sweat on her upper lip. "Is it hot in here or is it just me?" she asked with a shaky laugh, then wished she'd just kept her mouth shut when Jack gave her a slow once-over, his gaze traveling from the heels of her fuck-me boots up to the last strand of hair on her head, pausing at several sites of interest on the way.

"It's you," he answered, his voice low and gravelly.

Lainie was mesmerized as he pulled a straight-backed chair over, turned it around, and straddled the seat, resting his tanned forearms along the top. The movement was smooth, like he'd practiced it a thousand times to get it just right.

And, boy, did he get it right.

She gulped again, trying not to notice the way his thighs were pressed against the back of the chair, cradling it in the vee of his crotch.

Lainie shook her head to clear it. She was not here to think about thighs or crotches or—oh, my God—how much she envied that chair. She was here for a job. And if he knew about her petty thievery and wanted his money back . . . Well, good luck getting it.

Though the intriguing—and somewhat troubling—thought occurred to her that she could suggest that if he wanted payment, she'd be open to discussing, um, alternative forms of compensation. Of course, when one usually retired a debt, one didn't enjoy it as much as Lainie suspected she'd enjoy the "alternative form of compensation" she was envisioning right now.

Suddenly much warmer than she'd been even a moment before, Lainie fanned her heated face with one hand. "I'm here about a job. Lillian Bryson from next door thought you might have something for me. I'm very hardworking. And reliable," she assured him. Well, except for the occasional bout of theft. Lainie had the grace to blush.

"Uh-huh," Jack said.

"I'm organized, too. And good with computers." Lainie placed both her feet flat on the ground and leaned forward earnestly. "I can automate just about anything. Invoices to clients, vendor payment processing, mass mailings, monthly reports. You name it."

Jack cocked his head and half-lowered his eyelids so Lainie couldn't tell what he was thinking. Not that she was much of an expert at reading people's expressions to begin with.

But since he hadn't thrown her out yet, she figured she might as well continue her pitch.

"I've also done some database work, though I'm no data architect. Oh, and I've designed dozens of brochures. I even wrote the copy." That just about covered everything Lainie had been responsible for at her last job, where they were always understaffed and you could be designing an accounting system one day and unclogging the toilets the next.

"Uh-huh," Jack said again.

Lainie tried not to fidget when he didn't say anything more. Instead, she pasted a serene smile on her face and pretended she wasn't uncomfortable with the lengthening silence.

"So why do you want to work here?" he asked finally.

She released the breath she'd been holding and decided to tell the truth for a change. "Well," she said, "I could hand you the usual interview-speak and say that I've heard great things about your company and am excited about the opportunities here, but, frankly, I just moved back to Naples and I've never heard of Intrepid Investigations and I . . . I . . ." Lainie's voice trailed off and she had to swallow before looking Jack straight in the eyes and admitting, "I need the money. Which isn't to say that I don't have a lot to offer an employer," she hastened to add. "I just . . . Well, I'd pretty much take any job that was offered to me right now."

She held Jack's steady gaze as long as she could, but by the end of her pitiful speech, she dropped her head and was busy studying the worn traffic pattern on the beige rug at her feet.

Jack pushed back his chair and stood up, but Lainie refused to look at him, even when the toes of his brown loafers stopped less than six inches from hers.

"All right," he said. "You've got the job."

Slowly Lainie raised her chin, her eyes taking him in from his loafers to his well-worn jeans, to the flowered shirt that screamed "Tommy Bahama, 100-percent silk," up to the smattering of dark hair peeking through the unbuttoned neck of his shirt and stopping at his unreadable brown eyes.

Why? She wanted to ask, but didn't have the guts.

She needed this too badly—needed the money, the daily escape from her father, the hope that maybe, just maybe, her life wasn't a total disaster, that she could hide from everyone the awful failure she'd become, fix it before anyone ever found out. Lainie closed her eyes and took a deep breath.

"Thank you," she whispered. "This means so—"

"Eureka! I've got it!" the young man who had interrupted them before shouted from the doorway of the lunchroom, the rumpled piece of paper once again rustling as he held it in front of him and read:

> *Spouse got you down? Marriage in a rut?*
> *Think your wife's cheating?*
> *Feel it in your gut?*
>
> *Sir, don't despair. Don't get so depressed.*
> *Intrepid can help you,*
> *Find whatever she's repressed.*
>
> *So give us a call. Listen to our pitch.*
> *Our hidden cameras will catch*
> *That unfaithful bitch.*

Beside her, Jack snorted, and Lainie, feeling as if the black cloud that had been hovering over her head for the past twelve months had broken up just enough to let a weak ray of sunshine through, started to laugh. Then, because it seemed an appropriate thing to do, she started to clap.

"Bravo," she said as the young man took a bow.

Jack rolled his eyes. "Don't encourage him," he groused as he made his way back to his desk and sat down heavily in his leather chair.

But Lainie's good mood couldn't be squelched. "I thought it was great. What's it for?" she asked, ignoring Jack's warning.

Jack interrupted before the other man could answer. "This is my brother, Duncan. He's on a *Moonlighting* kick. Last month, it was *Magnum, P.I.*—that's why I'm wearing this stupid flowered shirt; he bought me a dozen of the damn things, and they must be mating in the closet at night because now I seem to have a hundred and can't find any of my regular shirts anymore. Before *Magnum*, it was *The Maltese Falcon.* I just got him to stop saying, 'I don't mind a reasonable amount of trouble' and laughing maniacally like Peter Lorre, so please, I beg of you, do not encourage him. The last thing I need is him dragging one of his sisters in here dressed in a kooky Agnes DiPesto getup to answer the phone with one of his ridiculous rhymes."

"You wound me," Duncan said, laying one hand over his heart.

"Stop it," Jack warned.

"Why? What's he doing?" Lainie asked.

"Herbert Viola. He's doing Herbert Viola."

"What are you talking about?" Lainie asked.

"Agnes DiPesto's love interest. He became a regular in the third season," Duncan answered.

"Well, Jack, if it's any consolation, I don't think Duncan's rhyme will work," Lainie said by way of a peace offering.

"Yeah? Why's that?" he asked.

"Because," she answered, with a conspiratorial wink at Jack's brother. "*Moonlighting* wasn't on cable. *Unfaithful bitch* would never have made it past the network censors."

{ seven }

Lainie let herself into her dad's house using the extra key Trish had given her last night. Her day, after leaving Intrepid Investigations, had been long and boring. She refused to come back here before Dad's shift started. Another run-in with him would have had her running for a drink, and she didn't have the money to invest in becoming an alcoholic. So with nothing else to do, she'd spent hours sitting on benches, watching the tourists go by.

"Makes me wish I'd taken up a hobby," she muttered to herself as she pulled the key from the front door and pushed it shut behind her.

Hobbies had never been her thing. She'd started working full-time during her junior year in high school and, once she got a taste of how good it felt to be needed, had increased her workload until there wasn't room for anything else in her life. She had often joked that she'd love to find a hobby . . . as long as it paid well.

And she'd admit that her attitude toward sports in general was tainted by her own lack of athletic ability, but, really, what was the point of it all? Golf, in particular, irritated her. It was so inefficient. If you wanted the ball in the hole, why didn't you just pick it up and put it there? Why waste hours whacking at it with a little stick? And don't try to tell her that it was about the exercise. She knew all about golf carts. Not to mention golf bags specially designed to keep a six-pack cold on the course.

Lainie went into the bedroom she was using—hard to think of it as "her" room when she'd only lived here for a short while so many years ago—and tossed her purse down on the top of the dresser. It was 5:30 according to the digital clock on the nightstand beside the bed.

5:30.

Lainie sighed and slumped down on the bed.

It would be at least six hours before she fell asleep. What was she going to do with all that time?

She leaned down to take off her boots, unzipping each one slowly and slipping them off. Then she lined them up neatly on the floor next to the nearest closet door and looked back at the clock.

5:32.

It was going to be a long night.

Well, she could kill at least half an hour making herself something to eat. She hadn't had a bite all day.

She was halfway to the kitchen when her dad's phone rang. Lainie frowned at the black cordless sitting in its charger next to the chocolate-brown leather—Dad always did have a thing for leather—sofa in the living room.

Should she get it?

It couldn't possibly be for her.

Or could it? Maybe Jack had gotten a really interesting case and wanted his newest employee to get started on a major investigation. Wouldn't that be cool? Not even her first official day on the job and already she'd be cracking high-profile cases.

"Hello," Lainie answered, eager for the opportunity to race off to some glamorous mansion where a betrayed young wife is found standing over the bloody bodies of her dead husband and his handsome gay lover or the backroom of a seedy bar where some local muckety-muck is rumored to be meeting with a Colombian drug supplier or . . .

"Hey, Lainie. It's Trish."

So much for glamour and excitement.

Lainie dropped into the recliner and tried not to sound too disappointed as she returned her half sister's greeting.

They chitchatted about their respective days—Lainie didn't mention that she'd gotten a job; she didn't want to make it sound like she'd been desperate—and then Trish got down to the reason why she'd called.

"Listen," she said. "I have some friends coming over in a little while for an impromptu girls' night in. Alan's working late, the kids won't be home for a few hours. It's gonna be a beautiful evening, and we thought we'd all just hang out by the pool and work on our tans. You up for it? It's not formal or anything. Everyone will bring a bottle of wine, I'll open up a couple bags of chips. It'll be fun."

Lainie contemplated the empty hours looming ahead and wished that she could say yes. She'd *love* to go hang out at Trish's. The only problem was, she didn't have a bottle of wine to contribute, and she couldn't afford to go buy one. She doubted Dad had one lying around that she could "borrow." He didn't drink wine.

At least, she didn't think he did.

But maybe she could go empty-handed. She hated to do it, but Trish probably wouldn't mind, right?

Her sister's next words killed that thought.

"The only thing is, I'm low on Chardonnay and—you know how it is when you're getting ready for last-minute company— I'm running around like a chicken with my head cut off. I don't have time to stop at the market. Would you mind going for me? I'll pay you back, of course."

And what could she say to that?

Can I get the money first because I'm flat busted?

Lainie slumped in her seat. "Gee, Trish, I'm sorry, but I already have other plans," she lied. Then, to make sure Trish didn't ask her to run to the store for her before she headed out, she added another lie on top of the first one. "As a matter of fact, I've got to run. An old friend of mine is picking me up in a few minutes"—which would explain why Lainie's car would still be sitting in the driveway if Trish happened to glance down the road—"and we're going to dinner at a restaurant on Vanderbilt Beach."

"Oh." Trish sounded genuinely disappointed, but Lainie wasn't sure if that was because she'd have to go get her own wine or because Lainie couldn't come to her party.

"Keep me in mind for next time, though," Lainie added, since she really would have loved to go.

"Sure. Of course," Trish said. "Well, I guess I'd better let you go."

"Have fun tonight."

"Yeah, you, too."

When her sister hung up, Lainie sat and stared at the phone in her hand for a long time. Something was niggling at her, some half-formed thought in her head that she instinctively knew was of vital importance but that she couldn't quite grasp. But the more she tried to figure it out, the wispier the edges of it became, until, finally, it disappeared completely.

With a sigh, she returned the phone to its charger.

Well, too bad. If someone wanted to tell her something, they were going to have to send down a stronger message.

Lainie's stomach grumbled just then and she couldn't help but smile. Maybe that was all it was—hunger pangs—and not some cosmic being trying to get something through her thick skull.

She got up and went into her dad's kitchen, which he'd remodeled three or four years ago. He hadn't gone high-end, which was no surprise. It wasn't like he made a lot as a cook—not a chef, but a *cook*—at the restaurant where he'd worked for nearly seventeen years. Besides, why bother stuffing the place with a commercial-grade stove, Sub-Zero fridge, or anodized aluminum pots hanging from a rack above the small, square island? Dad always said he got enough of cooking for other people at work. At home it was every man—or woman—for himself. It had been that way since Lainie was a kid, and, from the look of the passable-but-by-no-means-professional remodel he'd done, nothing had changed.

Fortunately, though, Dad kept his pantry well stocked.

Lainie was at that point on the hungriness scale that everything she spied made her drool. First, it was going to be a can of tomato soup and maybe a grilled cheese sandwich. Then Lainie opened the fridge. Ooh. Butternut squash and mascarpone cheese. She'd made this fabulous ravioli once with butternut squash, mascarpone cheese, and sage. It was one of the best things she'd ever eaten. But no, that would take too much time.

She opened the freezer.

Steak.

And not just steak, but gen-u-whine bacon-wrapped filet mignon.

Lainie swallowed.

Yes. She'd defrost it slowly in the microwave so it wouldn't start to cook. Then she'd season it with some garlic salt and pepper and pan-fry it in a little bit of butter.

Oh yeah. And she'd sauté some mushrooms. She loved sautéed mushrooms, and hadn't she seen some gorgeous portabellas in the produce basket near the sink?

In minutes Lainie had her steak defrosting and her mushrooms sizzling on the indoor grill, which she had missed noticing earlier because it was hiding beneath a metal cover. She inhaled the smoky, musty smell of the mushrooms, and put a hand to her stomach to stop it from rumbling.

"You'll be happy I made you wait," she told it, thinking about how fabulous that steak was going to taste right off the grill, the bacon crispy, the meat smooth and—

Damn!

There was Trish, coming up the driveway to their father's house.

Lainie jerked open the door of the microwave to make it stop and then glared helplessly at the mushrooms frying on the grill. She offed the heat and grabbed the plate she'd set on the counter for her steak.

There was no time to bother with finding tongs or something else to pull the mushrooms off the grill, so Lainie grabbed them with her fingers, wincing as they burned her flesh.

Then, with the sound of her sister's key sliding into the door, Lainie made a dash for it.

The door swung inward, blocking the view of the side of the house where she was staying, so if she could just make it to the hallway outside her bedroom, she'd be home free.

The doorknob rattled.

Lainie hugged the plate of mushrooms to her chest and leaped into the hallway.

The front door opened.

And Lainie pressed herself against the wall, her heart beating a thousand times a second.

Trish stepped into the entryway and stopped, her nose assaulted by an unexpected smell.

Lainie wasn't about to throw away that opportunity. She slunk silently backward, toward the open bedroom door. One more step. Then another.

Trish was on the move, heading—thank God—toward the kitchen.

Lainie hurried to the half-open closet door, pausing only for a second to grab her purse, which was sitting on top of the dresser in plain view of anyone who might just happen to poke her nose into the room. And Lainie knew there was no way she was lucky enough that Trish wouldn't do just that.

So she bundled herself—purse and half-cooked mushrooms and all—into the closet, scooting as far back into the darkness as she could. She got herself settled behind a hanging garment bag and did her best to close the folding door with her toe. There had been several hanging items and boxes in the closet that she'd pushed to this side to make room for her things last night. She hadn't bothered looking at any of them, assuming it was stuff her dad didn't have room for in his closet.

With nothing to do but sit and wait for Trish to get whatever she had come for and then leave, Lainie soon found herself wondering what was in the garment bag. Maybe her dad had a baby blue tux with a white ruffled shirt tucked away from the 1970s. If so, he could probably sell it for a small fortune at a vintage clothing shop.

The idea of her tall, beer-bellied dad trying to squeeze into a too-small tux from decades gone by made her smile. Somewhere in their boxes of disorganized family pictures, she seemed to recall a photo of him wearing that exact thing.

She set her plate down in the corner of the closet and twisted the garment bag so that its see-through side was facing her. It was hard to see much in the darkened closet, but she was certain whatever was in there was not baby blue.

No. It looked more like . . . red. A deep, rich red that was closer to burgundy than tomato-red.

Hmm, she wondered. What could it be?

But her curiosity was shoved aside when she heard footsteps coming down the hall. She let go of the garment bag, then winced when the hanger scraped the metal pole.

The footsteps stopped at the entrance to her bedroom.

"Lainie? Are you here?" Trish asked loudly.

Lainie held her breath.

"Lainie?" Trish said again.

Lainie was starting to feel light-headed, but didn't dare breathe. There was no way she could explain why she was hiding in the closet, no lie she could come up with, even if she had days to think up something instead of mere seconds.

If Trish flung open the closet door, Lainie would have no choice but to come clean.

So she sat there and did her best to make it seem as if she did not exist.

Finally the footsteps started again—this time heading back down the hall. Even then, Lainie didn't fill her lungs with much-needed oxygen. Not until she heard Trish mutter, "What *is* that smell?" just before the front door opened and then closed again did she risk taking a breath.

Whew. That had been close.

Lainie remained seated on the closet floor for a few more minutes to make sure that Trish wasn't coming back before she pushed at the hinged door and scooted out into the bedroom.

Starvation warred with fear as she thought about what to do

next. Cooking a steak would require more time in the kitchen, and what if Trish headed back over? No. She couldn't chance it. She was going to have to settle for a bowl of cereal that she could bring back to her room to be near her hiding spot, just in case.

Cautiously Lainie peered out into the hallway. Dusty sunlight filtered in through the gray glass sidelight next to the front door and lit a rectangle on the terrazzo floor of the living room. The house was quiet, as only an empty house could be.

Lainie kept one eye on the front door as she hurried into the kitchen, feeling like a secret agent. Her mission: capture the cereal and return safely to headquarters.

In minutes her mission was accomplished.

She sat on her bed, balancing a sweating bowl of shredded wheat with two scoops of sugar and skim milk in her lap, her ears attuned to alert her body if they heard anything besides the ordinary creaks and clicks of a forty-something-year-old house. When she was done eating, she set the empty bowl on the top of her dresser, vowing to return it to the kitchen later.

But then the thought that cockroaches might swarm the sticky goo left in the bowl during the night made her decide that risking another trip to the kitchen was worth it. When that, too, was accomplished successfully, she found herself sitting on her bed again, looking dismally at the clock on the nightstand and wondering if the numbers were stuck.

It was only 6:13.

Now what could she do?

Lainie looked around the room for some ideas, her gaze landing on the closet door, which was still crooked open.

Ah, the mystery of the garment bag. She could kill—What? Maybe five minutes?—checking that out.

She pulled the hanging bag from the closet, unzipping it as she transferred it to the bed. Only, when the clothes inside spilled out, all the blood drained from her face.

Memories—humiliating memories that she had long tried to forget—flooded her.

Why had her father saved these? Was it just an innocent mistake, or was this his way of reminding her that she was the same screwup now as she had been all those years ago?

{ eight }

Lainie stared at the red dress on the bed, with its thin spaghetti straps and smattering of beads on the skirt, the label still attached to the fabric under the right armpit. That dress had cost her twenty-five hours of working minimum wage at McDonald's back then. No way would she have asked her dad to help pitch in for the cost. If she had, he would have asked her if she even had a date, to which she would have had to reply, "No. At least not yet."

But when she'd seen the dress, two months before the prom, she'd had to have it. In a rare burst of optimism, she'd convinced herself that—surely—*someone* would ask her to the dance. She wasn't stupid. She knew that the one boy she'd had a crush on since moving to Naples the year before wouldn't be that someone, but she figured that maybe that geeky Mike from earth science or Chad from her computer lab might do it. Yeah, she was a nerd . . . and a little chubby . . . but they weren't exactly Homecoming Court material, either.

As the big day drew nearer, Lainie felt her optimism slipping away.

Finally, one week before prom night, she gave up. Because she couldn't stand the thought of sitting home that night, she'd volunteered to work. When one of her coworkers who had graduated the year before found out she hadn't been asked to the prom, he offered to take her, but Lainie politely refused. She figured it would be better to pretend that she'd rather be working than to be someone's pity date.

She was wrong.

She should have gone, pity date or not. She had regretted that decision for the last fifteen years, and seeing her sad, never-been-worn prom dress now brought the entire miserable fiasco of that night racing back.

It had been relatively quiet at McDonald's that night, which gave Lainie lots of time to think about the fact that she was wearing a ketchup-stained blue uniform while the other girls her age were dressed in frothy ball gowns. She was sweeping the floor; the other girls were being swept around the dance floor. But she was doing okay—really, she was—until ten minutes till midnight. The fast-food restaurant closed at twelve, and she was counting down the seconds until they locked the doors. She couldn't wait to be alone to indulge in some serious self-pity with the leftover soft-serve ice cream and a gallon of caramel topping, but fate apparently had other plans for her.

At 11:50 p.m., the front doors opened and a rowdy, laughing crowd of people bustled in—a rowdy, laughing crowd of Lainie's classmates, who had tired of the relative tameness of the prom and were out looking for some real fun. She could smell the liquor on their breath as they swarmed the front counter. The guys in the grill grumbled. All of the work they'd done to clean things up before they closed was for naught. Their spotless grills would soon be sizzling with a dozen Quarter Pounder patties and a handful of Big Macs.

After dumping a box of fries in the hot oil of the French fry machine, Lainie started taking orders, blinking back tears as the pretty girls with their expensive dresses ordered burgers, fries, ice-cream cones, and Diet Cokes. Finally, after what seemed like an eternity but was really only about eight minutes, all the orders were done and the lobby quieted down again. The prom-goers had congregated outside, taking over the playground. Lainie was glad that they weren't inside where she could see them and was just about to start locking up when it happened.

The doors opened again and Blaine Harper—the love of her pathetic teenage life—walked in. She'd had a crush on Blaine since moving to Naples in her junior year.

It had started in biology when they'd been paired up to dissect a cat. Lainie knew she couldn't do it, but she also knew that her dad wouldn't give her a note to excuse her from the task. It wasn't until her senior year that she got bold enough to start writing her own notes. She didn't know why it hadn't occurred to her earlier that the school staff wasn't exactly running a high-security operation there. It wasn't like they were going to send the notes in for handwriting analysis.

But she digressed. The short version of her falling for Blaine went something like this:

Lainie: "I can't cut open this cat."
Blaine: "Whatever. I'll do it by myself."
Lainie: "Thank you."

Blaine (to his best friend Tim): "Dude, there's a half-eaten bird in this cat's gut."

Yeah, it was love at first sight.

When Blaine walked into the restaurant on prom night, Lainie thought she was dreaming. He was alone and walking right toward her. Her silly romantic brain conjured up an image of him going down on one knee, reaching for her hand, and telling her what a fool he had been not to ask her to the prom. Of course, if Blaine had gotten down on his knee, she wouldn't have been able to see him over the counter. Which only showed how impractical fantasies really are.

Instead, Blaine looked deep into Lainie's eyes, licked his luscious, full lips . . . and ordered two McChicken sandwiches, two large fries, a vanilla shake, and a Diet Coke.

Then Shay Monroe—perfect skin, rich parents, head cheerleader Shay Monroe—came around the corner from where the bathrooms were and sidled up to Blaine. When Blaine put an arm around her shoulders and kissed her ear, Lainie's heart squeezed so tight she thought she was going to die right there.

No such luck, though. Instead, she got to endure a full five minutes of the Shay-Blaine lovefest while the chicken for their sandwiches was bubbling away in the hot oil. She watched them from beside the shake machine, wishing they would just go join the others outside, but they didn't. They stood in front of the counter, Shay looking gorgeous in a light pink dress that showed lots of cleavage and swished when she moved, and Blaine—Lainie's Blaine—in a black tuxedo with a daring black-and-pink polka dotted cummerbund.

As if frozen to the side of the shake machine, Lainie watched

Blaine tenderly wrap a lock of Shay's hair around his finger and give it a tug. Shay tilted her head back and let Blaine kiss her neck, then her shoulders, and then bury his face in her ample breasts.

Lainie looked down at her own chest. The new lower-cut uniforms her store had gone to actually looked pretty good on the girls with boobs. But they weren't as flattering on the then-flat-chested Lainie.

When the McChicken sandwiches were pushed over the top of the heating bin, Lainie bolted from her spot in her haste to get Blaine and Shay out of the restaurant as quickly as possible.

That was when disaster struck.

Later, after Lainie had rerun the whole nightmarish episode through her mind for the thousandth time, she realized that she must have spilled some ice on the floor when she was getting Shay's soda because her foot hit a puddle of water and she started to slip. She reached out to grab something to stop her fall, only her hand hit the lever that started the shake machine. It made this awful farting sound—it did that sometimes when air got in the line— and spewed strawberry shake mix all over her as she fell to the floor.

Lainie could hear Blaine and Shay laughing at her and, of course, all the rest of the kids chose that exact moment to come in from the playground outside. The only thing that could have made it worse would have been if her clothes had suddenly fallen off.

Fortunately, that didn't happen. At least, Lainie didn't think it did. Truthfully, though, she wasn't exactly certain what happened next. All she remembered was shutting out the sound of everyone's laughter as she ran into the walk-in fridge in the back of the restaurant. She sat down on a pickle bucket and bawled until she felt empty inside. When she came out, everyone was gone.

And she was certain that when she'd gotten home that night, she'd thrown that dress—the one now lying on her bed next to a clean and pressed McDonald's uniform from fifteen years ago—into the trash.

{nine}

What did private investigators usually wear?

Lainie pawed through her clothes, studiously ignoring the garment bag she'd shoved to the far side of the closet the night before. She had enough to think about this morning without dredging up bad memories from so long ago.

Hell, if she wanted to dredge up bad memories, she could pick a few more recent ones. No need to go back fifteen years when fifteen days was far enough.

She shook her head and sighed so loudly she was surprised it didn't wake her father, who was sleeping in his room on the other side of the house.

Back to the clothes issue.

Yesterday, Jack had been wearing jeans and an aloha shirt, while Duncan had on inexpensive-looking gray pinstriped slacks and a white, button-down shirt with the sleeves rolled up on his skinny forearms.

Lainie decided on a black skirt, knee-high black boots with a more reasonable heel than the ones she'd worn yesterday, and a red blouse with a square-cut neckline that was neither too conservative nor too revealing. She was going for hip and a little kick-ass, like Jennifer Garner in *Alias*, but not quite so sexy. This wasn't Hollywood, after all.

Though South Florida wasn't exactly known for its frumpy clothing, either. Skimpy, yes. Frumpy, no.

But this was work, and Lainie wanted to be taken seriously, so she'd keep the cleavage she'd have sold her soul for back in high school to a minimum.

She grabbed her black Coach purse and the sandwich and grapes she'd tossed into a bag for lunch earlier and let herself out of the house and into the cool morning air. After shooting a longing glance toward her convertible, she resolutely turned and started walking to town.

She'd be surprised if the car would even start, much less make it a mile without running out of gas.

Fortunately, the summer heat had not yet descended upon them. It was a fallacy that it was always hot in Florida. This time of year it actually cooled off at night, sometimes even getting down to the low seventies, which, okay, wasn't exactly cold, but wasn't blistering, either. Which meant that her walk into town—which would have been miserable in the middle of August—was actually quite pleasant at this time of year.

She arrived at the Intrepid Investigations office at a quarter to nine and was surprised to find the front door still locked. Cupping her hands around her eyes, she pressed her nose to the window and peered in, but there were no signs of life from inside the building.

Huh.

Somewhat put-out, Lainie stood frowning at the front door.

Yes, the office hours painted in white on the door said 9:00 a.m. to 5:00 p.m., Monday through Friday.

But she'd just come from Seattle, where *nobody* worked 9 to 5.

The Pacific Northwest was a workaholic's wet dream.

Lainie wasn't exactly sure why. Maybe it was the weather, which was so dreary much of the time that you might as well be indoors working. Or maybe it had started with Microsoft, where every hour you put in over the standard eight was rewarded with a hundred thousand dollars in stock options—at least in the beginning, before reality and the high-tech industry's stock prices collided. It could also have been "The Boeing Effect." The aviation giant that employed a huge number of people in western Washington was best known locally for its cyclical layoffs. Maybe the whole work-ninety-hours-a-week-and-maybe-you-can-keep-your-job-in-the-next-downcycle mindset had started the trend.

Whatever the reason, Seattle's attitude toward work was very different from that in South Florida, where the warm, sunny weather and beautiful beaches made every day (well, until the summer, when it got so hot that you wanted to be inside with the AC running full blast) a candidate for vacation.

Not that Floridians were lazy. Work just wasn't the entire focus of their lives.

Still, Lainie was more than a little relieved to see Jack step out of a black BMW sedan, his keys jangling in his hand as he headed toward the office.

What could she say? She'd only been here for one full day. Her transition from workaholic to well-rounded-person had not begun yet.

"Good morning," she said, eager to get inside and start her first day of work.

Jack dropped his keys and turned to look at her. His eyes were bloodshot, his hair sticking up as if he hadn't brushed it after rolling out of bed. He bent down to retrieve his keychain.

"You startled me," he said, juggling keys, a cup of coffee, and a magazine as he attempted to open the front door.

Lainie would have offered to do it, but she didn't want to seem smug.

"Sorry."

Jack grunted in response, then surprised her by holding the door open for her and waving her inside. He dumped his stuff on top of the desk he'd been sitting behind yesterday morning when she'd first come to see him about a job.

Lainie stood near the counter that ran half the width of the room, awkwardly shifting her weight from one foot to the other. The office reminded her of something you'd see if you went to renew your driver's license in a town with a population of less than ten thousand. There was a small table and two vinyl-seated chrome chairs off to the side—obviously what was supposed to pass for a waiting room—and a counter which someone could stand behind and tonelessly call out, "Number twenty-six. Twenty-six. Anyone have twenty-six?" to a crowd of one. Beyond the counter were four desks with fake wooden tops and metal sides that only went halfway down to the floor.

Several four-drawer metal filing cabinets stood along the far wall, with the requisite ficus in a terra-cotta pot between the filing cabinets and a door leading to what Lainie assumed was the lunchroom.

The carpet was your standard-issue beige indoor-outdoor stuff that could be purchased for ninety-nine cents a square foot. Installed. Including the pad.

The one word that came to mind to sum up Lainie's impression was *shabby*.

But Jack had the look of a guy with money, so maybe the business was making a fortune and he just didn't see the need to invest in making the place look glamorous.

She gave the room another once-over.

Yeah. That had to be it.

On second thought, the place had character. No cherry-wood, brass-and-glass office would say, "We're desperate for your business, so you know we'll work hard for you," like this did.

"So where can I put my lunch?" Lainie asked, when it became obvious that Jack wasn't going to give her the official welcome tour.

He had opened his top drawer and pulled out a value-size bottle of aspirin and was sitting there, just staring at it, as though willing it to open.

"Oh. Sorry. There's a fridge in the lunchroom," he said, waving toward the doorway Lainie had spotted earlier.

"Thanks." Lainie took pity on him and stopped in front of his desk to pop the top on his adult-proof bottle of aspirin before taking her lunch to the fridge in the equally unspectacular kitchen with its yellow vinyl flooring, card table and folding chairs, and coffeemaker that had once been white but was now stained to the color of hot chocolate.

That done, Lainie walked back into the main room. It appeared that two out of the four desks were unoccupied, so she picked the one across from Jack, nearest the front door.

"All right if I take this one?" she asked. She pulled open the top drawer and was pleased to find that it was empty—and clean.

"Sure," Jack mumbled.

She would have asked him if he'd had a late night, but she didn't want to seem overly nosy. Better to keep things on a strictly professional level until she had a better sense of the office politics.

Lainie stowed her purse in the bottom left-hand drawer and then, out of habit, powered on the computer sitting on her desk. She didn't know if she'd need it or not on her first day, but she felt better with its blueish light bathing her face.

One quick trip to the kitchen-supply room to gather some office supplies and back to her desk to arrange them neatly in her desk drawers, and she was all out of things to do.

"Okay," she said. "I'm ready to get started."

Jack stared at her as if he had no idea what she was talking about. Wow. He must have one hell of a hangover.

He cleared his throat. "Right. Started. Um. Give me about fifteen minutes, will you?"

Lainie arranged five blue pens on her desk so that all the caps lined up. "Sure," she said, though she had no idea what to do with herself for the next fifteen minutes. Maybe she could . . . she didn't know. Surf the Net for P.I. stuff, maybe?

She turned to the computer screen and frowned. It hadn't even asked for her user name and password. That wasn't good. Wasn't their network secured?

She took one of the pens out of the lineup and pulled off the cap. Then, at the top of a clean yellow legal pad, she wrote "TO DO" in capital letters. First item: Secure Intrepid's data from outsiders. Shouldn't be too hard. She'd learned how to do that back in high school.

When she looked up again, she realized that her new boss had disappeared. So, with nothing better to do, Lainie turned back to her computer and got to work.

$\mathcal{J}$ack sank down in the overstuffed red chair in Lillian Bryson's office and put his throbbing forehead in his hands. "Why do I keep doing this?" he asked.

Across from him, Lillian made the soothing sort of sound one would make to a toddler with a boo-boo on his knee. "Now, now, Jack," she said. "Everything will turn out all right. You'll see."

Jack glared at Lillian through his splayed fingers. She was up to her matchmaking tricks again, he could tell. That's why she'd sent Elaine (aka Lainie) Ames over to him yesterday. She couldn't help it. He'd known that for years. And he did have to admire her persistence. In the last three years alone she'd sent no fewer than a hundred women to Intrepid Investigations on the pretense of finding a job or hiring a P.I. to tail their cheating boyfriends or help get their kitties out of trees or whatever lame excuse Lillian could come up with to get Jack hooked up.

Like he needed her help.

He'd never told her this, but he actually kept a tally of the hopefuls Lillian sent to him. He'd been about to scratch another line on his list yesterday morning when in walked Lainie Ames.

And Jack, who always managed to turn Lillian's hopefuls in a new direction—away from him—found himself, for the first time, going along with her plan.

Why was Lainie different?

Well, for one thing, none of the other women Lillian ever sent him had stolen his credit card the night before asking him for a job.

Jack was a sucker for a good mystery.

He was also a sucker for the downtrodden, and the instant he'd seen the look in Lainie Ames's eyes when she realized who he was, he was hooked like a grouper on a forty-pound test line.

But now he was stuck with yet another employee he didn't need. Some days he felt like half the city of Naples was on his payroll. Virtually his entire family was on the Jack Danforth dole. Aside from his half brother Duncan, who worked (and Jack used that term very loosely) with him at Intrepid, there was half sister

#1 (Lisa)—his "housekeeper," who'd never cleaned a toilet a day in her life; half sister #2 (Kim)—his "cook," who couldn't boil an egg and who kept his fridge stocked with nothing but beer and Cheesecake Factory Snickers Bar cheesecakes; half sister #3 (Amy)—his "dog walker," who didn't seem to realize that HE DIDN'T HAVE A DOG; and half brother #3 (Trent)—who at least had the decency not to pretend he served a useful purpose as he collected his paycheck on the first and fifteenth of every month.

The only one on his father's side of the family who *didn't* collect a regular salary from him was the first half sibling he'd found out about at fifteen, also named Jackson Danforth III (it was a long story), who refused to ask for a cent of the enormous trust that Jack inherited from their grandparents. Nope, Jackson didn't want one cent.

He wanted the entire freaking thing.

But the courts had ruled that their grandparents had the right to give their money to anyone they chose. Hell, they could have given the entire hundred million to the Loyal Order of the Labrador as long as it could be proved that they were of sound mind. Which they had been. And they'd also been adamant that not one penny of their money should go to their "worthless" (their word) son—and the only way they could be sure that wouldn't happen after they died was to hand the purse strings over to Jack, who doled the money out to his half brothers and half sisters (quite liberally, he might add) as he saw fit.

If Jackson wasn't such an absolute turd of a human being, Jack might have felt sorry for him. He *did* feel sorry for all the rest of J.D. II's kids, which was why he allowed himself to be taken advantage of when they came calling for cash, why he let them hang out at his house whenever they needed to, and why he had stayed up too late last night when Trent had come around, nearly suicidal after yet another fight with their father, which led to yet another confrontation between Jack and J.D. and the Naples P.D. in the early hours of this morning, which made Jack feel like shit-on-toast, which was why he couldn't think straight when his newest charity case wanted him to make up something for her to do.

Jack closed his eyes and groaned.

He did not need the hassle this morning.

"Can't you have her revamp your filing system?" Lillian suggested. "Automate your billings? Get your Rolodex into Outlook?"

Jack splayed his fingers again. "Our filing system works fine. We're lucky to have two clients at any given time, so billings aren't exactly a problem. And my BlackBerry synchs with my contacts in Outlook."

"Hmm," Lillian said, frowning. Then her face cleared. "Well, you'll think of something."

"Gee, thanks for the help," Jack muttered. So much for hoping Lillian could get him out of the mess she'd landed him in.

There was nothing more he could do. His fifteen minutes were up. He was going to have to go over there and tell Lainie the truth— they really didn't need her. Intrepid Investigations had been dying when Jack had bought it from the father of a high-school friend seven years ago, and, to be quite honest, he hadn't put much effort into trying to keep it alive.

He'd never expected the place to roll in the cash. There just wasn't a lot of demand for investigative services in Naples these days. But owning the business gave him a nice tax write-off . . . and it provided at least one of his relatives with a job.

He snorted as he pushed open the door to the office, expecting to find Lainie filing her nails or cleaning out her purse or eating her lunch out of sheer boredom. Instead, she was frowning at her computer screen, a book that looked like it could have competed with *War and Peace* in the length department lying open on her desk.

"What are you doing?" Jack asked.

Lainie didn't look up from her computer. "Securing your network," she answered. "Right now your data could be accessed by any fifteen-year-old computer geek with wireless access and a few extra minutes on his hands."

Curious despite himself, Jack leaned his arms on the counter that overlooked the desk Lainie had staked out and studied her. He'd been so preoccupied with his trouble with his half brother and his lack of sleep this morning that he hadn't noticed much beyond the fact that she smelled really good when she leaned over to open his bottle of aspirin before sashaying into the lunchroom in those mind-blowing knee-high boots.

Jack cleared his throat. "Uh, we don't have a lot of data on our network," he confessed.

"Yeah, I noticed. That's the next thing on my list," Lainie answered absently, her fingers flying over the keyboard as she continued frowning at her computer screen.

"Excuse me?" Okay, he was glad he didn't have to make up things for her to do, but what was she up to?

"Automation. That's the key to not getting overwhelmed in business these days," Lainie said.

Yeah, and a lack of clients doesn't hurt, either, Jack thought.

"I've already checked to make sure software is available for private-investigations firms. Obviously, I haven't evaluated anything yet." She laughed and, because it seemed that it was expected of him, Jack laughed, too. "And, of course, I'm sure you'll want to be in on the development of vendor requirements and software selection criteria. We'll need to start with an end-user needs analysis, then I can move on from there."

Hmm. Jack wondered what foreign language this was that Lainie was speaking.

"End-user needs analysis?" he asked.

"Uh-huh. Oh, and you needn't worry that I'll keep scalability in mind during the process. Once Intrepid Investigations goes global, you'll be glad I did."

{ten}

Global? Hell, they were barely *local*.

Jack was about to admit that business wasn't exactly booming when Duncan made his appearance. As he had been yesterday, his younger brother was wearing a cheap suit that looked like it had been around since the eighties. Jack sighed and shook his head. Duncan changed his wardrobe with every new P.I. show he became obsessed with.

"Don't you have something from this century you could wear?" Jack asked.

"Do I? Do bears bear? Do bees be?" Duncan spread his arms wide, his joy at finding a way to work in a line from *Moonlighting* first thing in the morning as evident as the grin on his face.

Jack sighed again. "I can't wait until you get to *Remington Steele*. At least Pierce Brosnan was well-dressed."

"Bruce Willis was, too, if I remember correctly," Lainie said, finally looking up from her computer.

Right. She had to pick *this* conversation to engage in?

"I know, but I'm not the lead in this show. Jack is. I'm stuck doing the supporting roles, and all the unnamed employees who limboed with David Addison and hated Maddie Hayes wore cheap suits," Duncan said with a shrug as he ignored Jack and walked to his desk at the far end of the office.

"Do you really think they hated her?" Lainie asked, chewing on the end of her pen.

"Well, she did fire them all several times in the first couple of seasons," Duncan answered. "But I agree that they'd softened toward her by the episode when—"

"Stop!" Jack shouted. "You, back to work." He pointed at Lainie, who had turned and was looking at him with wide eyes. He couldn't take it. Duncan was bad enough. He didn't need *both* of them assaulting him with this *Moonlighting* crap. He glared at Duncan. "And you. Isn't it time for your morning coffee run?"

Duncan shrugged out of his cheap tan suit jacket and rolled up his sleeves. "Sheesh. What's up with you this morning?" he asked.

Jack pinched the bridge of his nose between his thumb and forefinger. "Sorry. I didn't get a lot of sleep last night."

"Yeah, I heard." Duncan visibly deflated, his slim shoulders hunching inward as he slumped over his desk.

Jack wanted to tell him to cheer up. Just because their dad was a jerk didn't mean they were destined to become one, themselves.

But he knew the best way to cheer Duncan up was to get back to their normal routine. Which meant Jack would have to endure another eight hours of random Bruce Willisisms from his P.I.-show-obsessed half brother.

"So, tell me, Duncan," Jack said as he resignedly headed to his own desk. "*Do* bears bear?"

Duncan blinked his watery brown eyes a couple of times. Then he looked at Jack and mouthed, "Thanks," before answering, "Yeah, I think they do."

"Good. Well, I don't know if bees be, but I do know that I need some caffeine in the worst way. And I think it's your turn to endure the Starbucks line. Would you get me a Grande latte with an extra shot of espresso?" Jack pulled a ten-dollar bill out of his wallet and handed it to Duncan, then turned to Lainie. "Do you want anything? It's my treat."

Lainie had been watching them with interest, but, for some reason, once they started talking about coffee, she had shifted uncomfortably in her seat and gone back to staring at her computer. "No, thanks," she mumbled.

Duncan raised his eyebrows, but Jack didn't know what was up, so he just shrugged.

By the time Duncan returned with their lattes and assorted breakfast pastries, Jack had forgotten all about Lainie's odd behavior.

Which was probably why he didn't notice the longing look she sent his half-full cup an hour later when he absently tossed it in the trash. How was he to know that our caffeine-deprived heroine had abstained from joining in the morning coffee pool because she feared that when her turn to buy came around, she'd have to confess to her new coworkers that she didn't have the money to chip in.

Time to call it a day."

Jack leaned back, yawned, and stretched his arms above his head.

Lainie made the mistake of looking up from her software analysis just as his black T-shirt cleared the waistband of his jeans, expos-ing smooth tanned skin and a smattering of dark hair just below his navel.

"Lainie, did you hear me?" Jack asked.

She had to look away so he wouldn't see the raw lust she was cer-tain was shining in her eyes. "Uh, I could keep working. Really. I don't mind."

"Naw, there's no need for that. We've survived for seven years without network security or file management software. I imagine we can make it one more day," Jack said.

Easy for him to joke about it. He didn't have nothing but an empty house waiting for him at the end of the day.

Or did he?

Lainie tilted her head and looked at him. She'd seen no evidence of a wife—no wedding ring or framed photos on his desk of a happy couple on their wedding day—but the idea that Jack didn't have a significant other was ludicrous. He was handsome, owned his own business, seemed to be financially well off, had a good sense of hu-mor, and appeared to be pretty nice.

So what was wrong with him?

Did he bite the heads off of small children or rodents? Have a secret fetish for women's panties?

"Why are you looking at me like that?" Jack asked.

Lainie struggled to wipe the grin off of her face. "Like what?" she answered, blinking innocently.

"Like you're wondering what I've got on under my clothes," he said.

Wow. He was good at that mind-reading thing.

"I'm not wondering anything of the sort," Lainie lied.

This was Duncan's cue to poke his head into the office from the kitchen, where he'd been hiding for the last half hour. "Hey, you guys are getting good at this *Moonlighting* stuff. That's just the sort of thing Maddie and David would have said."

Jack sighed. "We weren't acting."

"Could've fooled me," Duncan said.

"A gnat with a lobotomy could fool you," Lainie deadpanned. Okay, so when Duncan and Jack had gone out to lunch, she'd spent some time on the Internet and had stumbled upon some of the highlights from the popular 1980s TV show. She'd been waiting to use the "gnat with a lobotomy" line since she'd first read it.

Jack and Duncan both stared at her for a long moment, then Duncan walked over and patted her on the back. "Let's keep her," he said to Jack, as if she were a stray cat who had wondered in off the streets. Which, in a way, she guessed she was.

Lainie grinned. She couldn't help it. For the first time in months, she felt like someone actually liked her. Even if it was just Jack's goofy little brother, with his cheap suit and P.I.-show obsession, it still felt good to be appreciated.

She held up a bright yellow file folder. "I printed off a bunch of stuff from the fan sites and imdb.com. Some of it's really funny." She said this last to Jack, who rolled his eyes in return.

"Did you get to the 'Taming of the Shrew' episode?" Duncan asked excitedly.

Lainie opened her file and flipped through several pages before finding what she was looking for. " 'Pray sir, yea sir, I daresay I did say.' "

Duncan hooted and clapped, then leaned in to read over her shoulder. " 'Yea sir, you do say you did say?' "

" 'Yea, I say, but why do you pray? Do not gainsay what I say that we may make headway. I foray this way that I may be home ere midday.' "

" 'Hooray for this day and the words that you say and forgive my display, but I have something to say.' "

" 'Then without further delay, I say, fire away!' " Lainie finished with a laugh.

"What the hell did you two just say?" With a pained shake of his head, Jack ran a hand through his hair, making the short bits up front stand on end.

"I'm not sure," Lainie admitted.

"Yeah, I think that would be funnier in context," Duncan agreed. "Hey, maybe we could—"

"No! Absolutely not," Jack interrupted.

"What?" Duncan and Lainie asked at the same time.

"No costumes. No 'Taming of the Shrew' as played by the cast of *Moonlighting*. There will be no Shakespeare performed in this office. Do you two understand?"

Duncan and Lainie looked at each other and shrugged. "Okay," they answered in unison.

"I mean it," Jack warned.

"We get it, Maddie. Er, I mean Jack," Lainie said apologetically when Jack glared at her.

"Fine," he said.

"Fine," Lainie repeated.

"Good," Duncan said.

"Good," Jack said, then slammed his top desk drawer shut with more force than necessary. "I can't believe it. You two have got me doing it now," he muttered.

Lainie caught Duncan's thumbs-up from behind Jack's back.

"I saw that," Jack grumbled. Then he held the door open and waved to the sidewalk outside. "You can continue your effort to drive me insane tomorrow. Now get out there and enjoy this lovely evening."

Lainie felt her happiness deflate like a balloon losing its helium. She *liked* work. She had always liked work. And if some tiny voice inside asked if she were only using it to fill up the emptiness in the rest of her life, Lainie ignored it. Work made her feel important and fulfilled. What was so wrong with that?

Well, fine. Jack could insist that she leave the office at five o'clock, but that didn't mean he could stop her from working.

She grabbed a clean legal pad from her desk and tucked it under her arm along with her purse. Tonight, she could start writing up her ideas for a new marketing plan. She knew that Duncan and Jack had to be working on cases, but . . . Well, Duncan sure spent an inordinate amount of time hanging out in the kitchen or going for coffee runs or snickering at his computer screen while typing furiously. Maybe if he had a few more cases, all that goofing off would stop.

Though she had to admit that his *Moonlighting* shtick was kind of funny . . .

"Do bears bear? Do bees be?" She chuckled under her breath as she walked past Jack.

"Good night," Jack said firmly as he locked the front door behind them.

"Night," Lainie answered with an absent wave as she started off down the sidewalk.

"Hey." Jack's voice stopped her.

Lainie turned around. "Yes?"

"Where's your car?"

"It's so beautiful this time of year, I figured I might as well walk. Good exercise, you know?" Lainie said. Yeah, like she needed it. She'd lost twenty pounds since her ordeal began, and it suddenly occurred to her that she weighed less now than she had in high school.

Jack frowned. "You sure? I'd be happy to give you a ride home."

Lainie hastened to decline his offer. "No. Really, I like to walk." She could only imagine what he'd think of her father's shabby house. Most likely, he'd think she was exactly what she was—a girl from the wrong side of the proverbial tracks. She'd worked long and hard not to be that person anymore, and she wasn't about to let Jack see that side of her.

No, once she got her first paycheck, she'd be sure to drive to work in her fancy convertible and prove to him that she was somebody. Until then, he didn't need to know anything more about her than what she chose to let him see.

With another backward wave, she turned and started walking home. Jack let her go, but he couldn't help but think her feet were going to be killing her by the time she got to her father's house half a mile away. At least, that's where he assumed she was staying. She'd left her address blank on the application he'd asked her to fill out, and he assumed it was because she didn't have a permanent place to live in town yet. But because he was nosy—a good trait in a private investigator, Jack thought—he had driven by Lainie's sister's house, and then staked out her dad's place long enough to get a trace run on the license plate number of the cute silver Mercedes sitting out front.

So, he knew she had a car, and he knew where she lived. The only thing Jack couldn't figure out was how come it was so easy for him to tell that Lainie was lying about wanting to walk home.

{ eleven }

Network secured? Check.

Software implementation plan completed? Check.

Billing system automated? Check.

Advertising budget approved? Check.

Cases rolling in? Uncheck.

Lainie shoved a hand through her hair and stared, bleary-eyed, at her computer screen. She had the infrastructure in place, but the phones were not ringing off the hook. As a matter of fact, they weren't ringing at all.

Which might not be a bad thing since Duncan's latest rhyme ended with "two-timing prick."

But she didn't understand it. For a week—including taking her notepads to the beach on the weekend to avoid being home with her dad all day—Lainie had made plans, automated routine tasks, bought new software to help them run their business.

So where was all the business?

Jack wouldn't have hired her if there wasn't plenty of work to do. No sane businessperson overstaffed their company on purpose. That only led to layoffs, wrongful termination lawsuits, and expensive severance packages.

She had to be missing something.

It was about time she figured out what it was.

"Jack, could I have a minute of your time?" she asked.

"Take two, they're small," Jack muttered, without looking up from the latest issue of *Spy/P.I. Weekly*.

"No, I'm serious," she said.

Jack closed his magazine. "Sure, Lainie. What's up?"

"Well, I've been here for a week now, and I'm starting to wonder . . ."

"Wonder what?"

"Where are the clients? The phone calls? The cases?"

"Clients? Phone calls? Cases?" Jack repeated.

"Yeah."

"Um. We have clients. We have phone calls. We have cases."

"Where?" Lainie asked, glancing around the office at the empty waiting room, the silent telephones, and the more-than-half-empty filing cabinets.

"Where what?" Jack had wondered how long it would take for Lainie to figure out that he didn't need her, that Intrepid Investigations couldn't support one employee, much less three.

Sadly, the only cases here at Intrepid were *charity* cases.

But Jack didn't think Lainie would appreciate being considered a charity case, so he did the only thing he could think of. He stalled.

"You know *where what*," Lainie answered, giving him a stop-screwing-around look.

"Is that grammatically correct? 'You know where what'?" More stalling, while Jack tried to figure out what to say next.

"Come on, Jack. What's going on here? You don't care about grammar any more than I care about"—she fished around for a minute before finishing—"navel lint."

Jack raised his eyebrows. "You don't care about navel lint? Haven't you heard about proper belly-button care? You wouldn't want it to get infected. Things could get nasty."

"Jack," Lainie protested, and he knew the jig was up. He was all out of stalling techniques.

"Okay. Sorry. Uh, it's funny that you mention our clients today. We, um, actually have a new one coming in tomorrow morning. See, it's right here on my calendar." Jack held his BlackBerry up so Lainie could see it, knowing full well that the screen was too small for her to read from where she was sitting.

He *did* have an appointment tomorrow morning. With his half sister Lisa. Who was coming to ask for money, he was sure.

But Lainie didn't need to know that.

She had worked so hard over the past week that he hated to disappoint her by telling her that her efforts were completely wasted on this business. She seemed so . . . earnest, so worried that her contribution would make a difference to the bottom line (her words, not his). Jack had tried to tell her a couple of times that she should relax, have some fun with the job (while not going too far to encourage Duncan and his idiocy), but it was obvious that she took her position seriously, and there was nothing Jack could do to dissuade her.

He had known it would come to this.

Now he was going to have to tell her that there were no cases, no clients, no phone calls, and nothing that she could do was going to change that.

Jack opened his mouth to tell her the truth, but stopped when Lainie said, "That's great. My first case! I'm so excited. I mean, I *do* get to take part in it, right? You don't mind if I help?"

And what could he do? Crush her hopes like a swatter smashing a bug?

She was smiling at him with such unbridled enthusiasm, her brown eyes taking on a sparkle that Jack hadn't seen in them before. Not for the first time, he was struck by how pretty she was when she smiled, and he realized that he couldn't do anything that would make that smile disappear.

She'd find out soon enough that the client wasn't really a client. There wasn't much he could do to stop the inevitable. After all, it wasn't like he could start manufacturing cases out of thin—

Jack blinked.

No, he couldn't . . .

Or could he?

{ twelve }

So you know what you're supposed to do, right?" Jack asked.

Lisa—who was twenty-five now, but who Jack had trouble thinking of as anything but the cute little three-year-old he'd first met when he was fifteen—sighed loudly as she turned toward him in the passenger seat of his car.

"Yes, Jack, I think can remember the instructions you gave me less than two minutes ago."

"Sorry, Lise. It's the blond hair. Makes me underestimate your massive intelligence," Jack joked.

His half sister—who had gone blond this week—glared at him from under her lashes. "Very funny. Look, I get it. Go in, make up some story about wanting you to track down my cheating husband at some party at the country club tonight that I just happen to know you got an invitation to a month ago, and then hand you this wad of cash that you've just given to me."

"Perfect."

"What if I decide to just keep the money?" Lisa asked.

"Then you'll never get another dime out of me," Jack said.

"That's pretty harsh." Lisa didn't sound like she believed he'd really do it.

Jack wasn't sure he really would, either.

Yeah, he'd been the oldest kid that Jackson Danforth II had abandoned, but he wasn't the only one. And, not that it was any consolation, but at least he'd inherited more money than he could ever spend in one lifetime. His half siblings got nothing from their connection with J.D. other than a boatload of heartache.

"I can be mean when I have to," Jack said.

"Uh-huh."

Jack ignored her. "I sent Duncan to Miami on an errand this morning, so you don't have to worry about him blowing your cover. Just . . . you know . . . try to make the story sound good." He waved his hand as if giving some sort of vague stage direction and swallowed a premonition of doom when a sly smile crept over Lisa's mouth.

"I can do that. Anything else?" she asked.

"No. Just get it over with as soon as possible. And be vague if Lainie asks you any questions," Jack added.

"Sure." Lisa shrugged one slim shoulder. She'd do almost anything for what Jack was paying her. He was one of those rare good guys who'd give his last dime to save an ailing family member. Fortunately for her, though, he wasn't anywhere near to shelling out his last dime, and she wasn't above taking advantage of him when the need arose. Not that she thought she was that clever. Jack knew exactly what he was doing, and she had no doubt that if he thought she was getting into trouble by having things handed to her so easily, he'd stop the cash flow without feeling an ounce of remorse.

Which was why Lisa made sure she never got into trouble—or, at least none that her oldest half brother ever found out about.

With another sly smile, she patted her purse, where Jack's check for five thousand dollars was nestled safely next to her Gold AmEx and forty-dollar Lancôme lipstick.

Too bad everyone couldn't have a brother like Jack.

"See you in fifteen minutes," she said, pushing open the heavy door of Jack's Beemer so his new employee wouldn't see her getting out of his car. Briefly she wondered what Jack was up to with all of this, but the thought only lingered for about two seconds before she moved on to more important things—like whether any of her friends were up for a trip to the Keys now that her funds had been replenished . . .

Lainie was so excited about the prospect of meeting her very first client that she arrived at the office nearly half an hour early the next morning. Since Jack refused to give her a key—"I suspect you'll never leave this place if I do," he had said when she'd broached the subject—she had nothing else to do but wait. And pace.

She couldn't wait to try out the new software. You entered the data and—bam!—it set up a client contact sheet, a follow-up record, and an entry in their time-and-expense billing system. Lainie was dying to see if it worked as well as it had during the test phase.

Had she mentioned how much she *loved* automation?

She often looked back on her life and wished that she'd stuck with computer science, as she'd planned to do when she started at the University of Washington. Fifteen years ago she'd have been at the exact right place at the exact right time to make a killing on the computer boom. Instead, she'd dithered, changing her major so many times that she'd lost sight of the goal and had dropped out. A couple of jobs later, and she was back in the right place . . . just in time to watch the bottom drop out of every startup in town. Her company had actually managed to cling to life longer than most others, mostly by asking their employees to sacrifice portions of their salaries so they wouldn't go under. And, because all of them could look around and see the riches of the Microsoft millionaires, they remained blinded by their visions of wealth years longer than they should have.

Lainie shook her head to clear it of unpleasant memories.

All of that was past now. She had a new life to build, in a new town and a new industry. She was going to let the past go, move on, and prove to herself and everyone else that she had what it took to succeed.

She had the drive, the talent, the—

"Hey, Lainie, you want a cappuccino? The barista messed up and made me an extra one this morning."

Her mouth watered as she looked up to find Duncan bearing down on her with a brown paper cupholder in his hand.

She had the drive and the talent, but she was running low on caffeine.

"Um, sure. As long as it's an extra," she added. It wouldn't count against her if Duncan hadn't actually paid for it, right? She wouldn't be obligated to buy the next round in return. Right?

Lainie swallowed.

"Yep. Have at it." Duncan held the tray out to her and Lainie forced herself not to snatch the cup like a rabid squirrel after a toasted nut.

"Thanks," she said, sucking in the aroma of the drink.

They waited in companionable silence for Jack to pull up, and

Lainie was too preoccupied with her coffee to notice Jack's frown as he hauled himself out of his car.

"What are you doing here? I thought you were going to Miami," he said, sounding decidedly unfriendly this morning.

"Well, good morning to you, too," Lainie muttered.

"There was a bad accident on the interstate this morning, so I figured I'd give it a few hours to get cleared up. But I could leave now if you want." Duncan shot Jack a kicked-puppy look.

"No. I don't want you to get stuck in traffic." Jack sighed and seemed to be searching for something over Duncan's shoulder, but there was nothing there when Lainie turned to look. "Maybe you could go get some coffee," he suggested.

Duncan held out the paper tray he was holding. "I already did."

Jack pulled open the office door and Lainie could have sworn she heard him mumble "Of course you did" under his breath as she walked past.

Then, before Duncan even had time to shrug out of his hideous blue suit jacket, Jack said, "Can I have a word with you?"

And Lainie just managed not to say, "Take a dozen. There's plenty to go around."

Shaking her head at the ease with which she had settled into this banter, Lainie pulled open the bottom drawer of her desk and dropped her purse inside. Jack grabbed Duncan by the elbow and was leading him to the kitchen for a chat, but they'd only made it a few steps when a stunning blonde of about five-foot-ten pushed open the office door, paused dramatically to take a draw on her cigarette, blew the smoke out in a cloud, and then announced, "I think my husband is cheating on me, the dirty rat. But in order to twist his balls in a knot and feed them to him on a platter, I need pictures, and lots of them. Are you up for the job?"

The effect was ruined when Duncan said, "Lisa?" and then

squealed as if someone had pinched him, which made the woman gasp and start choking on her cigarette smoke.

"Would you get her some water?" Jack asked, directing the question to Lainie and ignoring the fact that he was closer to the kitchen than she was.

"Sure," Lainie said, her brow creasing as she moved to do what Jack had asked.

Something was going on here, but she had no idea what it was. As she got a shiny blue coffee cup out of the cupboard (she'd ordered nice new ones with the Intrepid Investigations logo on them and they'd just come in yesterday), she could hear the frantic whispering going on out in the office, like the skittering feet of mice in the attic.

When she had filled the cup from the water cooler, she hovered near the doorway of the kitchen, hoping to overhear what was being said. Holding the cup with one hand, Lainie leaned forward and brushed the hair away from her right ear . . . and nearly jumped out of her boots when Jack reached around the doorframe and took the cup from her nerveless hand.

"Thanks," he said with a wink that let her know that he knew she was eavesdropping. Or at least *trying* to.

"You're welcome." Lainie smoothed her hands down over her black skirt and stepped out of the kitchen as if nothing had happened. Out of the corner of her eye, she noticed that Duncan was doing his best to hide behind his computer monitor, his normally pale skin a ruddy color.

Hmm. What was up with that?

She forgot all about Duncan and his odd skin tone when Jack slid a hand beneath her elbow and guided her smoothly over to his desk. She felt her own skin prickle at the contact, her nerve endings instantly aware of even his slightest touch.

"I'm Jack Danforth and this is my associate, Lainie Ames," Jack said, thankfully unaware of the effect his touch was having on her.

"Lisa Sprick." The statuesque blonde held out her hand, knuckles up, as if she expected Jack to kiss them.

Jack deftly turned her hand and gave her a firm handshake.

Duncan made a strange noise as if he were being strangled, but when Lainie turned to look at him, he was back hiding behind his computer, so she couldn't tell what was going on. Ignoring him, she, too, shook Mrs. Sprick's hand and then waved at the chairs in front of Jack's desk, indicating that they should sit.

"So, would you like to tell us about your case?" Jack asked.

"Yes. It's about my husband. Bob. Bob Sprick."

Duncan made that noise again, and Jack cleared his throat, presumably, Lainie thought, to warn Duncan to be quiet. Didn't he realize they had a client here? A real, honest-to-goodness client?

She turned her attention back to Mrs. Sprick.

"Go on."

"Well, like I said before, I think he's cheating on me. He's not paying attention to my *needs* anymore. You're a woman. You know what I mean," she said to Lainie, reaching out to pat Lainie's hand with her own perfectly manicured one.

Lainie coughed, feeling the heat creep into her cheeks. "Um. Yes. Sure," she said. She was *not* going to look at Jack while they discussed a woman's *needs*. No way.

"But I'm not just going to lie back and let him stick it to me like this." Mrs. Sprick sounded outraged. "I've got our six children to think about here. What about their futures? Doesn't Bob care about that?"

"Six children?" Lainie squeaked. The poor thing. And she looked so young.

"Six children?" Jack repeated, shooting their client an unreadable look through his dark lashes.

"Okay, not six. There's just the one, but it feels like six some days. You know what I mean," she said, again patting Lainie on the hand.

"Uh, no, I don't. I don't have any kids."

"That's too bad. Children are such a blessing." Lisa Sprick smiled a beatific smile, and Lainie gasped as Duncan fell out of his chair with a loud thud.

"Excuse me. I've got to . . . run," he said, crawling out from under his desk, his face so red that Lainie feared for his health. Then he flew out the front door as if he'd been shot from a giant slingshot.

Lainie shook her head. What was wrong with him this morning?

"And you want us to follow your husband, is that right? Try to get some pictures? Didn't you mention something about a party this evening? At the country club? Where you suspect your husband has arranged a tryst with his paramour?"

"His pair of what?"

Looking frustrated, Jack rubbed his left temple. "His paramour. His girlfriend," he explained.

"Oh. Yes," Mrs. Sprick answered.

"And you brought the money to pay us our retainer. Five hundred dollars, is that correct?"

"Well, yes, but—"

"Good," Jack interrupted. "I'll just take down your contact information and you can be on your way."

Lainie shot Jack a quizzical look. Why was he rushing their client? It wasn't like they had anything more pressing to do, and it didn't seem like good customer service to shove clients out the door.

But maybe this was just something they did in the P.I. business.

Lainie shrugged. She'd ask Jack about it after Mrs. Sprick left. Until then, she'd have to sit back and let him take the lead.

{ thirteen }

What had he been thinking?

As five o'clock approached, the throbbing in Jack's temples increased until he felt like his brains were going to explode out his ears. This was the sort of thing that happened when you acted on impulse. You got bamboozled by little sisters with sick senses of humor—Bob Sprick indeed—who shot your good intentions all to hell.

What was that saying again? The road to hell is paved with good intentions?

Yeah. Hell. That's exactly where Jack would end up if Lainie found out that this case was nothing but one big joke.

This was what he got for trying to be nice. He should know better by now. Wasn't there another convenient saying for that, too?

Maybe it should be that nice guys ended up on the road to hell. Or being roadkill on Hell's Highway. Yeah. That was more like it.

But there was nothing he could do about it now, other than to go along with Lisa's story and head out to the country club. Who knew? Maybe everything would turn out all right after all. If nothing else, the food would be halfway decent. And the booze was free.

And it was all for a good cause—Save the Manatees, he thought it was, though after a while, they all kind of ran together in his head. It could be Save the Panthers, or Save the Turtles, or Save the Florida Residents Who Had Not Yet Succumbed to Plastic Surgery. He'd be sure to get a receipt for his donation when the night was over, which would make his accountant very happy.

First, though, he had to go home and get changed into appropriate cocktail party attire.

"Are you sure you don't want me to pick you up?" he asked Lainie as she set her purse on top of her desk.

Her gaze shifted to the left before she answered. "No, I'll meet you there. That way, if one of us sees Mr. Sprick leaving and can't find the other, we'll have a way to follow him."

A logical answer, and if Jack hadn't felt in his gut that she wasn't telling the truth, he might actually give her points for being so thorough. But other than confronting her about why she was lying, he didn't know what else to say, so he just told her to meet him in the country club parking lot at seven and they'd take it from there.

"Oh, and give me your cell number, just in case," he said, grabbing a Post-it note to scribble down the number.

Lainie paused by the front door and, had her back not been to him, Jack was sure he would have seen her gaze shift left again as she answered, "I dropped it in my dad's pool the other night and I'm waiting on a replacement. So for now, I'm afraid I'm a bit out of touch."

Jack tapped the end of his pen on his desk. O-kay. He was certain there was some explanation that would tie all these mysteries

up, but he sure as hell couldn't figure out what it was. "You can
just go down and get a new one at the Sprint store down the street.
Feel free to expense it. You need a cell phone on this job."

"Great. Thanks," Lainie mumbled absently as she left the office.
And if Jack watched her a bit too intensely before she disappeared
from view, Lainie was too preoccupied thinking about tonight's case
to notice. She was so excited to be going on her first stakeout that she
nearly skipped home in anticipation.

Finally she was getting to do some real private investigative
work! She was even going undercover as Jack's date. Not that anyone
would believe that Jack would ask her out if they knew who she really was. She'd spent all afternoon making up a history for herself—
a phony education at a private school in California, a family that was
heavily into almonds and oranges on the West Coast. And just in
case anyone had spotted her at Intrepid Investigations, some lame
story about her mom being an old college friend of Jack's mother and
how Lainie had used that connection to get a job with him here in
Naples. Just as a lark. Not that she needed the money, you see. This
last said with a roll of the eyes and a chuckle that would prove to
whatever socialite she was chatting with that she was above having
to actually earn a living.

She'd been surprised at Jack's reaction to her story, though.

"Why can't we just say you're my date?" he had asked after she'd
finished typing up all the details of her phony past and given him a
copy so that they'd be able to keep their stories straight.

Lainie had burst out laughing. "You're kidding, right?"

Jack looked at her as if she'd lost her mind. "No."

"No one would ever believe that you'd ask me out. Not as me.
I'm an employee," she'd patiently explained.

"What's wrong with that?"

"Nothing. But it's not like I have anything you'd want. I mean, you know, as a potential mate." Lainie suddenly felt very uncomfortable with this conversation. "Look, Jack, I just don't think—"

"That's okay, you look good," Jack interrupted with a grin that made Lainie's heart stop.

God, he was cute when he— No. Stop right there. Jack Danforth was out of her league. Hell, they weren't even playing the same sport. On the same continent.

Lainie shook her head to clear it. "Jack, focus. This story lends credibility to my cover. I think it's important that we stick to it."

"Okay," Jack said without further ado.

"Okay?"

Jack shrugged. "Fine."

"Fine."

And that was that. Lainie had gone back to setting up their accounting program to automatically create a profit-and-loss statement and Jack went back to . . . whatever it was Jack did all day.

Lainie turned into her father's neighborhood and fluffed her hair up off the nape of her neck. It was starting to get warmer in the afternoons. Thank God she'd have her first paycheck soon so she could start driving to work every day.

Which reminded her . . . She had no idea how she was going to get to the country club tonight. It was too far to walk, especially in high heels.

But could she count on the Mercedes to get her there and back without running out of gas?

Lainie chewed the inside of her cheek as she let herself into her father's house with her key.

This was what she got for being too proud to let Jack see where she lived. She was certain he already guessed that they didn't exactly move in the same social circles. She didn't need him staring at the proof of how far apart they really were.

Funny, but when she'd been at the top of her game—when she'd owned her nice house and had money to pay her bills and take vacations—where she'd come from had ceased to be important. It was almost as if that wasn't her past, like it was as unreal as the story she'd made up about Jack's fictitious date tonight. She wished it were that easy to rewrite her history now.

If only she could do that . . . Ah, but then where would she start? Would it be enough to rewind the past back to before she'd married Ted? No, she'd have to go further back. Before the doomed job she'd taken at that startup? No, further. Changing her college major? No. Not going to her prom? No. Not moving for the fifth time since her mother's death? No. To her conception?

Lainie closed her eyes for just a second and let the cool air coming from the vent in the living room ceiling wash over her.

Yes. Finally she'd come to the root of her problems.

Her mom had been so unhappy being a wife and mother that she'd killed herself. And her father? Well, he was better now, but for the first few years after her mom had died, he hadn't wasted any opportunity to let her know that he hadn't planned on having children and that he didn't appreciate being saddled with her.

He'd probably hoped her mother would leave him and take Lainie with her, just like Trish's mom had done.

A nice, clean break. He'd send a check every month, but he'd make sure to let Lainie's mom know that Lainie was *her* problem and that he was going above and beyond the call of duty by helping to pay for her mistake.

Lainie forced herself to open her eyes and unclench her hands.

"Enough," she whispered to herself. When would she learn that memory lane was peppered with land mines?

She was done thinking like a victim. It was time to get proactive.

Which meant she needed to think of a way to get to the country club tonight. But how? She couldn't afford a cab and, even if she took one there, she knew Jack well enough by now to know that he'd insist on driving her home after the party was over. So she had to drive herself.

She could ask Trish if she could borrow her car, but then what excuse would she give her sister about why she couldn't take the convertible?

Lainie peered out the kitchen window. Nope, not a cloud in the sky. She couldn't use the weather as an excuse.

Which left her where?

Nowhere.

Lainie sighed. If only she were a magician. Then she could wave her magic wand and—voilà!—create a gallon of gasoline out of thin air.

She leaned her elbows on the counter next to the sink and dropped her chin into her hands, trying to come up with a plan. But it was hard to think with the kid across the street revving up the engine of his father's leaf blower.

Typical teenager, Lainie thought, shaking her head as he held on to his pants with one hand and struggled to hold the blower with the other. Why the hell couldn't they buy pants that fit around their skinny little waists? Was it that this generation of boys had penises so enormous that they wouldn't fit in pants with crotches that didn't hang down to their knees?

Lainie rolled her eyes heavenward and then burst out with laughter when the leaf blower slipped out of the boy's grasp. Instinctively he let go of his pants in order to catch the blower and ended up tripping as his jeans slid down to his ankles, giving the entire neighborhood a nice view of his SpongeBob briefs when he, the leaf blower, and his pants all fell to the lawn.

Wiping tears of mirth from her eyes, Lainie turned away from the window and then gasped when she heard the leaf blower's motor die.

That was it! Her dad was sure to have *something* in his garage that ran on gasoline. If she was lucky—she didn't hold out much hope on this one, but she wasn't a complete pessimist, either—maybe he'd even have a spare gas can . . . with gas in it!

Lainie hurried out into the garage and hit the overhead light. The garage was cluttered, but not dirty, and she picked her way through the various bicycles that hadn't been used in years, assorted power tools, and miscellaneous small appliances, searching for anything that might be gasoline-powered.

Her heart leaped when she spied a red plastic gas can near the front of the garage, and then plummeted back to its normal position when she picked it up and realized that it was empty.

Well, that was fine. Good ol' Dad had a lawnmower. She opened up the tank and sniffed, then grinned when she discovered that it had plenty of gas.

Woo-hoo. She was on her way! Now all she had to do was to figure out how to get the gas from the mower into her car. It was way too heavy to pick up and try to pour the flammable liquid from one tank to the other.

Lainie scratched the side of her head as she looked around the crowded garage for inspiration. When she spied a length of green garden hose, she got an idea. She'd once spent the holidays with a college friend from eastern Washington whose parents owned a farm. One morning—so early that Lainie wasn't even sure it *was* morning—they'd gone out to set the irrigation hoses. It wasn't all that difficult once Lainie's friend had showed her how. What you did was to hold your hand over the metal, S-shaped hose and try to create a vacuum to pull the water up and over the lip of the irrigation ditch and get it flowing into the field. If the hand trick didn't work, you could also try sucking on the hose, but you had to get your timing just right or you'd end up with a mouthful of not-so-tasty ditchwater.

Surely she hadn't lost the knack for it. It had to be like riding a bicycle—one of those skills you just never forget.

And as Lainie opened the garage door so she could push her car inside, she silently uttered those five damning words, "How hard could it be?"

{fourteen}

Trish Miller was worried about her half sister, but every time she'd reached out to Lainie, she had been rebuffed. Her invitations to dinner had been refused, her offer to take Lainie shopping had been declined, and whenever she dropped over to visit, her sister seemed to be on edge. This was not the behavior of someone who had moved home to take it easy.

This was the behavior of . . . Trish frowned, the edges of her eyes crinkling. The teenagers in the high school where she was a guidance counselor behaved this way. They were secretive, guarded. If they had a problem, the adults around them were the last to know.

Some, of course, had the skills to meet life's troubles head-on. Most, however, did not. They danced around a problem, not trusting their parents to be able to help, but turning to their friends oftentimes made things much worse.

Trish had tried to broach the subject with Lainie, to ask her if something was wrong, but Lainie pretended that nothing was the matter. If that was the case, why was she creeping around and not telling anyone what she was doing all day?

Dad didn't know where Lainie spent her time. Trish knew because she had asked him.

Their father could be gruff sometimes, and she didn't envy her little sister having to grow up around him, but he *did* care. He just didn't know how to deal with people who cried or had emotional needs that he couldn't meet. He, too, was concerned about Lainie, but he figured he'd do what he had always done with her—leave her be until she asked for his help.

Trish wasn't sure this was the right approach. It certainly wasn't the way to go with the troubled kids she dealt with every day.

But she supposed her dad knew Lainie better than she did.

At least, she hoped he did.

Concern ate at her as she heaped a layer of instant mashed potatoes on top of the ground beef she'd browned and mixed with a can of cream of mushroom soup. The kids loved her shepherd's pie, though, like her, they probably could have eaten the ooey-gooey melted cheddar cheese off the top and forgone the rest of it.

Her husband, Alan, had become a bit of a food snob lately and had started turning up his nose at her old standbys like shepherd's pie or hot dogs wrapped in Pillsbury crescent dough. That's what success did to a person. Too many expensive dinners out and your palate couldn't help but change.

She'd bet one week of working at the high school and eating cafeteria food for lunch would change him back.

Though she wasn't sure she wanted him changed back. Since he'd started eyeing her meals with distaste, he'd suggested eating out a lot more.

Trish was all for that.

Fortunately, Alan was working late tonight, so she didn't have to worry about getting any comments about her artery-clogging food from him.

She eyed the nine-by-eleven casserole dish that was nearly overflowing with hamburger (or, rather, its politically correct cousin, ground sirloin), potatoes, and cheese. There was more than enough for the three of them. Maybe Lainie would like to join them? She'd seen her sister come home half an hour ago.

What excuse could she possibly give for not coming to dinner on a Thursday night?

Trish picked up the phone in the kitchen and dialed her father's number, then hit the Off button when Lainie didn't answer after six rings.

What the heck was up with her sister?

Dad had caller ID, so Lainie had to know that it was her calling. So why didn't she answer? Annoyed, Trish redialed her dad's number and let it ring until it rolled over to voice mail again.

That was it. She was going over there to find out—

"Hey, Ma. When's dinner?" Lucas asked, throwing his heavy half-boy/half-man arm over her shoulders and nearly crushing her in a hug. At fourteen Lucas was all goofy affection and practical jokes—mostly of the farting or diarrhea-noises variety. She prayed every night that he would never change, that he'd never hit that sullen, moody, rebellious stage that so many kids did.

If he could just make it through ninth grade like this, she figured she was home free. Eighth and ninth grades were the worst, both on the boys and the girls. For some reason—hormones were the likely culprit—these previously nice, normal kids just went all haywire for those two years. Some never made it back. But fortunately, most did.

"In about half an hour," she answered, blinking back the tears that were never far from her eyes where her babies were concerned. "I was thinking about asking your Aunt Lainie to come over, but she's not answering the phone. Would you mind going over there and seeing if you can drag her back with you? Not literally, of course," she added, just in case.

Lucas shrugged and grabbed a handful of shredded cheese that hadn't yet made it onto the top of her shepherd's pie. "Sure. But you know I could really do it," he said, grinning as he fisted his hands in the air and did his Hans-and-Franz "pump you up" impression from the old *Saturday Night Live* reruns she and Alan had just started letting him watch.

Trish laughed. He was such a goofball.

"Thanks," she said, and then went back to sprinkling cheese over her casserole.

When Lucas hadn't come back after ten minutes, Trish's mom-radar went off. Why hadn't he come to tell her what Lainie had said?

She wiped her hands on the dishtowel she'd been using to pat lettuce dry for the salad she'd just finished. She walked out into the living room, where Heather was curled up on the sofa, reading a book.

"Hey, honey, have you seen your brother?" she asked.

Heather looked up with that "huh, I'm in another world" look she got when she was really into a book. "He went up to his room, I think," she said.

Trish hurried up the carpeted stairs of their remodeled home. They'd added nearly a thousand square feet to the first story of the house and then put on a second-story addition about ten years ago, when Alan had gotten his first big promotion. Trish had never wanted expensive cars or jewelry (though she wouldn't turn down either), but a nice home had always been important to her. She wanted enough room for friends and family to come visit, for the grown-ups to hang out in the kitchen and family room watching the Super Bowl while the kids were up in the second-floor bonus room—still within shouting distance, but far enough away so that they could enjoy their own video games or movies without any adults yelling at them to be quiet.

Lucas's room was down the left hallway, the farthest room on the right.

Trish knocked—she wasn't above snooping, but allowed both her kids the illusion of privacy—and waited for Lucas to tell her it was okay to come in before pushing the door open. She ignored the mess—some battles just weren't worth fighting—but was concerned when she found her son sitting at his desk with his head in his hands.

"Lucas, what's the matter?" she asked, all of her protective-mommy instincts going on alert. Had Lainie said something to upset him? How *could* she? Trish found her half sister to be a little . . . distant, maybe, but she'd always been nice to the kids. More than nice. Loving, even. Kind and generous. Never forgot a birthday or a holiday.

So maybe she should calm down and not jump to conclusions.

Trish took a deep breath and pushed aside a pile of questionably clean clothes from the corner of Lucas's bed before sitting down.

Lucas was silent for a long moment. Then he lifted his head and turned troubled eyes to her.

"I don't know if I should tell you this," he said, though he clearly wanted to.

Hmm. Maybe he'd caught Lainie coming out of the shower or something. That was certainly not good, but at least it would explain why she hadn't answered the phone.

"Is it something that might hurt someone if you don't tell?" Trish asked. If it *was* the shower thing, Lainie and Lucas could work it out for themselves. There were some embarrassing things that everyone in your family didn't need to know.

"I think so," Lucas answered.

Damn. Trish rubbed her mouth. "Then you have to tell me."

Lucas nodded, but didn't say anything at first. Then, just as Trish was about to prod him, he blurted, "I caught Aunt Lainie huffing gas fumes in Grandpa Carl's garage."

[fifteen]

Lainie grinned at her reflection in the rearview mirror, inordinately pleased with herself for managing to get the gasoline out of her dad's riding lawnmower and into her Mercedes without spilling—or swallowing—a drop. It had taken longer than she'd expected, though, so she had to rush through a shower, makeup change, and blow-dry before flipping through her meager wardrobe to find the black wraparound dress she had on now.

It was a nice enough dress with a label she wouldn't be ashamed for anyone to see, and she liked the way it swished around her knees when she walked. She'd gone bare-legged, hoping that going without panty hose was still the trend as she slid her feet into a pair of three-inch-high pointy-toed pumps.

She checked her makeup in the rearview mirror as she pulled through the gates of the country club, half-expecting some power-hungry guard to tell her she didn't belong here.

"Like I need someone to tell me that," she murmured as she cruised past the valets and headed to the far corner of the lot, where Jack was standing next to his black sedan.

"Right on time," he said with approval as she pulled her key out of the ignition and slid it into the cute-but-cheap piano-shaped cocktail purse she'd salvaged from the Garage Sale from Hell.

Jack opened her door for her and Lainie felt a little bit like Cinderella as she swept out of the car. She'd never been inside the country club, so why not let herself feel like a princess, just for tonight?

"Here, let me pin this on you," Jack said, holding up a black, flower-shaped pin.

"What's that?"

"Hidden camera. Just in case we catch our subject in flagrante. If you want to take a picture, you just push the top petal."

"Oh. Yes. Of course," Lainie said, then awkwardly pushed out her left shoulder so Jack could pin the corsage-like brooch to her dress.

In seconds he was done and had stepped back to admire his handiwork.

"You're pretty good at that," Lainie said, wondering if she had just imagined the barest brush of his palm over her breast.

"I've had lots of practice," he told her with a lopsided grin.

"I'll bet," Lainie muttered under her breath. The girl he'd been with the night she'd first seen him at the Ritz had been so young, it wouldn't surprise her if their next date was to her prom.

Jack's grin widened as if he knew exactly what she was thinking. "You ready?" he asked without further comment about his prowess at pinning corsages on women's bosoms.

Lainie fiddled with the two swathes of fabric tied together at her hip until she felt certain they were secure. Then she nodded once, took a deep breath, and straightened her shoulders. "Ready," she announced.

Jack looped his arm around hers as he pulled her away from her car. "Into the lion's den we go, then."

His arm was firm and warm beneath her fingertips and Lainie had to fight the urge to step a little closer to him. Jackson Danforth III was out of her league, she reminded herself. *Way* out of her league. He was debutantes and Gulf Coast mansions and lifetime appointments to the Art Museum's board of trustees. She was . . . Nothing. A rootless wanderer who'd lived in Naples for just over a year, fifteen years ago; a failure who'd come crawling back after Seattle's gloomy gray skies—and fatal downturn in the high-tech industry—finally did her in.

No, she was definitely not Jack's type. And wouldn't he get a laugh out of knowing that for a brief second she had actually wondered if he'd been attracted to her, too?

Lainie snorted silently to herself, then focused her attention on the reason they were here at the swank country club this evening.

"Did you get a photo of our subject?" she asked as Jack nodded to a tuxedoed footman acting as a human doorstop outside the massive wooden doors flanking the entrance of the stone building. The sound of her heels hitting the polished marble floor echoed loudly through the hall, making Lainie feel as if she were clomping like a mule. She tried to lighten her footfalls, but it was no use. The sound followed them even as they turned the corner toward a crowded ballroom on the left.

Jack paused just inside the doorway, his fingers tightening on hers when he pulled her up against his side as another couple pushed past them and entered the ballroom. After scanning the room for a moment, he leaned down and said something softly in her ear. It took every ounce of Lainie's willpower not to shiver as his warm breath tickled her skin.

"He's over there. The unfortunately named Bob Sprick," Jack announced.

"So what are we looking for? Do we just stand around and wait for Bob Sprick to get caught doing something he shouldn't?"

Jack coughed and covered his mouth with the back of his hand, and Lainie began to worry because when she glanced up at him, she found that his face had turned an odd shade of purple.

Thinking he might be choking, she patted him on the back and asked, "Are you all right?"

"Fine," Jack managed to spit out between another bout of coughing.

While Jack recovered his composure, Lainie studied their subject—a medium-tall man with light brown hair who appeared to be in his mid-thirties and looked vaguely familiar to her. But she'd remember if she'd ever met a man with that name before. It wasn't something you'd easily forget.

Mr. Sprick seemed completely innocuous, but Lainie knew his type could be the worst. Embezzlers, bigamists, sexaholics, gamblers, liars, and cheats. They came in all shapes and sizes, but it was the normal-looking ones that surprised everyone, as if only the heinously ugly were capable of evil.

"So, what should I be on the lookout for?" she asked again once Jack had caught his breath.

"I'm not sure exactly," he answered. "We'll just have to keep our eyes on Bob Sprick and see what arises."

Lainie squinted up at Jack. Okay, now he *had* to be joking.

But before she could call him on it, a tuxedoed waiter stepped in front of them and shoved a tray of heavenly smelling delights under her nose. "Crab puff?" he asked.

Lainie swallowed the lake of drool that had pooled in her mouth at the smell. Never one to resist temptation, Jack grabbed a handful of crab puffs and popped two of them into his mouth like popcorn before lifting the last one to her lips. When Lainie opened her mouth to decline, Jack slipped the crunchy hors d'oeuvre onto her tongue, where the delicate puff pastry spread with layer after layer of salty butter melted.

Lainie closed her eyes in ecstasy. *God, that was good.*

"Do you know how many calories are in those things?" she protested after taking a long moment to recover from her near-orgasmic experience.

Jack eyed her up and down and then up again before responding. "Why do you care? You look great."

Yeah, well, she should. The hit-rock-bottom diet was certainly working for her these days, though she usually had to struggle to keep that extra ten pounds from turning into twenty. She could just imagine what she'd look like if she made a regular diet of the crab-stuffed puff pastry and filet mignon bites with Roquefort dipping sauce and key-lime tartlets that were on the menu this evening.

Lainie shuddered at the thought. She didn't have to work too hard to imagine what she'd look like if she packed on a few extra pounds because she'd struggled with a weight problem all throughout her high school years. She *knew* what it was like to be unattractive, to be invisible to all the pretty people of the world, to feel as if—to yourself as much as to them—you might as well not even exist.

The buttery taste that lingered on her tongue suddenly made her feel sick, as though she'd just eaten an entire pie or box of doughnuts instead of one bite-size crab puff.

Smoothing her palms over her hips, Lainie mentally shoved all those worms from her past back into the ooze-filled pail where they'd come from. They had no place in her life anymore. She was a smart, competent, attractive woman—no longer a dumpy, overweight teen without a shred of self-esteem.

Now if only she could find a way to get rid of that kid once and for all . . .

"Lainie, did you hear what I said?"

Jack nudged her shoulder and Lainie blinked herself back to the present with an inarticulate, "Huh?"

"I said, 'We should mingle.' You know, find out who else is at this shindig; keep an eye on Bob to see if he slips someone a steamy love note or something."

"Oh. Right," Lainie said as Jack put a hand on her lower back and guided her into the ballroom. In what seemed like seconds, a glass of champagne had magically appeared in her hand, and, without stopping to think how it had gotten there, Lainie took a sip.

Jack introduced her to a couple he knew—Sylvia and Paul Newman (not *that* Paul Newman, but Jack probably knew *him*, too)— and Lainie absently made small talk while watching Bob Sprick out of the corner of her eye.

She took another sip of her champagne as Jack excused himself to go say hello to someone else that he knew and the Newmans drifted away. She knew she should "get out there" and make contact with others while she was here—networking was crucial to growing a business like theirs—but schmoozing wasn't exactly her strong suit.

She leaned back against the wall and watched the partygoers kiss one another's cheeks or clap each other on the back. The conversations all sounded the same to her—can you believe the upcoming hurricane season is almost upon us?; summer just seems to come earlier and earlier every year, doesn't it?; so glad the tourist season is over and all the traffic is gone; it was getting so that I couldn't even find a parking space outside my favorite shops. Blah blah blah.

Lainie basked in the inaneness of it all as she idly searched for Jack's head of thick, dark hair in the crowd. Suddenly she straightened, spilling a tablespoon of champagne down the front of her black dress.

"Damn," she muttered, wiping at the liquid as she hurriedly set her glass down on a passing tray.

Bob Sprick had disappeared.

The last time she'd glanced his way, he'd been talking to a blond woman and gesturing toward the hallway. Maybe they'd gone outside for a tryst?

There was no time for her to find Jack in the crush of bodies filling the ballroom, so instead, she headed toward the hall alone, side-stepping chatting groups of three or four and nearly colliding with a waiter carrying a tray laden with more heavenly smelling nibbles as she scurried to catch up with their subject.

After narrowly avoiding disaster—and, yeah, wouldn't it just be *hilarious* if she ended up with ten pounds of chicken satay down her dress and peanut dipping sauce dripping from her hair?—Lainie dashed out into the hall just in time to see Bob's suit-clad back disappear around the corner. Skidding a little on the smooth marble floor, Lainie charged after him. Her hand flew to the black flower-shaped pin that Jack had pinned to her dress earlier.

A surge of excitement buzzed through her at the thought of finding Bob Sprick engaged in some sort of illicit behavior. Her first case and already she was catching people with their pants down. So to speak.

Lainie's grin widened as she flew around the corner, her fingers already tightening on the camera's shutter. Then she gasped and windmilled her arms backward in an attempt to slow her forward momentum as she realized that the hallway ended abruptly about five feet from the corner Bob had turned moments ago.

She took a step back and scowled at the dark, eight-paneled door. Bob Sprick had gone into the men's room.

And she had no way of knowing whether or not he was alone. Maybe he and Blondie were going at in the restroom. Wouldn't be the first time a public bathroom was used in such a private manner.

Damn. She should have tried to find Jack before racing out to follow their subject. Now what was she going to do?

She raised her thumb to her mouth and absently gnawed at her fingernail.

She couldn't go into the men's room. Getting kicked out of the country club would definitely not be good for business.

But how else could she find out if Bob was in there alone? What if, at this very moment, he was slipping Blondie his Sprick?

With a glance behind her to make certain she was alone, Lainie did the only thing she could think of: She pressed her ear against the door in the hopes that she might be able to overhear whatever might be going on inside.

But all she heard was the sound of a toilet flushing.

Good. So that meant that Bob was—

Lainie nearly choked on her own hastily indrawn breath when she heard the sound of footsteps approaching the men's room.

What now?

Desperately she glanced around the alcove, looking for a place to hide.

There was a life-sized statue of a man with a fig leaf just barely covering his impressive marble package to one side and a low table with an arrangement of fresh flowers on the other. The table was too small for her to hide beneath, so Lainie did the only other thing she could do—she ducked behind the statue, squeezing herself in between the statue's smooth, firm buttocks and the hard wall at her

back just as a tall, black-haired man came around the corner and
headed into the men's room.

"Whew. That was close," Lainie whispered to the statue's un-
moving back as she closed her eyes with relief.

That was it. She'd had enough of loitering around the men's
room like a pervert. No, she'd just go back to the party and find
Jack and let *him* handle this type of thing from now on.

Lainie rolled her eyes at herself as she thought about how ridiculous she had to look standing here fondling the ass of a marble
statue. Okay, so maybe her love life wasn't exactly what you'd call
robust, but she wasn't so desperate that she'd been forced to get her
thrills by feeling up inanimate objects.

She had to get out of here before Bob and that other guy came
out and spotted her.

Only . . . when she tried to move out from behind the statue,
she felt a curious tugging at her waist.

Dang. The ties of her dress must have gotten caught on something.

Without an inch of extra space in which to turn around, Lainie
sucked in her breath to give herself a little room. But it was no use.
She was trapped.

With a loud sigh she closed her eyes and rested her forehead just
above the curve of the statue's left butt check, the marble cool beneath her heated skin.

Great. This was just great.

She kept her eyes closed as the men's room door opened and
Bob Sprick and the other man exited talking about one of the three
acceptable topics of conversation: this year's upcoming hurricane
season.

Once the men's voices had faded away, Lainie opened her eyes
and tried to shift her body to the right so she could assess the prob-

lem. She was able to move far enough to see that the ties of her dress were indeed tangled up in something—the thick fingers of the statue's right hand. It was almost as if the thing had come to life for just a second and grabbed her dress as some sort of joke. She'd never admitted this, but Lainie secretly suspected that statues came alive when people weren't watching.

She managed to pop her right arm free and, somewhat embarrassed, slid her hand up the statue's thigh toward the spot where its wrist was joined to its right hip. Her fingers skimmed over the fig leaf, then jerked back as if they'd been burned when an amused voice from out of nowhere said, "A little up and to the left and you're going to make somebody verrrrrry happy."

{ sixteen }

Lainie peered out from behind the statue to find Jack watching her with amusement.

"He was hard as a rock before I even touched him."

"I know how he feels," Jack said, raising one eyebrow suggestively.

Lainie rolled her eyes. "Could you help get me out of here? My dress got caught and I can't get loose."

"What were you doing back there anyway? Or should I ask?"

Forcing herself not to blush, Lainie removed her hand from the statue's firm butt cheek. "I'll tell you later. Right now I'd appreciate a little assistance."

She tugged at her dress, humiliated that Jack had discovered her in this predicament.

"All right. Just hold on a second," he said, frowning thoughtfully at the statue for a moment.

Lainie waited for him to figure out some brilliant solution, then rolled her eyes again when he pronounced, "It looks like you're pretty tangled up back there."

"Yes, I had pretty much figured that out for myself," she said.

"Right. I guess you'll just have to take it off."

"What?" Lainie yelped.

"I think once we've got some slack, we might be able to get it loose," Jack said.

"*Might* be able to?"

Jack shrugged. "No guarantees in life, you know."

"Easy for you to say. You're not the one doing a striptease at the country club," Lainie muttered as her hands went to the side zipper of her dress. In order to shimmy out of this thing, she was basically going to have to kiss the statue's ass before slithering down its legs. With Jack watching.

Fab-u-lous.

Her long, drawn-out sigh could be heard all the way to Miami.

Well, at least she'd worn decent underwear, she thought as she yanked at the back of her dress. She managed to drag it up so that her nose was caught in the plunging neckline, the fabric at the back bunched up behind her head. She could feel a draft in the rear, the hemline of her former knee-length dress now skimming the tops of her thighs.

"Give me a hand here, would you?" The scowl she threw Jack's way did nothing to stop his shoulders from shaking with laughter. The bastard.

"Sorry," he said, without sounding the least bit apologetic. He reached around the back of the statue and attempted to get a hold of the back of her dress, but the angle of the statue's arm made it impossible for him to reach.

"Put your arm around his waist," Lainie suggested as Jack's hand dangled uselessly six inches from her shoulder.

Jack stepped back and frowned at the statue. "I'm not putting my arms around him. He's a guy."

Lainie snorted. "He's not even a *he*. He's an *it*. And I'm going to be stuck here all night if you don't."

When Jack hesitated, Lainie shook her head with disgust. *Men.* "Come on, Jack. Don't be such a baby."

"Fine. But you're going to owe me for this," he muttered, sliding his arm around the statue's waist and cringing as one sculpted marble nipple dug into his cheek. He pulled his head back as far as it would go without snapping his neck, and Lainie had to bite the inside of her lip to keep from laughing.

Jack grabbed hold of the right shoulder of her dress. "There. Now slide out of it," he ordered.

Lainie tried. Really, she did. But all she managed to do was to get the neckline to move out from under her nose and get stuck on her ear.

"You need to hold on to both sides," she mumbled through the fabric of her dress.

It was Jack's turn to utter a wall-shaking sigh. This was *so* not going to look cool. He glanced behind them to make sure the hallway was empty. Then, with a distasteful curl of his lip, he slid his other arm around the statue's waist.

"This is gonna cost you, Lainie," he muttered into the statue's chest as he grabbed the other shoulder of her dress and held it steady while she struggled to extricate herself.

"Give me a break. You're not the one standing half-naked outside the men's room door," Lainie groused.

Okay. He'd give her that. Still . . .

An idea suddenly struck him—and, no, it didn't leave a bruise—as he twisted his head to peer at Lainie from beneath the statue's underarm. Then he forgot what he'd been about to say as her head came out from under her dress and Jack saw that she was wearing nothing but a pair of black silk panties and matching bra.

"Nice," he whistled, before good sense had a chance to stop him.

Lainie was tempted to clap her hands to her chest in an attempt to cover up, but then she thought better of the idea. What was the use anyway? Her bra and panties covered more than her hands would. *Just pretend you're wearing a swimsuit*, she silently ordered herself as she ducked out from behind the statue.

Now if she could just get her dress free before anyone else walked by . . .

"Close your mouth," she said to Jack as he continued to stare at her as if he'd never seen a woman in her underwear before. Ha. Right. Jack Danforth was one of Naples' most eligible bachelors. She was certain that he saw plenty of women—with and without their underwear on—every week. Which meant that he could stop gaping at her and help her get her dress back on before they both got tossed out on their ears.

She bent over the statue's fingers where her dress was tangled, ignoring the heat coming off Jack's body as he stood next to her, leaning nonchalantly against the wall as if the last five minutes had never occurred.

"So anyway, I figured out how you could repay—" Jack began, but stopped when the unmistakable sound of high-heels clicking on the marble floor reached their ears.

Lainie looked up, desperate, and their gazes slammed together.

Damn. Someone was coming.

Her fingers tightened on the fabric caught in the statue's hand. She tugged, trying to pull it free.

Meanwhile, Jack shrugged out of his suit jacket. "Here," he said, holding it out. "Put this on and stand behind me. I'll cover you."

Lainie gave her dress one more frantic jerk, and it finally came free. Only, the footsteps were just outside the alcove. She didn't have time to turn her dress right-side-out and tug it on over her head before whoever was out there rounded the corner. So, instead, she slid Jack's jacket over her shoulders and wrapped it around her like a cocoon as he put himself between her and the intruder.

She found herself once more trapped between the wall and the hard, muscled back of a man. Only this one was warm and smelled like heaven.

Lainie inhaled deeply and nearly passed out from ecstasy. Man, he smelled good. He must have rubbed cologne on the back of his neck, right there where his thick dark hair came to a V.

The temptation to stand on her tiptoes and bury her nose in the skin at the base of his neck was so overwhelming that Lainie jerked her head back to make sure she didn't do anything she'd later regret. But she forgot how close she was to the wall, and her head hit the dark mahogany paneling with a surprisingly loud *thunk*.

"Ow," she grumbled, reaching up to rub the back of her head.

"Shh," Jack whispered, as if she'd done it on purpose. Then he took a step backward, pressing himself even closer to her as whoever was out in the hall stopped at the entrance to the alcove.

Oh, this was hell. Jack's firm butt was pressed into her hips, her breasts smooshed against his back. And she was *surrounded* by his smell. It invaded her nostrils and sucked all the extra air from the atmosphere. Lainie tried to get a grip on herself. It was just cologne, for God's sake! And it wasn't like she'd never noticed how good Jack smelled before.

But he'd never been this close before, either. The combination of heat and that smell and—okay, okay, she'd admit it—pure animal lust was making her a little crazy.

Lainie shivered. She wondered if Jack would notice if she "accidentally" brushed a hand over his butt. And squeezed. Oh, how she loved a nice, firm set of buns on a man. These days, with all those baggy pants guys wore, her butt obsession was a bit starved. You never knew if a guy was packing a cute ass until . . . well, until he was standing in front of you, buck naked, and at that point it was a little too late to be critical of the merchandise.

Of course, it figured that Jack would have a great butt. He had everything: good looks, wealthy family, straight, white teeth.

What more could a guy—

"Why, Jack Danforth! I've been looking all over for you," a woman trilled.

Lainie recognized the voice immediately and froze, all thoughts of Jack and his nice ass and lust and even that heavenly smell scattering from her mind like rats fleeing from an alley cat.

Shay Monroe—even the thought of her old nemesis's name made Lainie cringe—wasn't in quite the same financial stratosphere as Jack, but she wasn't exactly poor, either. It was inevitable that at some point she'd attend one of the same social functions that Jack did.

But why did it have to be tonight?

And, even more important, why did she have to show up at this exact moment?

Lainie already knew why. It was because whatever force ruled her world had a sick sense of humor. She'd known it since she was seventeen, on the absolute worst night of her life, when she had thought things couldn't get worse . . . and then they did.

Lainie closed her eyes at that thought. She was *not* going to think about that night right now. The situation was bad enough already without dragging up that painful memory again.

No, instead she had to figure out a way to get her dress back on before Shay realized that Jack was not alone. She was not going to face her demons wearing nothing but her undies.

Although, at least they were her *good* undies . . .

Lainie shook her head. That didn't matter. She had to get dressed. Which meant that Jack had to give her a little room to move around in. She pushed against his back in a subtle attempt to tell him to step forward a bit, but he only pushed back.

"Shay, it's nice to see you again," he said, with seemingly genuine pleasure.

With a scowl Lainie jabbed her chin between Jack's shoulder blades. Yeah, it just figured that he'd be happy to see someone like Shay.

Not that there was anything wrong with her. She was just so freaking *perfect*.

You know how in high school there was that one person who seemed to have it all together? Who stopped wearing her Calvins the day Guess came into fashion? Who knew that curly hair was on its way out just as the female cast of *Melrose Place* straightened their spiral perms and went for that sleek, shiny look instead? The girl all the guys—nerds and jocks alike—fantasized about as they began their lifelong obsession with masturbation?

For Lainie, that girl had been Shay Monroe. Shay, with her bouncy blond hair, her never-rumpled, always-in-style wardrobe, and her long, slender body that was perfectly showcased by her cute red-and-white cheerleader uniform.

Shay, who never had to work an after-school job to pay for her own car insurance. Shay, whose Christmas presents never came from Goodwill. Shay, whose family owned a string of fast-food restaurants that paid for her invisible braces, bought her expensive attire, ensured that the cheer squad was able to attend the National Cheer-Off every year on Maui, and funded her Ivy League education. The same fast-food chain where Lainie worked the closing shift, five nights a week (six, if somebody called in sick), from five p.m. to one a.m. her last year and a half of high school.

Yes, back in high school, Shay Monroe had had it all.

And if Lainie's guess was correct, fifteen years after graduation day, Shay Monroe *still* had it all. Even worse, fifteen years after graduation day, Lainie still felt like the geeky girl from high school who'd had a huge crush on Shay's boyfriend and humiliated herself in front of them both on prom night.

Ugh. Lainie grimaced. She was not going to be disgraced like that again.

Lainie straightened her shoulders and shoved against Jack's back, forcing him to take a step forward. She ignored his cough of disapproval as she fumbled to find the opening of her dress.

"So, you mentioned that you were looking for me?" Jack asked as if it were perfectly normal to stand in front of the men's room and have a leisurely conversation.

"Yes," Shay answered with a frown in her voice.

Lainie could just imagine the tiny, nearly invisible line on Shay's forehead that would accompany her frown. The bitch probably didn't even need Botox injections like normal people did.

"Is there someone behind you?" Shay asked.

Lainie's eyebrows shot up as she realized that Shay was just about to peer around Jack's back. In desperation she shoved her head into the neck of her dress and tugged it down as Jack's suit jacket fell to the floor at her feet. Then she put one hand against the wall, leaned back nonchalantly, and kicked the jacket into the corner just as Shay's perfectly coiffed blond head came into view.

Shay speared Lainie with her crystal clear blue eyes.

"Who are you?" she asked.

Before Lainie could answer, Jack turned around, his eyes widening slightly when he caught a glimpse of her. Lainie thought that perhaps he was just surprised that she'd managed to get her dress back on, but then she made the mistake of looking down at herself and nearly groaned aloud.

Her dress was on inside out. Of course. She'd had a 50-percent chance of getting it right, which meant that the bastard running her life had an equal chance of making a fool out of her.

"Thanks a lot," she muttered under her breath.

Jack squinted at her strangely, but didn't ask what she was talking about. Instead, to Lainie's surprise, he put an arm around her shoulders and said, "This is Lainie Ames, my date."

"Your date?" Shay's gaze bounced from Lainie to Jack and back.

"Not really. We work together. Our mothers were friends," Lainie hastened to add, though she should have kept her mouth shut and let Shay think that she and Jack *were* dating. Wouldn't *that* take the glossy shine off her pearly whites, to think that this once-chubby geek had landed Naples' most eligible bachelor?

Only, when Shay held out her hand and introduced herself, Lainie realized that she had no idea that Lainie was *that* Elaine Ames, the one who had made herself into a human Popsicle on prom night in front of Shay and all her friends.

No way was Lainie about to remind her.

Instead, she pasted a serene smile on her lips and gave Shay's hand a limp shake. "Nice to meet you," she said.

"Hmm," Shay answered absently before turning her attention back to Jack.

Lainie relaxed, figuring that in Shay's mind, she had just been dismissed, but then felt every hair on her body stand on end when Shay tossed her mane of blond hair behind her shoulder, dug a piece of paper out of her purse, waved it at Jack, and said, "This is why I was looking for you. I saw your ad in the *Naples Weekly* this morning. I never knew you were a private investigator." Another hair toss. "Anyway, I want you to find out everything you can about this man. Blaine Harper. *Doctor* Blaine Harper. He's back in town for our fifteen-year high school reunion. And I plan to get him back for good."

{ seventeen }

*B*laine Harper was back in Naples.

Lainie had thought of nothing else for the past twelve hours. She'd fallen asleep with those words ringing in her ears and woken up to them this morning when her alarm clock buzzed.

She sat on the bench outside the office, waiting for Jack to arrive with his usual jangling of keys and juggling of coffee and mail, and tried to loosen the grip of whatever it was that was squeezing her lungs so tight that she could hardly suck in a breath.

She tried telling herself that she didn't know why it bothered her that Shay Monroe was using their reunion as an excuse to get Blaine back, but she knew it was a lie. It bothered her because she knew Shay would be successful.

Women like Shay always were.

Lainie squinched her eyes shut on a vision of Shay sliding out of the backseat of a black stretch limo, putting her dainty, newly manicured hand in Blaine's as he helped her out of the car, her expensive red heels tapping the sidewalk as all of their classmates stopped to watch her alight from the vehicle.

No. It wasn't fair. That was supposed to be Lainie, wowing her graduating class with her fabulous clothes, her fabulous guy, her fabulous life.

Once again, Shay Monroe was stealing Lainie's dream.

"You gonna sit out here all morning?" Jack asked.

Lainie forced her eyes open. "I didn't hear you drive up."

"I put 'er in stealth mode this morning," he said, nodding toward a black convertible that was different from the car he had driven last night.

"It worked."

Jack grinned and leaned against the door as if he were in no hurry to move inside, but Lainie needed something to do, something to get her mind off of her shattered dreams, so she hurried inside to boot up her computer and get back to the case they'd started working on last night.

"How do we get the pictures off of this?" she asked and held out the black pin she'd unclipped from her dress this morning.

Jack took it and slid behind his desk. "I've got a cable that connects right to the computer. We'll have them downloaded in no time."

"I don't think I got anything more than a photo of Bob talking to a woman at the party, but maybe you could identify her. That would at least give us one lead."

With an incomprehensible grunt, Jack turned to his computer, leaving Lainie with nothing to do but wait. Fortunately, Duncan came in just then. He was always good for a little comic relief.

"Morning, Duncan," she said.

"It is indeed, Ms. Ames," Duncan replied. "That is, until 12:01, when it will become afternoon. Been that way for years, as I understand it."

Lainie chuckled. Duncan was certifiable, but he was kind of cute with his twinkling brown eyes and shabby suits.

He paused in front of Jack's desk. "By the way, I picked this up at the coffee shop this morning. Thought you might find it interesting."

Jack stopped clicking his mouse and absently picked up the flyer that Duncan had dropped on his desk. "A Doctor Diet seminar? Are you trying to tell me something?" he asked, raising his eyebrows at his half brother.

"Certainly not, Boss," Duncan said. "Why, you're as fit as a fiddle. Healthy as a horse. Robust as a . . . uh, a ratchet."

"A ratchet? Are ratchets robust?" Lainie asked.

"Of course they are. You ever seen a limp ratchet?" Duncan said.

"Not since Viagra was invented," Lainie quipped back.

"Good one." Duncan shot her a look that told her he was impressed at her improvisational skills, and Lainie had to admit to feeling a little bit proud.

"Thanks."

Across the room, Jack rolled his eyes. "So . . . About this brochure?"

"Right. Back to business. No time for such foolishness around here. That, my dear brother, is an announcement for a seminar this afternoon at the Ritz-Carlton Hotel given by none other than Doctor Diet himself," Duncan announced.

"And I would care about this why?"

"Did you not tell me this morning that we have a new case?"

"Yes. I mean, no. I didn't *not* tell you— Oh, screw it. You know what I mean."

Jack grumpily hid behind his computer screen, and Duncan grinned at Lainie as if to say, "Ha, I won!"

Then he took pity on Jack and explained, "Doctor Diet is none other than Blaine Harper, the man our new client wants us to check out."

Lainie blinked. What? Blaine Harper was some sort of diet guru?

She was dying to know more, but no way would she let on to Jack and Duncan that she was interested in this as anything but just another case. So she tilted her own computer screen toward the front of the office so no one could see it and then opened her Internet connection and googled Blaine Harper in private.

The Doctor Diet site was first on the list of results. Before Lainie clicked the link, she peered out around the edge of her monitor to make sure her coworkers were occupied with their own work. Duncan had disappeared into the lunchroom, where he spent most of his day, and Jack had pushed the flyer to the corner of his desk and was clicking away at something, so Lainie pulled her head back into her bubble and surfed to the site.

Then she nearly screamed when a man's voice said, "Do you struggle with your weight? Doctor Diet can help!"

Criminy.

She randomly poked at the buttons on her computer until the man shut up. She *hated* websites with those annoying sound clips.

"Jumping right into our new case, I see," Jack observed mildly without looking up from his screen.

Lainie rubbed her forehead. "Just trying to do my part," she mumbled.

When Jack just grunted, she made sure her speakers were muted and then turned back to the Doctor Diet website. She closed the Flash introduction—another thing she hated on a website; after the first visit, it got really annoying—and went into the main site.

The first thing she saw was Blaine Harper's face smiling out at her. And, oh, wasn't he even more handsome than he had been in high school?

Lainie swallowed her sigh and guiltily looked around the office to make sure no one was paying any attention before raising her hand and touching the strong line of Blaine's jaw. His hair was darker than it had been back then, the blond deepening to a streaked mix of brown and gold. His hazel eyes were more green than brown, his nose a bit crooked from where it had been broken during the last football season.

She pressed her fingers to the cleft in his chin, just like she'd dreamed of doing back in high school, and then let out an involuntary scream when a rectangular foil packet sailed across the room and hit her in the middle of her chest.

"That'll take that spot off your monitor. Rubbing it will just leave fingerprints," Jack said.

Lainie touched the dent in her chest with her index finger. "That hurt," she protested, though it hadn't really.

"Want me to kiss it and make it better?" Jack raised his eyebrows suggestively.

"No. I'm sure it will heal fine on its own."

"Really, I'll bet I'm more effective than that Doctor Diet guy you're so busy checking out."

Lainie scowled, hit the minimize button on her web browser, and twisted around to figure out how in the world Jack had seen what she was doing. "I wasn't— I mean— How did you— Is there a camera over here or something?"

She got up and started turning over the items on her desk to see if Jack had rigged her area with spyware. Jack grinned and let her continue until he'd had his fill of fun for the morning. Then he stood up, stretched, and said, "Naw. There's nothing over there, Lainie. I just got lucky. I mean with my guess."

Lainie glared at him. "That's the only luck you're ever going to have with me," she muttered.

"Aw, come on, Lainie. I was just having some fun."

She plopped back down on her chair. "Fine."

"But you *were* googling this guy, weren't you?" he asked, holding the flyer between his thumb and forefinger.

"What if I was?"

Jack shrugged and grinned—and damn that devilish grin that made Lainie forget for just a moment that no way, NO WAY, was Jack Danforth flirting with her—and said, "Just remember to wash up when you're done."

"Grr."

"Did you just growl at me?" Jack and his unholy grin came to lean against her desk, and Lainie refused to notice the way his jeans clung to his thighs—no baggy-ass pants for Jack Danforth, thank God—or how his polo shirt lay against his flat stomach or how his sleeves ended right at the thickest part of his biceps and made Lainie want to—

She dragged her gaze away from him.

"Don't worry. I've had my shots," she said, smiling sweetly.

"I usually prefer to progress from growling to licking and leave the biting for at least a third date. But, hey, if you want to just jump right into the good stuff . . ."

Okay. She was waaaaay out of her league here. "Jack, could you get serious?"

He chuckled and pushed himself away from her desk, which left Lainie with a conflicting sense of regret mixed with relief.

"Have it your way. But when you're done checking out the Diet Dude, come over and see the pictures you took last night. They're pretty . . . um, enlightening."

Lainie pushed her chair away from her desk. "It's Doctor Diet, not the Diet Dude," she grumbled.

Jack lifted one shoulder in a "whatever" gesture. "Well, I say we go one better than looking him up on the Internet. Why don't we trot on down to the Ritz and size him up in person?"

"What do you mean?"

"I mean, let's go to his seminar. See what all the fuss is about. If nothing else, we can grab some lunch beforehand. I understand they make a mean grilled veggie dish. And their key-lime cheese-cake is worth stealing for," he added with a sidelong glance that made Lainie stop in her tracks like a wolf that had just stepped in the middle of a trap and knows that if he lifts his paw, the trap will spring shut.

"Sounds great!" Duncan yelled from the lunchroom. "When are we leaving?"

And Jack just grinned at her as if he were the devil and she'd just put a big ol' discount sticker on her soul.

Then the phone rang and Lainie nearly flattened Jack in her haste to grab it and avoid the inevitable discussion about why she'd taken his credit card that night and, why, if he knew that she had done it, he had even hired her in the first place. Because, really, she didn't want to know.

"Intrepid Investigations," she answered the phone's insistent summons.

"Hello? Lainie? This is Maddie Case. From next door. Lillian has a background check she was hoping you all could do. The file's ready if you want to send Duncan over to pick it up."

"I'll be there in a second," Lainie said, silently sending up a prayer of thanks for the interruption.

She hung up the phone, backing toward the front door as she explained that she'd be back in a minute. And if that minute just happened to turn to thirty . . . well, Rules of Engagement was a client. What could she do?

{ eighteen }

Maybe she was overreacting.

Trish rubbed her chin as she reread the U.S. Department of Justice's intelligence brief on huffing—subtitled "The Abuse of Inhalants."

There were eight signs of abuse: drunk or disoriented appearance; paint or other stains on face, hands, or clothing; hidden empty spray paint or solvent containers and chemical-soaked rags or clothing; slurred speech; strong chemical odors on breath or clothing; nausea or loss of appetite; red or runny nose; sores or rash around the nose or mouth.

Had Trish noticed any of these?

No.

Well. Wait a minute.

The night Lainie arrived in town and they'd gone to dinner at the Ritz, she'd barely eaten a thing. Even when Trish had offered her a bite of her dessert, Lainie turned it down. And Lainie loved sweets.

Come to think of it, hadn't Lainie refused every one of Trish's dinner invitations? And she was so thin. She had to have lost nearly twenty pounds since Trish had last seen her.

But maybe there was another explanation.

Like . . . Um . . .

Trish frowned at her computer screen as an appointment reminder popped up. She had a meeting in five minutes with Mike Spencer, the head of the science department and one of the high school's top teachers. He had some ideas about how to get the boys of this generation re-engaged in learning by getting them involved in science projects geared toward their gender (read: those that produced bad smells and explosions).

She printed off the Department of Justice's brief, vowing to keep a close watch on her sister to see if she exhibited any other signs of chemical abuse.

Because there was one thing Trish was sure of. If her sister needed help, she was going to get it for her . . . whether Lainie liked it or not.

$\mathcal{N}$ever offer to help."

Lainie raised her eyebrows at Rules of Engagement's receptionist as Lillian Bryson's words drifted out of the hallway and into the waiting area.

"She's in the middle of a class," Maddie whispered, pointing to the back of their office as if Lainie couldn't figure out where the noise was coming from.

"What's she talking about?" Lainie whispered back.

"Rule number four. If a man asks for your phone number and

then fumbles around like he can't find anything to write with, don't help him out. The key is, you've got to make him work for it. Otherwise, he won't see you as a challenge."

Lainie squinched up her face. "Aw, come on. That stuff doesn't really work, does it?"

Maddie shrugged. "I don't know. I'm afraid to try it. The last thing I need in my life right now is a man."

Boy, could she relate. Although the thought of walking into her fifteen-year reunion on the arm of Blaine Harper wasn't exactly unappealing . . .

Lainie took the file folder that Maddie held out and stood there for a moment, thinking. Wouldn't that be a shocker? If she somehow managed to catch Blaine's attention before Shay Monroe got her hooks back into him? And then, by some miracle, if she managed to get him to ask her to the prom—er, the reunion, that is?

Wouldn't everyone look at Lainie Ames differently, then?

Like, maybe she wasn't a total failure?

Like, maybe the last fifteen years hadn't been a complete waste?

Like, maybe she was somebody important, after all?

Lainie sighed and shook her head. Yeah. Like, maybe she had woken up this morning under the spell of the Miracle Fairy.

Nothing was ever that easy for her. What she wanted, she didn't get. If someone wanted to write a tagline on her tombstone, that would be it.

Yeah, yeah. Poor baby.

She rolled her eyes at herself. Enough whining. Time to get back to work, and hope that Jack had forgotten all about her stealing his credit card to pay for dinner at the Ritz.

Uh-huh. Like that was going to happen.

Lainie straightened her shoulders as she entered the Intrepid Investigations office.

Beg. That was her strategy. If Jack planned to hold her little, teeny, tiny transgression over her head, she'd hit the carpet and plead with him to forgive her. She'd promise to pay him back out of her very first paycheck if only he wouldn't fire her. She needed this job too badly, and—she was surprised to realize—she liked it here. She'd never worked somewhere this . . . not serious, before.

She'd been here a week and no one had left the office in tears.

No one had missed a kid's school play (okay, so none of them actually had kids, but still). No one had had to reschedule a dentist appointment for the fifteenth time because some urgent meeting had suddenly come up. No one had to stay until two in the morning to meet a deadline or get up at three-thirty to catch an early morning flight.

It was kind of . . . nice.

"You ready? 'Cause I'm ready," Duncan said as Lainie set the file containing the info for the background check on her desk.

"I'm ready. You ready?" she absently asked Jack.

"Lady, I was *born* ready," Jack answered. Then he threw one arm around Duncan's shoulders and the other around Lainie's and added, "Come on, kids. We're off to see the Wizard. The Wonderful Wizard of Loz. Weight loz, that is."

And Lainie couldn't help but smile because, for all the other things that had gone wrong in her world lately, it was nice that work at least seemed to be going right.

[nineteen]

Lainie ate so much at lunch that she was afraid she was waddling as she, Duncan, and Jack made their way down the stairs to the ballroom of the Ritz-Carlton Hotel.

It was all Jack's fault. She had planned to order the smallest salad she could find, along with a glass of ice water, even though Jack had made it clear that he was going to pay for their lunch. Or, rather, Duncan made it clear that Jack was going to pick up the tab.

"He always does," Duncan assured her as he ordered himself the seafood special, an iceberg-wedge salad, a cup of lobster bisque, and a side order of fries. And a Coke.

"I'll just have your house salad," Lainie told the waiter.

Jack eyed her over the top of his menu. "You're not one of those women who's on a perpetual diet, are you?"

Lainie glanced down at the prices next to the items on the

right-hand side of the menu. The cheapest thing there was a pulled pork sandwich, and it clocked in at $12.95. Her salad was half that.

"No. I just don't like to eat a big lunch," she lied. The truth was, she didn't really like to eat breakfast, so lunch was her big meal of the day. But she'd already taken enough advantage of him, so she'd just stick with her salad.

"Have it your way," he said. Then he went on to order two lobster bisques, a chicken Panini with sweet-potato chips, the grouper special, and two iced teas. "If there's anything left over, you're welcome to share," he said after the waiter had left.

And Lainie had blinked back an unexpected rush of tears, tears that threatened again when Jack nudged a heavenly smelling cup of soup under her nose and said, "You gotta try this. It's amazing."

He was right. It was amazing.

As were the key-lime cheesecake and chocolate turtle pie that they shared among the three of them after their meal.

Lainie put a hand over her distended belly and groaned. "I can't believe we're walking into a diet seminar after eating that lunch. They're going to smell the chocolate on our breath and start some kind of riot. Our likenesses will be burned in effigy at all Doctor Diet workshops from now on."

Jack laughed and threw a friendly arm over her shoulder. "Stick with me, kid. I'll protect you."

Then Lainie smiled up at him and, in that moment, everything changed.

It wasn't a subtle shifting of emotion, or the kind of thing that you didn't recognize until later, after you'd had time to think it all over and analyze it from all angles.

No. This was a lightning bolt. Accompanied by a thunderclap.

A whack upside the head with a cast-iron frying pan.

Complete with cartoon stars whirling around her head.

In that second, Jack stopped laughing, his dimples fading as his eyes darkened. The air around them stilled, as if someone had spun an invisible cocoon around them. Lainie felt the hair on her arms sizzle with the electricity passing between them.

Then Jack raised his hand to her mouth.

And slowly, her bones melting with each passing second, he dragged his thumb along her bottom lip.

And when Lainie felt like she was about to drop to the floor in a boneless heap, Jack slipped his thumb into her mouth. She tasted . . . salt. Chocolate.

Heaven.

"You had some chocolate on your lip. I had to get it off so the dieters wouldn't attack." His smile was back. Or half of it was. But that look in his eyes was not the same old look. He was looking at her as if he'd like nothing more than to . . . What?

Kiss her?

No. More like *consume* her.

Lainie shivered.

No one had ever looked at her like that before, and Lainie wasn't sure she liked it.

Hell, who was she kidding? She definitely liked it. She was just having a hard time *believing* it.

She licked the chocolate off of Jack's thumb and then—terrified that she was about to burst into flames right there in the hallway of the Ritz-Carlton Hotel—she stepped back. Away from the source of the heat. Like any sane person would do when she was about to get burned.

Lainie wiped a hand across her forehead.

How many times did she need to remind herself that Jackson Danforth III was out of her league? Yeah, he might find it amusing to play with the hired help for a while, but she was not the sort of woman his type stuck with for the long-term. And, frankly, her heart wasn't up to playing Jack's game.

She wasn't foolish enough to think that Blaine Harper was going to meet her and fall instantly and forever in love with her, either, but at least with Blaine, she had a chance to get something out of it for herself.

With Jack, she'd end up losing her job—or, even worse, her heart—when it was all over and he moved on to someone in his own social circle.

Lainie took another step back and bumped into Duncan, who had been gaping at a pair of hotel guests on their way to the swimming pool wearing identical dental-floss bikinis and had missed Jack's little show.

Grabbing Duncan's arm, she turned him away from the beautiful people and marched him down the hall, too much of a coward to dare glancing back to see if Jack was following.

"This amazing little pill holds the secret to permanent weight loss."

The former prom king and captain of the high school football team paced the front of the packed ballroom with all the energy of a late-night infomercial host. He was good, too, Lainie had to admit. He had that charisma, a passion for what he was selling, though Lainie guessed that it was the selling itself, rather than the product, that really turned him on.

"Now, I could show you a lot of complicated charts and graphs, put up a bunch of scientific mumbo jumbo to explain how it is that the CR-252 compound works, but I'm guessing that you all are not interested in a complicated biology lesson."

"Wouldn't want to clutter our pretty little heads with real information," Jack muttered under his breath.

Lainie refused to look at the man standing next to her in the back of the ballroom, his heat crowding into her space. "Shh," she whispered back.

"Let me just give you a quick demonstration of how CR-252 works. You, ma'am. There in the back by the door. Could you come up here for a moment?"

Lainie turned to see who he was talking to. She hadn't thought there was anyone else here by the door but them.

She froze and slowly turned back to the front of the room.

Blaine chuckled. "Yes. You. In the black-and-white top."

"This ought to be good." Duncan rubbed his hands together.

Jack folded his arms over his chest. "Yeah. Go for it, Lainie."

Lainie gulped. This was it. She was going to be close enough to Blaine Harper to reach right out and touch him. Had he chosen her because he recognized her from fifteen years ago?

No. Surely not.

She slowly made her way up the aisle between the folding chairs where the mostly female Doctor Diet audience was seated and then mounted the steps to the left of the stage where Blaine was standing.

"There, that wasn't so difficult, was it?" He smiled and took her hand.

Lainie waited to feel something—some electricity pass between them, some spark now that she was within feet of the man she'd felt so strongly about over a decade ago. There. She felt something. Wasn't that— She covered her mouth with her free hand as a tiny burp escaped.

Must be the key-lime cheesecake.

"What's your name, miss?" Blaine asked, pulling her behind him to the center of the stage.

"L-Lainie. Lainie Ames," Lainie answered. The heat from the lights overhead was making her sweat. She looked out over the crowd of expectant faces, surprised that most attendees ranged from wafer thin to only slightly overweight. They didn't look like they needed a miracle. A few laps around their neighborhood gym would do the trick.

"Nice to meet you." Blaine squeezed her hand and then let it drop. "I wonder if you wouldn't mind doing me a favor. I'd like to show these fine people how CR-252 works."

Lainie glanced over at Jack, who hadn't moved from his post against the wall, and then blinked to clear her head. She didn't need Jack's permission for this or anything else. She turned back to Blaine and smiled her most flirtatious smile. "Well, sure. I'd be happy to."

"That's wonderful!" Blaine clapped his hands as if she were a child who'd just taken her first steps. Then he turned to the audience. "Now, first, I want you to assure these fine people that I'm not paying you to endorse my product in any way. Is that correct?"

"That is correct," Lainie said.

"We've never even met before this afternoon."

"Uh . . . It's true that we don't know each other," Lainie answered.

What? That was true! So maybe it wasn't exactly the answer to his question, but she was standing here, next to her high school crush, and he was nodding approvingly and smiling at her—two things he'd *never* done fifteen years ago. She figured she deserved to be cut a little slack.

"Great. So here's what I'm going to have you do, Miss Lainie Ames from— Where did you say you were from?"

"Um, I didn't. I just moved to Naples from Seattle," she said.

"Seattle. That's a great town. As is Naples, of course." He grinned at the crowd to show that he wasn't playing favorites.

"That's true," Lainie agreed.

"So, Lainie, here's what I want you to do. It's very simple." As he talked, he walked to the side of the stage, where a young brunette with her hair in a ponytail and a headset on her head was holding a plate with a silver cover over it. Blaine took the plate from her and paced back to Lainie. "I want you to take the lid off of this and tell the audience what you smell."

Lainie hesitated. What in the world—

Blaine laughed and looked out at the crowd. "She must think I've got a rabbit under here."

"I was more afraid it might be a rat," Lainie blurted.

"Ah, not to worry. That's the whole point of this exercise, so no one will leave thinking they smelled a rat."

"Ba dum bum." She mimed a drumroll, and then turned to the audience. "He's a doctor *and* he's got a sense of humor. And I'm not seeing a ring on his finger. What's wrong with all of you single girls out there? You're falling down on the job."

"Believe me, you're all doing fine." Blaine sent the crowd a mock put-upon look and everyone laughed.

And when he glanced back at Lainie, his over-the-top infomerical-Doc smile was gone and a real one was in its place. For the first time since she'd stepped onstage, Lainie felt the flutter of butterflies—and this time it wasn't the key-lime cheesecake—in her stomach.

"All kidding aside, Lainie, would you do the honors?" Blaine held out the plate again, and this time she didn't hesitate.

She put her index finger through the hole on the top of the lid and pulled it off. The aroma of freshly baked bread wafted up into her nostrils. Despite the fact that she was so full she couldn't eat another bite, her mouth watered.

"Yum. Bread. It smells so good," she said, without being prompted.

"Exactly!" Blaine punched the air with one fist. "That's what makes CR-252 so effective. You see, studies have shown that people who are overweight tend to eat—*even when they're not hungry!*—because their noses tell them that there's something good available."

He tapped Lainie's nose with a finger when he said the word *nose*, and she couldn't help but notice how nicely manicured his hands were.

"CR-252 blocks the stimulation of the olfactory receptors, so you only eat when your body needs nourishment. No longer are you a slave to your sense of smell! You eat less and—without feeling deprived, without having to go on some complicated diet or join some expensive gym—you lose weight!"

Blaine turned back to her, setting the plate of warm bread on a stool that sat across from another stool bearing a glass of water and a green-and-white bottle of what Lainie could only assume was the miracle pill he was pushing.

"Now, can I ask you to do one more thing for me, Lainie? Would you mind?"

"No. Sure," Lainie answered. He was actually quite cute this close up. His skin wasn't nearly as smooth as it looked on his website. In person, he looked more . . . real. Which, she supposed, only made sense.

"Would you take one of these? The effect is immediate. I promise it won't hurt."

"Yeah, I've heard that one before," Lainie deadpanned, waggling her eyebrows at the audience, who got a good laugh.

Blaine chuckled and held out a white capsule and the glass of water. Lainie shrugged. Might as well do it. What could it hurt?

She took the pill and chased it with half a glass of water. "Done," she announced, handing him back the glass.

Blaine put the half-empty cup back on the chair next to the bottle of pills. Then he picked up the plate of bread again and held it under her nose. "What do you smell now?" he asked.

Lainie sniffed. Hmm. She leaned closer to the bread and sniffed again.

"Nothing," she said. "I don't smell a thing."

"And this bread, it's not appealing to you now, is it? You're not even slightly tempted to break off a piece and slather it with hundred calories per tablespoon, hundred-percent fat, salted butter, are you?"

"No," Lainie admitted, without adding that she hadn't really been tempted to do that even before taking the pill.

"There you have it, ladies and gentlemen," Blaine said, pointing to her with both hands. "What more evidence do you need that CR-252 works? You have my guarantee that it will work for you."

The audience applauded and Blaine took a bow, then turned to her with a grin, took her hand, and pushed her forward so that she could also take a bow. Lainie laughed as she straightened up.

"That was kind of fun," she whispered out of the side of her mouth.

Blaine covered the mike clipped to the neck of his silk shirt. "I've got another show in an hour. Want to do it again?"

Lainie blinked at him, wide-eyed. Did he really mean it?

"No, I'm kidding." Blaine laughed. "I really can't do that. You never know when you're going to get a repeat attendee, and they'll nail you on that sort of thing."

Right. Of course he hadn't meant it. Lainie forced herself to keep smiling.

"But this was fun. Probably one of the best shows I've ever done. You were great."

Blaine turned to face her, then looked over her shoulder as the audience dispersed—some of them going directly to the sales displays set up around the perimeter of the room, but some heading toward the stage. "Look, I don't have a lot of time. It's normal, I guess. Everyone wants to meet me. Ask questions. You know." He shrugged, and then surprised Lainie by reaching out and taking hold of her left hand. "But I'm in town for a while. I'm actually from Naples originally," he said with a snort, which Lainie couldn't interpret. "Anyway, what I'm trying to say is, can I have your number? Your phone number, I mean. I'd really like to give you a call sometime, Lainie Ames from Seattle."

{ twenty }

She hadn't given him her number.

Lainie groaned and banged her head on the dashboard of Jack's black BMW. Her high school crush—the one man who could redeem her in the eyes of her classmates—had asked for her number. AND SHE HADN'T GIVEN IT TO HIM.

Instead, Lillian Bryson's Dating Rule #4 had popped into her head.

Why? She didn't know.

It wasn't like she believed in that sort of thing. Dating wasn't a game. There were no rules.

It was ridiculous to even think that there were.

But for some reason, when Blaine had asked for her phone number, all she could think was "Make him work for it." So instead of just reeling off those seven little digits, she'd winked at him (and,

oh, wasn't she just the *picture* of sauciness?) and said, "I work at Intrepid Investigations. We're in the book."

Then—and the only way to properly convey her horror at what
she had done was to shout—SHE HAD TURNED AND WALKED
AWAY.

Without making sure he had heard her. Without checking to see
that he'd spelled it correctly. Without even watching to make sure
that he'd written it down.

Lainie banged her head on the dashboard again.

She was such an idiot.

"Um, you know, I hate to pry, but would you like to give me a
clue as to what's wrong here? If you keep that up, you're going to
dent my car."

"Don't you have insurance?" Lainie muttered.

"It doesn't cover intentional acts by the criminally insane," Jack
quipped back.

Lainie sighed and covered her face with both hands. She'd had a
chance at maybe, just maybe, getting her life back on track and she'd
blown it. What was wrong with her?

No wonder Fate was such a cruel mistress. Every time she handed
Lainie something she claimed that she wanted, Lainie threw it back
in her face.

"Aargh," Lainie groaned, the sound muffled by her hands.

"At least she's not banging her head anymore," Duncan said from
the backseat.

"No, but this wailing and teeth-gnashing is going to get old
pretty quick," Jack said as he slid the car into a spot near the front
door of the office. He turned off the engine and twisted in his seat
to face Lainie. "Come on, Lainie. Give me some answers."

"Delaware, all of the above, ninety degrees," she mumbled
through her fingers.

"Very funny."

"That's it. She's the one and only woman for me. Can I have her?" Duncan asked.

"Don't you have some copies to make?" Jack said.

"No." Duncan leaned forward and rested his elbows on the backs of their seats.

"Some people to call?"

"Uh-uh."

"An unemployment form to fill out?" Jack warned.

"Right-o, Boss. I'm outta here." Duncan started whistling as he exited the car.

"I'm not telling you what's wrong," Lainie said. "It's a personal matter." There. Maybe he'd think it had something to do with her hormones or something. Guys never wanted to hear about that.

"Oh. Well . . ." Jack paused, obviously uncomfortable. "Look, I don't know what's going on here, but . . . If there's anything I can do. Or if you just want to talk. Well. I just want you to know that I'm here. For you. You know. As a friend."

O.

K.

Jack's speech surprised her so much that she dropped her hands from her face.

"A friend?" she repeated.

He cleared his throat and loosened his collar, obviously not realizing that he was wearing an open-necked shirt. "Yeah. A friend. Why not? Just because I sign your paychecks, that doesn't mean we can't be friends, right?"

Lainie shook her head. "Of course not. It's the twenty-first century."

"So it is. So it is. And men and women can be friends in the twenty-first century. Can't they?"

"S-sure," Lainie stuttered.

"I mean, wasn't that the whole point Meg Ryan's character was trying to make in *When Harry Met Sally*?"

Um. Where exactly was this conversation going?

"I think so."

"But then, of course, there was Billy Crystal and his theory that men and women can't be friends because, inevitably, the guy's going to be thinking about sex, and that ruins the friendship."

"You're not going to make me start talking with a funny accent or something, are you?" Lainie asked, shooting him a sideways glance.

"No," Jack answered absently. "I mean, not unless you want to. But I don't suppose . . ."

"Suppose what?"

"Naw, nothing."

"What?" Lainie asked, then bonked her head on the window as Jack speared her with a grin that could best be described as wicked.

"You wanna get naked and see if I can tell whether or not you're doing that thing Meg Ryan was doing in the deli? That would certainly test the theory of whether or not we could be friends."

Lainie rolled her eyes. She was *not* going to fake an orgasm in Jack's car. Or anywhere else, for that matter. "Jack, get serious."

"Get serious? Lainie, I just propositioned you. If I get any more serious, they're gonna have to move us to the erotica shelf."

"Jack," Lainie warned.

"Lainie." Jack grinned. "Sorry. But at least you're not upset anymore."

And as Lainie pushed open the car door, she realized that he was right. She wasn't going to tell him that, though. Wouldn't want him to get a big head.

"Has anyone ever told you you're a nice guy?" she asked as they walked into the office.

"Me? Hell no. I'm not nice. I'm eye crust. I'm navel lint. Haven't you read the script?"

"Expensive navel lint, though, right?"

Jack shot her a lopsided grin. "Exactly."

God, he was cute when he smiled like that. He was even cuter when he leaned down and kissed her on the tip of her nose and said, "I like you, Lainie. I'm glad you're here."

Lainie swallowed heavily. Uh-oh. What was that she just felt? Was it her frozen heart starting to melt?

She stepped back, her hip bumping into the top of her desk. "I'm glad I'm here, too. At work, I mean. I've got a lot to do. Uh. I never did get a chance to see those pictures from last night."

Jack leaned back against his own desk, his jeans stretching across his muscular thighs as he crossed his arms over his chest and watched her for a long moment in silence. "I'll e-mail them to you Monday morning. Why don't we call it a day? It's Friday night. I'm sure you've got plans, and so do I."

Lainie tried not to look desperate as she glanced at the clock. It was only four-fifteen. She couldn't go home now, not and face another seven or eight hours of emptiness. "I don't mind working," she said.

"Aw, come on. Go." Jack waved toward the front door, then suddenly straightened. "It looks like my date is here already. Now we can both get head starts on our evening."

A stunning woman with shiny, waist-length brown hair and the tiniest hips Lainie had ever seen pushed open the door to their office. She had exotic, almond-shaped brown eyes, a blinding smile, and cheekbones a model would sell her soul—or at least this season's latest handbag—for. A pair of red stiletto's encased her size-four feet, and matching red ribbons wound around her calves like snakes. Her dress was red, shimmery, and clung to every curve of her size-one body.

In short, she was every real woman's worst nightmare.

"Jack, honey. You're not ready." She pouted, giving his jeans and polo shirt a disappointed once-over.

"We're headed to Miami," Jack threw over the woman's teensy—yet perfectly toned and tanned—shoulder.

Well, of course. Who *didn't* go clubbing in South Beach on a Friday night?

Lainie shoved the jealous beast that was trying to come out of her mouth like that creature from *Alien* back down into her throat where it belonged. She knew women like this existed in real life—how else would fashion designers stay in business?—but she'd never actually met one until now.

And here she had been feeling pretty good because she was back down to a "skinny" size ten again.

Not anymore.

She pushed her own—dull, lank, and mousy by comparison—brown hair out of her eyes, then quickly hid her hands behind her back when she realized how awful her nails looked. She hadn't been able to afford a manicure in ages. And her feet! Since moving back to Florida, she'd stopped wearing shoes at night and the skin on her heels was like plywood.

She couldn't imagine the woman currently curling her arm around Jack's had ever had a blister between her toes, much less ever experienced dry, cracked heels or even had a hangnail. Her skin wouldn't dare rebel against her like that.

Lainie pasted on a wobbly smile as she forced herself to walk past the perfect couple. This was the picture she would keep in mind whenever she started thinking that Jack's teasing was anything besides his way of taking pity on her.

That's all that it was. Nothing more.

{ twenty-one }

And then, you will never guess what she did. Come on. Guess."

Jack absently rubbed his right ear, which was feeling abused after being chewed on for the past half hour by his half sister, Amy. "Uh, she scratched you? Pulled your hair? Flipped out a knife?"

Amy's sigh rocked the car. "No. That would be *Lisa's* mom, not mine."

His father, J.D. Junior, had fathered seven children, all with different women—three of whom he'd married, and four of whom he had not.

Jack couldn't wait to see when kid number eight would show up. He knew, with 100-percent certainty, that there would be a number eight. Since Dear Old Dad had only turned sixty-five last year, Jack figured he'd be firing live rounds for a good ten years yet. Maybe even twenty.

Jeez. So that could mean there might be an eight, nine, ten, and eleven still to come. Then, knowing Dad, he'd probably shoot for an even dozen.

Which was exactly why Jack Danforth II's parents had set up a skip-generation trust. Even before they'd passed away a decade ago, they'd seen the path their only child was on, and they hadn't wanted the fortune they'd worked so hard to preserve to end up being doled out to every woman who fell into their son's web.

Jack wasn't angry at his dad anymore. J.D. was just . . . well, J.D.

A lying, cheating, lazy, worthless bum who sometimes slept with nice women and broke their hearts when he knocked them up and walked away, and sometimes slept with pain-in-the-ass women and broke their hearts when he knocked them up and walked away.

Jack's mom was the former variety. His half brother Jackson's was not. Neither was Duncan's, Lisa's or Trent's.

But Amy's and Kim's moms weren't so bad. At least not that Jack could tell, though Amy certainly had a bug up her rear about her maternal parent this evening.

Sometimes he felt that his life was more like old reruns of *Dallas* or *Dynasty* instead of *Moonlighting*. Though he had to give both Duncan and Lainie credit there. They were working damn hard to fit at least one joke from that old show into every day.

"All right. So tell me. What did she do?"

Amy's mother had apparently not approved of her daughter's attire this evening and had expressed her displeasure in a manner to which Amy took offense.

"She tried to put some old Chinawoman curse on me. Told me a good daughter would do as her mother said."

"Isn't your mom Vietnamese?" Jack asked blandly.

"So what? You know what I mean. She tries to use all that 'old country' shit on me whenever she wants me to bend to her ways.

I'm not going to do it. I'm an American. I've never even *been* to Vietnam. What does she want, for me to dress like I'm going out to some fucking rice paddy or something? I've seen the movies. Those clothes are ugly. Where do they get them? Burlaps 'R' Us?"

Jack swallowed a snort of laughter. Encouraging Amy would be a mistake. "Well, did you ask your mom what she had in mind? I really doubt she expects you to wear something that bad." As a matter of fact, Mai was one of the most beautifully dressed women he knew. She probably just wanted her daughter—who could have passed for Mai's twin—to wear a dress that wouldn't make it quite so clear that Amy preferred Brazilian bikini waxes to regular ones.

"No. I left as she was in the middle of putting some sort of hex on me. I'll probably end up having frogs appear in my bathwater or something."

Jack chuckled, then fiddled with his rearview mirror as the setting sun did its best to blind him. They were still about half an hour from Miami, where Jack was meeting with contractors to discuss their progress on the conversion of an apartment building he owned into a condo-hotel. He knew Amy loved Miami with its anything-goes and party-till-dawn attitude, so he'd invited her along for the weekend when the meetings had been set up.

As much as he rolled his eyes and griped about them, he loved his half brothers and half sisters. Well, except for Jackson. Jackson made it hard for anyone to love him. Still, they were family. A kooky, mixed-up, cheaper-by-the-dozen family, maybe, but a family nonetheless.

"So, what's up with the new girl in your office?" Amy asked, interrupting his thoughts about J.D. and his miscellaneous progeny.

"Lainie? Nothing's up with her. Why do you ask?" Jack shifted his gaze from the road to his half sister and back. Amy was usually so self-centered that she didn't notice anyone else but herself.

He was surprised she'd registered Lainie's brief presence in her world.

"Duncan likes her. He says you do, too. Says he can *feeeeel* the chemistry between you two."

"Duncan should be careful what he says. His job is expendable."

Amy socked him with her small yet bony fist. "Stop threatening to fire Duncan. We all know you'd never do it."

She was right.

They both knew it.

"Yeah, I like Lainie," Jack said, changing the subject. "She's got a good sense of humor, even though she's suffered some setbacks lately. And she has a great work ethic, which is more than I can say for anyone else in my employ."

Amy shrugged off his insult. "Some of us don't have to have work ethics. Some of us were born lucky."

"When you fall from that pedestal you've put yourself up on, it's gonna hurt. The drop is long and, let me tell you, the landing is a bitch."

"Oh, what do you know about it? You're the one with control of all the cash. You wouldn't know a hard landing if it smacked you on the ass."

Yeah, right. Jack knew a thing or two about what it was like to fall on your face with what seemed like the whole world watching. That was why, after he'd done some digging and unearthed a few things about Lainie's past, he'd begun to think of her as more than just the cute mystery woman who'd had the balls to steal his credit card that night at the Ritz.

As a matter of fact, he was beginning to suspect that he and Lainie Ames had more in common than she would ever know.

* * *

$\mathcal{A}$nother Friday night alone.

Lainie stood on the porch and stared at her father's front door. Then she took a step back and looked down the block at her sister's house.

Trish and Alan had put a lot into remodeling their place, and, for the first time, Lainie realized that they were not alone. Most of the houses on this block had gone through facelifts; some—like her sister and brother-in-law's—had added second stories. Others—including her father's—remained the original square footage, but had new roofs, fresh coats of paint, and had been professionally landscaped.

The neighborhood wasn't nearly as shabby as she'd remembered it being in high school. But when had it changed?

It wasn't like she hadn't been back in fifteen years. Why hadn't she noticed the metamorphosis before?

Standing on the porch with the sun beating down on her shoulders, Lainie shrugged. It didn't matter. She was glad for her father and sister that the neighborhood had improved, but that didn't leave her any less alone this evening.

With a resigned sigh, she put her key in the lock and pulled open the front door. She was greeted with a refreshing blast of cold air, but crinkled up her nose when she stepped inside.

"Smells like gas in here," she muttered as she closed the door behind her.

She wondered if maybe she'd left the lid off the tank of her dad's riding mower, but when she opened the garage door and sniffed, she realized the smell wasn't coming from there. She walked through the house to see if she could identify the source of the smell, but thought that maybe she had just imagined it . . . that is, until she opened the door of her room and was assaulted by fumes.

Lainie pinched her nose shut. Whew. Someone could lose a few hundred thousand brain cells after breathing that in.

She opened the two windows that ran the length of the room to try to air it out.

Then, with the sneaking suspicion that she'd found the culprit, she lifted the top of the wicker clothes hamper, and then hurriedly clamped it back on when the odor of gasoline wafted out.

Damn. She must've gotten gas on her clothes last night when she'd been siphoning it from the mower into her car.

"That's it. Into the wash you go," she said, picking up the hamper—lid and all—and carrying it to the laundry room. She threw everything—whites, darks, and in-betweens—into the wash. It was going to take at least two cycles to get that smell out. Might as well do the first run as quickly as possible.

That done, she went back to her room to change, but noticed as soon as she stepped into the room that the gasoline smell had been masking another, mustier odor.

Wrinkling her nose with distaste, Lainie went on another sniff hunt. This time the unpleasant stench led her to the closet. She stood in front of the slatted doors, her hands on the faded brass knobs, and inhaled.

Yes. It was coming from in there, all right.

She pulled open the closet doors and peered inside. Her clothes were still hanging on the left, her shoes neatly arranged below them on the floor. Unless the Florida heat and humidity was causing her stuff to mold, Lainie didn't know why any of that should stink. She bathed every day. Took her clothes to the dry cleaner at the first hint that they were no longer fresh. Put talcum powder in her shoes to soak up any moisture.

Lainie leaned in and sniffed.

No, it wasn't her clothes.

She bent down and smelled.

Nope. Not her shoes, either.

She stepped over to the other side, trying to ignore the garment bag that had brought back such bad memories. There was nothing else hanging on that side of the closet, so Lainie crouched down to see if there was something on the floor that reeked of mold.

There were several old shoeboxes on the floor. Lainie pulled the lid off the first one and frowned. What was all this stuff?

She pulled the box out into the light.

It was full of papers and yellowed photographs. She lifted the first item from the box and skimmed the faded handwriting.

Her first-grade report card.

Lainie's eyes narrowed. Where had they been living back then? In some Navy town in California, if she remembered correctly.

She glanced at the date. December ninth. End of the first quarter, her first year of school.

She wasn't sure how it worked now, but at her school—at least back then—everything you did was either satisfactory or unsatisfactory. There were no grades, no graduation ceremonies for six-year-olds who had learned how to say their ABCs and tie their shoes in order to pass on to the second grade.

Lainie read through the report card and couldn't help but smile. The teacher's comments seemed so serious.

"Elaine seems to have a difficult time concentrating."

"Elaine sometimes has trouble controlling her temper."

"Elaine does not participate in class activities as much as I would like."

She'd earned satisfactory scores in all categories—including penmanship, which made her laugh, because she was left-handed and had been a messy writer until she'd finally figured out that if she turned her paper to the right, she could print her numbers neatly without running her hand over what she'd just written.

Lainie turned the report card over then and her smile froze. There, clipped to the back, was a note written in the same handwriting as on the report card. It was addressed to her father.

"Dear Mr. Ames," it began. "I struggled with Elaine's student evaluation because the girl who began my class back in September is not the same one that I'm teaching today. Elaine started out this year as a bright, cheerful child who was helpful and kind to others, if maybe a bit overbearing when things weren't going her way. More recently, however, she's been moody and withdrawn, barely participating in class discussions even when called upon directly. Obviously, your wife's tragic and unexpected death in October—"

Lainie stopped reading and dropped the report card as if it were a purring cat that had suddenly turned and bit her.

She put the lid back on the box and shoved it back into the closet, eyeing the other two boxes warily. On the one hand, she was curious to know what was in them. On the other, she didn't want anymore unpleasant surprises.

Tipping her decision in favor of hand number one was that she still had to find the source of that musty odor. If there was something nasty in one of those boxes, she needed to get rid of it. She wasn't going to be able to sleep in this room otherwise.

Lainie pulled the second box toward her and cautiously lifted the lid to peek under it. This one was full of ribbons—green ones, red ones, a few blue ones. They seemed harmless enough, so she dragged the box out of the closet to get a closer look.

"Fourth place in the fifth-grade three-legged race." Lainie chuckled as she pawed through the silly ribbons.

It was an overachiever's worst nightmare. She'd forgotten that, even back then, schools had tried to raise their students' self-esteem by giving them ribbons for everything from placing ninth in the crab-walk race to participating in the third-grade spelling bee.

Satisfied that nothing was amiss in this box, Lainie put the lid back on and pushed it back into the closet.

Then she peered into the last box and frowned. This one was full of photos—more recent ones than in the first box, their colors not quite as faded as the others. But as she started to pull the box out, she spied the edge of a plate stuck in the corner of the closet.

Oh, geez. She smacked her forehead with the palm of one hand. It was the mushrooms she'd halfway cooked the night Trish had invited her over for an impromptu party. And, ugh, did they smell ripe.

Squinching up her face, Lainie grabbed the rim of the plate with two fingers.

Yep, that was definitely the source of the musty smell.

Keeping her nose plugged, she took the plate into the kitchen and ran some water over it, but the mushrooms seemed to have attached themselves to the ceramic so she filled a mug with water and zapped it in the microwave for two minutes, and then poured the near-boiling water over the mess in the sink. Satisfied that would at least soften up the grime, Lainie set the cup next to the plate, started the washing machine again, and then went back to her room.

She hauled the box out of the closet and plunked it down on her bed. Then she pulled off her shoes and clambered on top of the quilt, crossing her legs pretzel-like as she settled in to find out what memories the box held.

The photos were like a reverse-time history of the friends she had known and the places she'd lived. She wasn't sure—had she been the one to keep the box or had someone found these pictures in her room after she'd moved out? And why hadn't she taken them with her to Seattle?

Probably because she'd moved enough times to know that everywhere you went, you started over with a new set of friends, a new life. It might sound glamorous, but Lainie knew it wasn't.

Maybe some people were cut out for the nomadic life, but not her.

She'd forgotten how painful it was to leave old friends behind.

She blinked back tears as she gazed at a picture of her fourteen-year-old self. For some reason, she'd gotten chubby between her thirteenth and fourteenth birthdays and that chubbiness had lingered until Lainie hit nineteen. Even then, no one would ever have termed her slender or svelte, but she'd lost that all-over pudginess that had come upon her so unexpectedly in her teens.

Or . . . maybe it hadn't been so unexpected.

Lainie looked at the picture again. She looked sad, this girl who was half-Lainie and half-someone she didn't even recognize anymore.

Fourteen.

She would have been starting ninth grade that year.

Had they just moved again?

Lainie could almost answer yes without even doing the math. Weren't they *always* moving again?

She forced herself to try to remember. Her fourteenth birthday. August sixth.

Yes. They'd moved that summer and all the neighborhood kids warned her how awful the high school in this blue-collar town was rumored to be. She didn't remember much from that move—she'd learned well the power of forgetfulness over the years. The quicker you forgot your friends from the last town, the less saying good-bye hurt.

But what she did remember was that the neighborhood kids were right. That school was awful.

The tenth-graders picked on all the younger kids, leaning against the walls that led to the cafeteria to harass them as they went in to lunch. They'd hurl insults, somehow instinctively knowing the barb that would get under your skin and hurt the most. You needed a gas mask to go to the girls' bathroom because the cigarette smoke was so thick. And the bus ride home was torture. A particularly tough tenth-grader chose newcomer Lainie Ames to harass. No one would sit with her for fear that they, too, would become Rita's target, which meant that Lainie had to suffer the sharp pencil jabs and insults about her weight, her clothes, her hair, and anything else Rita could think of, all by herself.

And there was no point trying to talk to her dad about it. She'd tried that once, when he'd overheard her crying and asked her what was the matter.

"Well, you *do* eat a lot for a girl," he'd said, when she blurted out that Rita had said she was fat.

Of course she did. She was a lonely kid with no one to turn to for comfort. Cinnamon toast heaped with butter had become her new best friend.

Lainie put the picture back in the box and started flipping forward, stopping when she found a photo that made her smile. This one was taken in Naples, a few months after they'd moved here. This move wasn't quite as difficult as others in the past, maybe because Trish had been here to help ease the transition. It was still tough facing that first day of school, but at least Lainie had known *someone* in town.

Her stomach grumbled just then, and Lainie was stunned to realize that she was hungry. How could she possibly be hungry after the lunch she'd eaten?

Obviously her stomach didn't care about logic. It wanted food, so Lainie took a handful of photos from the top of the shoebox and went to the kitchen to forage for something to eat, stopping on the way to toss her clothes in the dryer.

She opened the fridge and contemplated her choices. She wasn't *hungry* hungry. She really just wanted a snack, something comforting to curl up with while she looked at the rest of her pictures.

"Ooh, is that crème brûlée?" Her stomach gurgled in anticipation. She loved crème brûlée with its smooth eggy custard topped with that warm, crisp toasted sugar crust. Dad had probably brought these home from the restaurant last night.

Lainie pulled out one ramekin and held it up to her nose. The effect of Blaine's miracle diet pills obviously didn't take long to wear off, because she could definitely smell the crème brûlée, though at this point it was just the crème and not the brûlée.

That was easy enough to fix. Hadn't she seen a hand-held torch in the drawer with the waffle iron?

She sprinkled a spoonful of sugar on top of the custard and then set it on the counter next to the toaster before going in search of the brûlée torch. She'd had one just like this back in Seattle. You filled it with butane and clicked the igniter and—voilà!—instant burnt sugar.

Lainie grinned wryly as she took the torch from the drawer. She'd sold hers for fifteen bucks (original price $39.95) at the Garage Sale from Hell. At the time she'd reasoned that a brûlée torch wasn't exactly a necessity. You could achieve the same result by broiling the sugar-topped dessert under a broiler. But that exposed the entire custard to heat, while this method only warmed the top. Plus, it was easier to control. With the broiler, one second your sugar hadn't even melted and the next second it was burned.

Blech.

There was nothing worse than the acrid taste of overly burned sugar on top of an otherwise perfect crème brûlée.

Lainie twisted the nozzle on the torch to get the butane flowing and then clicked the igniter several times.

Hmm. It wasn't lighting.

She grabbed a pack of matches from the junk drawer and lit a match, holding it to the hole in the torch where the butane should be flowing.

When that didn't work, Lainie blew out the match and tossed it in the disposal side of the sink. Then she closed the gas line on the torch. It must be out of butane. Fortunately, she'd seen a white canister with red lettering in the junk drawer next to the matches.

Silently thanking her dad for being prepared, Lainie pulled the butane cartridge out of the torch and, out of idle curiosity, sniffed it to see if she could tell if it was empty.

She had no idea what had made her do that.

Nor did she have any idea what made her look up at that moment.

Perhaps it was the odd feeling that she was being watched. Or maybe it was just that her neck was tired and needed a stretch. Whatever it was, Lainie chose that moment to glance up . . . and then dropped the canister of butane as her gaze met Trish's in the window above the sink.

{ twenty-two }

What a weird weekend," Lainie muttered to herself as she turned down Sunshine Parkway and headed toward the office. On Friday night she had finally told Trish about her new job, which she thought would make her sister happy. But it seemed that every time she turned around, one of her family members was standing there watching her. Like they were afraid she was going to make off with the family silver or something.

"I don't know why they'd bother. There are no family heirlooms to steal."

"Pardon me?"

Lainie blinked and realized that she'd been just about to run into a man on the sidewalk. "Nothing. Sorry," she said.

"No problem," the man answered, then asked, "Do you work here?"

"Where? At Intrepid Investigations?" She eyed the guy. Was he a potential customer? Could be. He had on blue pants and a white shirt with the name Dave embroidered on the right side of his chest.

"Yeah," the man confirmed.

"Yes, I do."

Ooh. This was so cool. Her first solo client! Too bad she didn't have a key to the office to let them in. She couldn't wait to set up her first client file using the new software she'd—

"Good. Then I can leave these with you," the man said. Then he opened the door of the van he was standing next to and pulled out an impressive arrangement of colorful mixed flowers. There were white roses, pink gerbera daisies, some purple flowers that Lainie didn't know the name of, all set off with a nice mix of greenery.

"They're beautiful," she said, all the while thinking that Jack must have been pretty amazing this weekend to impress his young hottie enough to send flowers.

Figured. She'd spent the weekend under the curiously watchful eyes of her family while Jack had been having a wild time in Miami with a hot babe. Once again, just went to show how far apart their worlds were.

"You got me flowers? How sweet. I'm sorry, but I didn't get you anything. Is it our anniversary? I always forget that sort of thing," Jack teased as he slid his car into the parking spot the flower delivery van had just vacated.

Lainie rolled her eyes. "Why would I give you flowers? You've never even bought me dinner."

Jack pointed his keychain at his car, and it chirped cheerfully as the doors locked. "That's not exactly true," he said with a grin.

Lainie had the grace to blush, but she hid behind the bouquet so Jack wouldn't see. "Well, they're not from me."

He opened the door to the office and held it open for her to precede him inside. Lainie put the heavy vase on his desk before turning to head back to hers, startled to find Jack blocking her way.

He looked happy this morning. Relaxed. No bloodshot eyes or frown hovering about his mouth. And why not? He'd probably spent the last two days having sex, hanging out at the beach with the amazing female specimen he'd left with on Friday night, having more sex, eating in swank restaurants, having even more sex . . .

"Looks like you had a great weekend. What's it like dating Miss Teenybopper 2005?" The words were out before Lainie could stop them. Oh, jealousy. She was a vicious mistress.

Jack put a hand to his heart and shot Lainie a wounded look. "Ouch. That hurt."

"Uh-huh."

"She's actually Miss Teenybopper *2006*. I know I'm not quite the man I used to be, but I've not yet been reduced to having to settle for last year's model."

Lainie shook her head and wondered what it was that attracted Jack to such young women. Then she gave herself a mental slap upside the head and told herself to stop being so naïve. What appealed to him was cellulite-free thighs. Flat stomachs. Probably tongue-piercings. Yeah, she might be over thirty, but she knew what tongue-piercings were good for.

To a guy like Jack, regular blow jobs had probably become boring. De rigeur. Passé.

He was probably so oversexed that nothing short of trapeze-swinging, latex-wearing, whip-wielding acrobatics did it for him anymore.

If she wasn't so jealous, she might even have felt sorry for him.

With a sigh, Lainie sidestepped her boss. *No more pining for things you can't have*, she scolded herself.

"I'm just kidding. Amy's my sister. Well, my half sister," Jack corrected. "Even if she weren't, I'd never date someone like her. She's way too wild. I'm looking for someone a little more grounded. Someone who's experienced a few hard knocks and had to get back up on her feet again. Someone who appreciates that life isn't always easy."

Lainie swallowed as Jack's words washed over her. She could feel his gaze on her back, could almost touch the connection hanging between them.

Why would he say something like that to her? He couldn't possibly—

"Morning, guys," Duncan said, oblivious to the charged air in the office as he clattered in from outside.

"Has anyone ever told you that your timing sucks?" Jack said.

"Nope. Consider yourself the first."

Lainie shivered, still half under Jack's spell. She turned to find that he was watching her, his dark eyes full of an emotion she couldn't name.

She pulled her bottom lip into her mouth to moisten it. Why was her mouth so dry all of a sudden?

Jack noticed the gesture and his eyes darkened even more. He took a step toward her and reached out, his warm, strong fingers caressing the bare skin of her upper arm.

"Lainie," he began.

"Hey, nice flowers. Who are they from?" Duncan asked as he walked around the back side of Jack's desk on the way to his own.

"Would you—"

Lainie leaned forward. *Yes*, she wanted to shout, without even hearing the question.

"Lainie, they're for you," Duncan interrupted.

Ask the question, she silently urged, ignoring her clueless coworker. She didn't care about the flowers. What was Jack about to say?

"Wow, you must have made quite an impression on this guy. Not only did he send flowers, but he promises to call you this morning. In two hours. Go figure. He's making a date to ask you out on a date."

Jack's teeth snapped shut as he narrowed his eyes on Lainie's face. *Please, just ask*, Lainie begged silently.

"Who are the flowers from?" he asked without turning his head.

"Blaine Harper," Duncan answered. "Looks like I've got competition for our little Lainie's affections. Doctor Diet's got the hots for her. Isn't that sweet?"

Jack dropped his hand and took a step back. "Yeah. That's . . . sweet," he agreed.

Lainie closed her eyes, her emotions in a turmoil. Wasn't this what she'd dreamed of? Blaine Harper—popular, handsome, and now rich—was interested in her. *Her.* Elaine Ames. Outsider. Former chubby geek. A woman whose life, even now, was a mess.

She should be elated. Lillian Bryson's rules of engagement had worked. Because of Lillian's advice, Lainie had snagged Blaine's attention. There was no guarantee that he'd ask her to be his date for the reunion, to give her the second chance at wowing her classmates that she so desperately wanted. But now, at least, there was some possibility that it might happen.

Why, then, did she suddenly feel so disappointed?

{ twenty-three }

After about fifteen minutes of moping, Lainie decided to stop being such a whiner and use this opportunity for all it could be worth. Blaine Harper was going to call between 11:30 and noon and she had no idea what to say to him.

Should she just make small talk?

Giggle coquettishly?

And what if he didn't come right out and ask her on a date? Should she bring up the topic herself?

Lainie tapped a pen on the file folder in front of her. She needed help. But who could she ask?

Certainly not Jack. Or Duncan. Even the thought of broaching the subject with them made her snort with laughter. Trish might be able to help, but Lainie doubted it. Her half sister had been married for nearly fifteen years. What did she know about the rules of today's dating game?

No. Lillian Bryson was the only one Lainie could turn to. But she didn't have the money to pay for Lillian's advice.

Lainie had no other choice. She was going to have to try eavesdropping.

Who knew? It had worked for her last Friday. Maybe it'd work again today.

Now all she needed was an excuse to drop by Rules of Engagement.

Lainie frowned and tapped the folder again. What reason could she use to go over there again? It had just been luck that had brought her to Lillian's office last week.

Well, that and a background check, Lainie amended.

Then she straightened up in her chair. That was it! The background check.

Lainie grabbed the file folder from her desk and stood up.

"I'm going to run the results of this background check over to Rules of Engagement," she announced.

Jack looked up from whatever he was busy working on at his computer. "It's not done yet. I'm still waiting on the results from the credit bureau."

"Oh." Lainie sat back down. Narrowed her eyes. Thought for a moment. Stood up again.

"Okay, then I'll just run and get some coffee," she said. They wouldn't see her going into Rules of Engagement . . . unless they were spying on her.

"Great. Get me a mocha, would you?" Jack asked absently, returning to his work.

"And I'll take a caramel macchiato. Extra whip!" Duncan hollered from the kitchen.

Uh-oh. She didn't have any money.

But she couldn't tell them that.

Great. Now what was she going to do?

Lainie sighed. Well, this was her own fault. She should know by now that her lies always snowballed until she was overcome by the avalanche.

She shook her head and grabbed her purse. She'd think of something. But first, she had to figure out what to do about Blaine.

She headed out into the warm spring sunshine. A couple meandered by on their bicycles as a large brown butterfly landed on some pretty yellow flowers that spilled out of a planter a few feet away. Springtime in South Florida and color was everywhere. Even the trees were gloriously decked out in brilliant red, purple, orange.

In Seattle trees bloomed in three colors: white, light pink, or pale yellow. It surprised her to see anything else after so long in the Pacific Northwest.

But her mission this morning was not to catalog the differences between the northern and southern climates, so Lainie hurried next door, looked behind her to make certain Jack and Duncan weren't watching, then pulled open the door and slipped inside.

She expected to be greeted by Rules of Engagement's receptionist, and was pleasantly surprised to find the waiting area empty.

Yay. This might be easier than she had anticipated.

Lainie tiptoed down the hall, pressing her back to the wall as she stopped outside Lillian's office and cautiously peered in. She could hear voices coming from the classroom at the end of the hall, and hoped that she could get away with eavesdropping for a few minutes. Really, all she needed was a few words of advice. Armed with that, she might feel more comfortable taking Blaine's call.

After ascertaining that Lillian's office was empty, Lainie continued tiptoeing down the hall.

With a guilty glance behind her, she pressed her ear to the door.

"—tell me why you should never accept a date without forty-eight hours' notice?" Lainie overheard Lillian say.

"Because you don't want to be his booty call?" a female answered.

"That's one reason, yes."

"You don't want him to think you're just sitting around waiting for him to call?" another woman said.

"True. But, more important, you *don't* want to be sitting around waiting for him to call," Lillian said. "Your life should be full enough that you know what you're doing forty-eight hours from now—even if it's just scheduling some time for yourself to relax or clean your house. That man should not be the number-one priority in your life. If he is, you've given him way too much power, and I can guarantee that he's going to make your life miserable."

Lainie snorted. Yeah, well, they could make your life miserable even if they weren't your number-one priority. Ted had proven that to her.

Oh, what was the use? This wasn't going to help her—

"Lainie? What are you doing here?"

Lainie spun around so fast that she whacked the side of her head on the doorframe. "Maddie. Hi. Uh, what am I doing here?"

Yes. Exactly. What was she doing there?

"Uh . . ." Come on. Think.

She rubbed her ear and floundered desperately for some plausible excuse. When her gaze hit upon a door on the other side of the hall marked "Restroom," she stopped rubbing and smiled.

With a silent apology to Duncan for throwing him under the bus, she said, "Um, I wondered if it would be okay if I used your bathroom. Duncan went into ours ten minutes ago. With the latest issue of *Spy/P.I. Weekly* under his arm." She waggled her eyebrows at Maddie. They were both women. They knew what that meant. But just in case, Lainie added, "It's not going to be safe to go in there for another hour, if you know what I mean."

Maddie crinkled her nose. "Yeah. I know what you mean. Feel free to use ours anytime. I don't envy you, having to share with two men."

Actually, Jack and Duncan weren't bad, and Lainie felt a little guilty for insinuating that they were. Not guilty enough to retract her statement, mind you, but guilty enough to feel a twinge as she thanked Maddie and slipped into the bathroom to make the illusion of her lie complete.

What is taking Lainie so long with that coffee?" Jack grumbled as he slammed the door of the cupboard in the lunchroom after taking out a mug.

"Somebody's in a bad mood all of a sudden," Duncan observed mildly from behind his magazine. He loved *Spy/P.I. Weekly*. All those stories of real detectives—mostly embittered ex-cops or hardened military guys—going up against embezzlers or kidnappers. And they had the greatest toys.

Duncan read the specs for the latest miniature high-powered weatherproof 95-NM IR LED illuminator with the ninety-foot range and sighed.

Why couldn't they get one of those?

But he knew why. Because they weren't a *real* detective agency.

Because Jack really didn't care if they had any cases or not. He'd only bought Intrepid Investigations to bail out a friend's father and had ended up liking having an office downtown.

This place, like Duncan's job, and Kim's job, and Amy's job, and Lisa's job—and now Lainie's job—was just a charity case; something Jack did out of pity.

Lainie hadn't figured that out yet, though. And Duncan had to give her credit. She was trying to revamp this place, make it a real business instead of the joke it was now.

Duncan, for all his obsession with all things P.I., was no idiot. He'd noticed the way his older half brother looked at Lainie when she wasn't watching. There was definitely some chemistry between the two—chemistry that Duncan had thought was about to explode this morning when he'd walked into the office.

"Seems to me that it's not the coffee that's got you acting like a bear whose honey's been stolen right out from under his nose."

"What are you talking about?" Jack asked, banging his cup down on the table, which only made half the water he'd just poured into it slosh over the rim.

"I'm just saying, I think someone's upset because someone else got flowers from someone who isn't you."

"Right. That's it exactly, Duncan. I have never met anyone who could put two and two together faster than you," Jack said, with all the disgust he could muster.

"What can I say? Math was always my strongest subject," Duncan quipped. Then, ignoring Jack's frustrated growl, he went back to drooling over his magazine and dreaming of one day becoming a real private investigator.

This is another fine mess you've gotten yourself into," Lainie grumbled, realizing that she was spending waaaay too much time talking to herself lately.

With two coffee orders and no money, this had been the only plan she could come up with.

She let herself into her dad's house, praying that he would still be asleep. Her lie supply was running dangerously low today, and she was already going to have to make up something to explain why she was taking her espresso machine to the office when there was a perfectly good Starbucks half a block away.

She was also going to have to waste some of her precious fuel. No way was she going to lug that espresso machine for half a mile. Not only was it heavy, but it would take her forever to get back to the office. As it was, she'd already been gone too long. She was certain Jack would notice her long absence.

She only hoped he didn't insist again that she get a cell phone so that he could keep tabs on her. She was going to need every cent of her first paycheck to get caught up on her car payments, and she had no idea how long it might take him to reimburse her for the expense.

Lainie winced as the heels of her shoes clunked against the terrazzo floor. She froze for a long moment, listening to hear if her dad had noticed the sound.

When no one stirred, she let out a relieved breath.

Okay. Just get the espresso machine and the coffee beans from the freezer and she'd be home free.

Lainie walked into the kitchen on the balls of her feet, trying her best not to make a sound. Grabbing the espresso machine under one arm, she carefully unplugged it, pleased with herself that she'd remembered to do so. She could just imagine getting halfway to the door and being yanked back by the cord.

With the cord wrapped around her arm so she wouldn't trip on it, Lainie went to the freezer and slowly pulled open the door.

Please, she prayed, *don't let a bag of frozen peas or pound of butter fall out.*

For once, her prayer was answered.

The door *whooshed* open quietly and Lainie gently wrestled the bag of gourmet coffee beans out from between a box of chopped spinach and a brown-paper-wrapped piece of meat.

Her mission accomplished, she let go of the door and heard it close with a satisfying *snick*.

Almost there, she told herself as she tiptoed to the front door.

And then she was outside. Soon the espresso machine was safely stashed on the passenger seat with the coffee nestled beside it. Lainie pushed the car door closed with her hip.

She couldn't believe it. This had been so easy!

She tried to contain her glee as she let herself in the driver's-side door. She'd be back in the office in less than ten minutes, doling out lattes like—

Ugh.

Lattes. Mochas. Caramel macchiatos.

She needed milk. And chocolate syrup. And caramel.

With extra whip.

Double ugh. And whipped cream.

Lainie rested her forehead on the steering wheel. She couldn't just make regular coffees. That would never satisfy Duncan and Jack. They'd send her back down to Starbucks, and this time she'd have no excuse. She'd have to admit that she didn't have any money, and that was the last thing she wanted to tell them. Especially Jack. The chasm between them was already Grand Canyonesque. She didn't need to widen it any further.

"All right. I'm going back in," she said to her reflection in the rearview mirror. If the circumstances hadn't been so dire, she might have laughed at herself. She was making this sound like some sort of Special Forces reconnaissance mission.

"All right troops, we're not leaving without the two percent."

Okay. So it was a little funny.

Lainie rolled her eyes as she stepped back out of the car. This *was* another fine mess she'd gotten herself into.

And she was lucky, at least, that her dad kept his pantry pretty well stocked. In no time she was loaded down with a carton of milk, a squeeze bottle of Hershey's chocolate sauce, and a jar of caramel sauce. Now, for the whipped cream.

Lainie pulled open the freezer. She'd searched the fridge for a spray can of whipped cream, but had only found the unwhipped variety in a one-quart carton. With her fingers crossed, she scanned the freezer shelves, hoping to find some Cool Whip.

But, at last, her luck had run out.

Lainie closed the freezer door.

Well, this was just going to have to do. So Duncan wouldn't get any whipped cream on his caramel macchiato. He'd survive. She'd bring along the cream so he could get the smoothness of it in his drink, even without the foam that whipped cream would provide.

She made another trip back out to the car and added her find to the growing stash on the passenger seat.

Then, as she was walking around the hood of her car, she stopped. Wait a second. Didn't Dad have one of those stainless-steel whipped-cream makers, the kind you filled with cream and then pressed a lever and it infused the cream with some sort of gas that whipped it instantly? Hadn't she seen it in the pantry, right next to the canned pumpkin?

Lainie glanced toward the house.

Should she risk it?

If she didn't, was there a chance that Jack and Duncan would send her to the market to get some real whipped cream?

Yes. It was possible.

Better to brave waking up her dad than having her plan fail because she'd neglected this one little thing.

Lainie tiptoed into the kitchen one last time, wincing when the panty door squeaked as she pulled it open. She reached inside. Wrapped her fingers around the cool metal. Pulled it out. Winced again as she slid the door closed and heard it pop into place.

Then she turned around, guiltily hiding the whipped-cream maker behind her back as she crept toward the front door . . . and never noticing that her father was standing in the shadowy hallway, watching her go.

{twenty-four}

*B*ack at the office, Lainie had her lie all prepared.

Fifteen years in Seattle had turned her into a major coffee snob. Even Starbucks wasn't good enough for her anymore.

Right.

She *loved* Starbucks. Once she got some money and could start buying their four-dollar cups of coffee again, she was going to have to come up with another lie to reverse this one. Maybe she'd say that, with nothing else available, she was forced to lower her standards.

She mentally shrugged as she juggled her espresso machine with the other supplies she'd taken from her dad's house.

Whatever. She'd come up with something. She was fast becoming quite a good liar, it seemed.

She had a feeling that might come in handy as a private investigator.

Yeah. So maybe she should just think of it as on-the-job training?

"Sorry it took me so long," she said as she pushed open the front door with her hip and dropped her stuff on the counter.

Jack sent her an unreadable look, while Duncan got up from behind his desk to help her carry her load to the kitchen. "What is all this stuff?" he asked.

Lainie gave him the story she'd come up with about preferring her own coffee to Starbucks', which he appeared to swallow without question as she got set up. In no time she had milk frothing, water caffeinating, and cream whipping.

She came out of the kitchen and set Jack's mocha on his desk. "I hope you like it," she said, surprised to realize that she really meant it.

Jack just grunted and didn't look up from his computer.

"Well, then, if you don't want it . . ." She bent down to take the cup back, but stopped when Jack speared her with his dark eyes.

"Oh, I want it all right," he purred.

Lainie tried forcing a laugh out of her suddenly constricted throat, but it sounded more like a choke. "I meant the mocha."

"I didn't."

"What do you mean, then?" Lainie asked. He was acting so weird today.

"I—"

Jack cursed when the phone on his desk rang, then he cursed again as he looked down at the caller ID display.

"You'd better get it," he said.

"Why?" Lainie crossed her arms over her chest and frowned. She was tired of this. If Jack had something to say to her, he could—

"It's *Blaine*. Make sure to thank him for the flowers."

Lainie let out a frustrated sigh. "I will," she said. Then she hurried over to her desk and picked up line one before it rolled into voice mail.

"Hi, Lainie. It's Blaine. Blaine Harper," he said with a laugh, as if he thought maybe she wouldn't remember.

And Lainie, feeling like Donna Reed in *It's a Wonderful Life* where she's talking to Sam Wainwright on the phone while Jimmy Stewart stands there oozing jealousy, laughed a phony laugh and answered, "Yes, Blaine. Hello. How *are* you?"

And just like in that movie scene, she barely heard what Blaine—who was the one guy she actually had a chance with—was saying.

She couldn't seem to look away from Jack, who was staring at her with open hostility.

"What? Um, yes, fine. And you?" she said when that seemed like the appropriate thing to say.

Blaine answered, but Lainie had no idea what he said.

"Oh, yes. Uh-huh. They're beautiful. Thank you."

Jack shoved his chair back with so much force that it careened into the filing cabinet behind him with a loud crash.

"No. No. Everything's great here. What? Tonight?"

Lainie shook her head and turned her back on Jack's glare. She had to pay attention here. Blaine was the one she wanted, not Jack. Jack was unattainable. Jack was beyond her reach.

Yes, maybe they shared an attraction to each other, but that was it. Once their lust was satisfied, there would be nothing left. And by then Lainie would have missed her chance at Blaine, her chance to redeem herself and prove, once and for all, that she wasn't a failure.

"No, I can't tonight," she lied, Lillian Bryson's advice ringing in her ears. It had worked once. Please. Please, let it work again, she prayed.

"No, not tomorrow, either. I'm afraid I've got to work late. Big case, you know," she said softly so Jack wouldn't overhear and call her on her lie.

Lainie squeezed her eyes shut. *Come on. Ask again.*

"Oh," Blaine said, sounding disappointed. "That's too bad. I'm afraid my timing is terrible. I'm booked the rest of the week, and then I have to head out of town on Saturday morning."

Lainie's fingers grasped the phone so tightly, she was afraid it might crumble to dust in her hand. She wanted so badly to change her answer, to tell him that she'd rearrange her schedule to accommodate his plans, but Lillian had sounded so sure . . .

"Well—" Blaine began after a long, uncomfortable silence.

Lainie opened her mouth to tell him that she'd just rechecked her schedule, and, imagine that, she was suddenly free this evening.

"How about Wednesday? I think I could move a few things around and free up my evening."

She felt like crying with relief. "Yes. Wednesday's great."

"Wonderful. Shall we meet somewhere? Say seven o'clock? Do you have any suggestions?"

Lainie opened her eyes to find Jack glowering at her from across the room. She didn't know what devil prompted her to do what she did next, but she found herself steadily returning Jack's gaze as she answered, "The restaurant at the Ritz is amazing. I think it would be the perfect place for our first date."

"Don't you have work to do?" Jack asked irritably as Duncan followed him out of the office.

"Do I? Do ducks duck? Do flies fly?"

"Don't start with me," Jack warned. "I'm not in the mood for it today."

"Why? Because you've got competition for Lainie's affections? Jack. Man. You are looking at this all wrong."

Jack stopped on the sidewalk with one finger pressed to his

keychain and wished he could shut his brother up as easily as he could lock and unlock his car.

He'd had to get out of there. He couldn't listen to Lainie cooing over that slimy diet pill doc anymore. *He* should have been the one to send Lainie flowers. Why hadn't he thought of that?

Jack had never been good at this stuff. He never seemed to know the right thing to do until it was too late.

He had to figure out a way to keep Lainie out of Blaine Harper's clutches. But what was he supposed to do?

"Are we going to lunch?" Duncan asked from the passenger seat of Jack's car, looking very much like an eager puppy hoping for a ride.

Jack just scowled at him from the sidewalk. Going to lunch with Duncan wasn't going to fix this situation. Of that much, he was certain.

He tossed Duncan the keys. "You go. I've got something I need to do."

Jack ignored Duncan's whoop of joy—he didn't usually let anyone else drive his cars, especially not Duncan who wasn't exactly the safest of drivers. But this was an emergency.

He headed to Rules of Engagement. Lillian Bryson would know what to do.

Hadn't he overheard enough of her lectures from between the thin walls separating Intrepid's kitchen from Rules of Engagement's classroom? He knew all about not saying yes to a date within forty-eight hours, about not having sex within the first month, about always letting the guy do the calling. Hell, over the last seven years, you'd think he might have actually learned something that would have improved his own dating life, but no. He didn't date much.

His father's antics had left him with few illusions about romance.

And when you approached dating with such a jaded attitude, it wasn't surprising when things never seemed to work out.

But the way he felt about Lainie was different. He liked her in a way he'd never liked any other woman before. He knew it sounded crazy, but from the minute she'd walked into his office that morning after stealing his credit card at the Ritz, Jack had known she was it. *The one.*

And he wasn't going to just sit back and let the diet doctor have her. Not without a fight.

He shoved open the door to Rules of Engagement, startling Maddie, who stared at him, wide-eyed.

"I'm here to see Lillian. Is she free?" Jack asked. Even if she wasn't, he wasn't going to take no for an answer. He needed help, and he needed it now.

"Sure, Jack. Go on back," Maddie said.

Jack nodded once, then headed down the hallway toward Lillian's office. He caught her in mid-bite of what appeared to be a turkey sandwich.

"Sorry to barge in like this. I need some advice," he said, stepping into her office and shutting the door behind him.

"This is a surprise. What can I do for you?" Lillian asked once she'd rinsed down her sandwich with a sip of water.

"I've met someone I really like, but I think I may have made a mistake by waiting too long to tell her. Now there's another man in the picture, and I'm not sure what I should do to get him out."

Lillian rewrapped her sandwich in the plastic wrap it had come in. "I see," she said, drawing out the words so they lasted a good thirty seconds. "So, this woman doesn't know how you feel?"

Jack scratched his head. "She knows I'm attracted to her. I mean, she has to know. And she's . . . Well, I think she's attracted back." God, he sounded like such an idiot.

"You have actually *talked* to this woman, haven't you?" Lillian asked with a little frown creasing her forehead.

"Of course I have."

"That's good." She sounded relieved.

"I mean, we haven't been on a date or anything. Not officially." Jack closed his eyes and rubbed his temples. No wonder he sounded like an idiot. He *was* an idiot. He was acting just like David Addison in that stupid *Moonlighting* show Duncan was always quoting, dancing around his feelings for Lainie without once telling her how he felt. No wonder she was going out with Blaine Harper. The diet doc had actually had the balls to *ask* her.

"Uh—" Lillian began.

Jack held up his hand to stop her. "Right. I see the problem. I've got to get her out on a date, show her what a great guy I am. Woo her. Charm her. Lock her in an ivory tower so no one else can have her."

"Jack—"

"I'm just kidding." Jack sighed. "But she's going out with him on Wednesday. I heard her make the date. I've got to get to her before that, so mine will be the date she compares everyone else's to. Unfortunately, she knows about your forty-eight-hour rule."

"She does?"

"Uh-huh."

"How do *you* know about it?"

Jack pointed to the left. "Thin walls," he answered.

"Ah."

"So what can I do? If I ask her out for tonight or tomorrow night, she'll think she has to say no."

"Lie," Lillian said.

"Lie?" Jack blinked. Had she just said what he thought she had said? Sweet Lillian Bryson?

Lillian got up and walked around her desk, where she leaned

against the top and speared him with her motherly gaze. "Yes. Lie. Cheat. Don't steal, but do whatever you have to do to make an impression on her before she goes out with this other guy on Wednesday night. Otherwise, he'll be the one to set the standard. If this woman is that important to you, you'll think of a way to get her to go out with you before then."

"Okay," Jack said, somewhat bemused by Lillian's take-no-prisoners approach to the dating game.

"Okay."

"Good."

"Good." Lillian grinned. "I told you how to make her love you, now get out."

{twenty-five}

"Well, there's certainly nothing incriminating here," Lainie said as she flipped through the pictures from their surveillance at the country club last week. Jack had downloaded them off the camera pin and e-mailed them to her this morning. She hadn't realized that she'd inadvertently snapped several photos when she was pressed up against the rear of that statue. There were photos of the statue's lower back, of the dimples above its butt cheeks, and a few butt-crack shots that would have made even the most hardened plumber envious.

Lainie frowned when she came to a picture that was unlike the ones before it. Rather than the cool gray marble of the previous shots, this one was a sort of pinkish color with a flash of black. She squinted and clicked the button to zoom in on the photo, then zoomed back out in an attempt to figure out what it was.

Comprehension struck, and, with her cheeks on fire, Lainie deleted the photo from her inbox.

It was cleavage. *Her* cleavage, to be more precise. The camera must have gone off when she'd tugged her dress on, inside out.

"Looks like you're well on your way to becoming a first-class private investigator," she mumbled as she looked at the previous picture.

Hmm. Wait a second. There was more to it than just the marble statue's butt cheek. There was a flash of something over there, to the left.

Lainie blew up the photo, then cropped all but the area she was interested in and zoomed in some more.

She narrowed her eyes. What was that? It looked like a man's hand holding a baggie filled with something white.

She must have taken it when Bob and the other guy were coming out of the men's room. With a click she moved back another photo. In this one the camera had been pointing down, toward the floor. When she enlarged this picture, she saw two men's shoes— one brown, the other black. Yes, that's it. It must have been when the two men were coming out of the bathroom.

Lainie opened another picture and discovered a flash of green. Money. Moving from one man's hand to the other's.

So what could the white stuff in the baggie be?

Lainie's eyes widened. Omigod. Lisa Sprick thought her husband was cheating on her—which he might very well be doing—but it also looked as if he were buying or selling drugs on the side, too.

This was awful.

No way could they tell Mrs. Sprick about the drugs. Not without more evidence.

They needed to get back into this case, set up a round-the-clock surveillance schedule.

At least, that's what *Spy/P.I. Weekly*'s "Ask the Expert" guy said when Lainie e-mailed him for advice . . .

The first thing she needed to do was to call Mrs. Sprick and find out where her husband would be this evening so they could set up a tail. The file should have Lisa's number, as well as information about where Bob worked, so they could arrange surveillance for tomorrow as well.

Lainie double-clicked the icon for their new case management software and entered her user ID and password at the prompt. She had full access to all of their cases, so she didn't have any trouble opening Lisa Sprick's file.

She frowned when she realized that Jack had done a haphazard interview with their client. He hadn't gotten Bob's place of employment, information about where he spent his free time, or anything. Well, she'd fix that.

Lainie dialed the contact number that Jack had typed in for Lisa Sprick.

"Big Tow Towing," a man answered on the second ring.

What? Lainie hurriedly checked the number she'd dialed against the one in Mrs. Sprick's file. Yes. She'd dialed the right number.

Lainie cleared her throat. "Um, yes, is Lisa Sprick there?" she asked.

"Right lady. Pull the other one," the guy said, sounding like he was going to hang up on her.

"No. Wait. What about Bob?"

"Bob Sprick?" She could just imagine the man's expression as he asked that question.

"Yes."

The guy on the other end of the line sighed so heavily that Lainie's hair stirred. "Look, lady, nobody's prick is here, got it?

And no, my refrigerator ain't running. What are you, fourteen?"

"No. Wait," she said again. "I can explain."

"Yeah. Explain it to somebody else. I ain't got time."

Lainie stared at the dead receiver in her hand. That hadn't gone the way she'd expected. Now what were they going to do? Jack must have written the number down wrong. They had no way to contact Mrs. Sprick. No way to—

Wait a second.

Wasn't the first rule of investigating: Never give up?

With nowhere else to focus her attention for the next two days, Lainie figured she might as well throw herself into her job. Her first order of business was to find Lisa Sprick. How hard could it be?

There's something going on with your sister."

Trish sighed and pushed a lock of blond hair behind her ear. "What makes you say that?" she asked. She didn't want to tell her father what she suspected yet. Not until she was sure. Lainie and Carl's relationship was already strained at best. Trish didn't want to make things worse by voicing her fears without any hard evidence to back her up.

Yes, there was the gasoline incident that Lucas had witnessed. And, okay, on Friday night when she'd gone over to check on Lainie, she'd seen the mushroom tea in the sink.

And smelled an unmistakable chemical odor when she'd walked in the door.

And caught her sister sniffing a canister of butane.

Trish's shoulders drooped. Of the twenty or so inhalants specifically listed on the Department of Justice website, they'd caught

Lainie with three. The mushrooms weren't commonly used by huffers, but she suspected that it wasn't a giant leap from getting high using common household substances to moving on to hard-core drugs like shrooms, LSD, heroin.

Oh. This was awful.

Where would it all end? With Lainie homeless, lying in a ditch, her needle-scored body bruised and battered? Would she start turning tricks to earn enough money for her drugs? She'd gotten a job down at that investigations firm, but everyone knew that drug abusers couldn't hold down jobs for long. Maybe . . . Oh, no. Maybe that's what had prompted her little sister's move to Naples in the first place. Had she lost her job and her home in Seattle because she couldn't kick the habit? Was she here, not to start a new life as she'd told them, but because she had nowhere else to go?

Trish took a deep breath and tried to calm herself down. Maybe there was another explanation. As damning as the evidence was, maybe—

"She took my whipped-cream dispenser," Carl said, interrupting Trish's thoughts. "It's not like I care if she borrows it. It's just . . . weird. She came tiptoeing in this morning while I was asleep, and I woke up and heard her rummaging around. I got up to say hello and I see her sneaking out with the whipped-cream dispenser behind her back, like she's some kind of criminal. I don't get it, Trish. Maybe all that rain in Seattle addled her brain."

Trish blinked back tears as she put an imaginary red X through another substance the DOJ listed at their website. Nitrous oxide. Abused more frequently than any other gas. Easily obtained from—drumroll, please—whipped cream dispensers.

There was no other explanation. Lainie was a drug addict.

"I'm so sorry to tell you this, Dad. I've felt that something was wrong, too, but . . . Well, now I'm sure." She took a deep breath, and then blurted, "Lainie needs our help. She's addicted to huffing."

{ twenty-six }

*B*ob Sprick wasn't in Naples.

As a matter of fact, there were no Spricks in Naples at all. Or in the surrounding areas, according to her online phone directory. So now what should she do?

Cautiously Lainie peered out from between her computer screen and the bouquet sitting on the corner of her desk. Jack had come back about an hour ago, his bad mood apparently having subsided.

He'd even brought her a sandwich, which she'd eaten while throwing suspicious glances his way. Why was he being so nice after nearly biting her head off earlier?

It didn't matter. She had a job to do.

If only she could figure out how to do it . . .

She opened her mouth, intending to ask Jack for his help, but the ringing of the phone cut her off.

She glanced at the caller ID and frowned. Golden Gulf High School? What could they want?

"Intrepid Investigations. Lainie Ames speaking," she answered.

"Hey, Lainie. It's, um, Trish," her sister said hesitantly.

"Oh, hi. How are you?"

"Good. And you?"

"Fine. Thanks." So much for brilliant repartee.

"Good. Um. I'm sorry to bother you at work . . ."

"It's no bother," Lainie said, surprised to discover that she really meant it. Used to be, she hated getting personal calls at work, probably because she was so busy that she knew any time spent on nonwork-related activities would have to be made up in the wee hours of the morning or late at night. It was kind of nice to have a job that didn't require you to check your soul at the door.

"Good," Trish said, making Lainie think she needed to buy her big sister a thesaurus one of these days.

"Yes. We've established that," Lainie joked, but it must have gone over Trish's head, because her sister just said, "Um-hmm."

"Look, uh, I was wondering if you had a chance to maybe come down here for a half hour or so. There's something I wanted to discuss with you. You know, away from Dad and the kids and any disruptions."

Lainie clicked on the calendar section of her e-mail program. What do you know? Her schedule was completely empty. Today. Tomorrow. Pretty much all week.

"Just a sec," she said, then held her hand over the mouthpiece of her phone. "Hey, Jack, do you mind if I run out for about an hour? My sister wants to see me."

"You're planning to come back, right?" he added, though Lainie had no idea why it mattered.

"Yeah."

"Go ahead then. I think I can manage to keep everything under control until you get back."

Their gazes skipped around the empty, silent office before meeting back at the middle of the room. They shared a rueful smile.

"I'll be there in about fifteen minutes," Lainie told Trish, who, not surprisingly, answered with yet another, "Good."

Lainie hung up and grabbed her purse from the bottom drawer of her desk. She pulled her keys out, but then decided she might as well walk. It was a gorgeous day—the temperature hovering just below eighty, humidity at a hair-curling 85 percent, but quite pleasant with the soft breeze blowing in off the Gulf—and after so many days of being forced to exercise, Lainie was discovering that she actually enjoyed it.

"I'll be back," she called to Jack as she headed outside into the sunshine.

"I'll be front. That's where all the good stuff's located," Jack called back, making Lainie chuckle.

She was on the sidewalk outside the high school in less than fifteen minutes. A chain-link fence ran around the perimeter of the school—whether to keep the kids in or out, Lainie had never been quite sure. The parking lot was crowded with a mix of expensive imports and midpriced sedans. Naples was a wealthy town, but even wealthy towns had their regular folk. Besides, most of the really rich kids—kids like Jack Danforth III—went to Gulfside Prep, where no Toyota or Honda dared to go.

She turned into the parking lot and stood for a moment, studying the school she'd graduated from. It looked much the same as it had fifteen years ago, though there were a few more rectangular outbuildings dotting the perimeter than there had been back then. The white stucco of the main building was almost blinding in the midday sun, while the red roof lent the school a Spanish air. The grounds were well maintained, the lush lawn kept green by daily sprinklings of reclaimed water.

Lainie waited for the unpleasant sensation of being back here to rush through her, and was surprised to remember, instead, how relieved she'd been to move to a school where she wasn't being tormented by bullies every day. She'd forgotten that. It wasn't like she'd made instant, lifelong friends here, but her days had mostly passed in peace.

Her unrequited love of Blaine Harper notwithstanding.

Lainie smiled to herself as she started toward the entrance to the school.

Her gaze was caught by a movement to the left and Lainie froze midstep.

It was Bob. Bob Sprick.

Instinctively Lainie darted between two vehicles and crouched down so he wouldn't see her. She couldn't believe her luck. What were the chances that she'd find her subject here at the high school, of all places?

She crab-walked around to the front of one car, then peered up over the hood to keep her subject in view. He was whistling off-key, his arms loaded down with stuff—papers and other things Lainie couldn't identify from here. She had to get closer.

And, dang! Why hadn't she thought to bring a camera?

She darted down two rows of cars, then flattened her back against a blue-green Mercedes and held her breath as Bob crossed the same row.

Whew. That had been close.

She got on her hands and knees and peeked between the tires to see that her man had stopped near an older, silver Chrysler. She heard the jingle of keys, then a car door squeaked open and slammed shut. Then footsteps rang out on the pavement.

Bob had put whatever he'd been carrying in the car and now he was coming back this way.

Lainie gasped. She had only seconds before he caught her.

Just as his white tennis shoes rounded the corner, Lainie rolled under an enormous Toyota Land Cruiser that was big enough to mount an invasion of Canada all by itself.

She held her breath and pressed her nose to the pavement as the shoes passed her by.

The sound of footfalls faded away and Lainie shivered. This private-investigator stuff was a lot more dangerous than she'd ever guessed it would be.

She rolled out from under the Land Cruiser.

Now to see if she could find out what Bob had put in his car. If nothing else, she could get his license plate number and track him down that way. How cool was that? She had another lead.

Warily Lainie poked her head above the hood of the SUV. Bob was heading back toward the school, his empty arms swinging at his sides.

What was he doing here? Buying drugs? Selling them?

It seemed that today's high school kids had so much more exposure to drugs than Lainie's generation had, fifteen short years ago. It was awful how many of them got caught up in it, smoking pot to ease the pressure momentarily, then sliding deeper and deeper into the habit as everything around them fell to pieces.

Lainie shook her head sadly. If Bob was involved in selling drugs to kids, she'd do everything she could to make sure he got busted. This was more important than just some scumbag cheating on his pretty young wife. Kids' lives could be at stake.

She sidled over to the Chrysler, all the time watching Bob to make sure he didn't turn around.

Her eyes narrowed as she glanced into the car. There was

something white there on the seat, beneath a brown file folder and several yellow pads of paper.

She looked back up at Bob, who had stopped on the sidewalk and was talking to a brown-haired boy of about fifteen or sixteen. Lainie gasped as she saw the boy reach into his pocket and draw out a green bill.

Omigod. She was witnessing a drug deal. A real drug deal.

She cursed herself again for not thinking to bring a camera. Damn. If she could just have gotten this on film.

Bob and the boy started toward the school.

Lainie didn't know what to do. Should she tackle the guy? He was bigger than she, but she had anger—and surprise—on her side. But hadn't she read that a P.I.'s first responsibility was to gather the evidence? She couldn't bring Bob to the police's attention with nothing but a few blurry pictures from last week showing money changing hands. She needed more than that if she hoped to help the police get a conviction.

But, that said, no way was she going to let him sell whatever it was that was sitting in near-plain-view in the front of his car.

Slowly Lainie pulled up on the door handle of the Chrysler, praying that Bob hadn't locked it again . . . or activated an alarm. Not that anyone would pay it the slightest attention. People had gotten so jaded about car alarms these days that nobody even bothered to see if it was their own car's alarm going off when the alert sounded. Still, it would probably give her a heart attack.

She breathed a sigh of relief as the door clicked open without an accompaniment of screeching alarms.

Her hand snaked out to grab the block of white powdery substance, and she half-expected someone to lurch up from the backseat and grasp her wrist.

But no one did.

Lainie didn't bother closing the door. So what if his interior lights drained Bob's battery? That was the least the drug-dealing bastard deserved.

With the package under her arm, she jogged away from the Chrysler as quickly as she could. When she'd gotten a safe distance away, she glanced around to make sure no one was watching. Then, just like she'd seen a thousand cops do on a thousand TV shows, she opened one corner of the bag, licked her pinky, stuck it in the bag, and pulled out a fingerful of white powder. She sniffed it, but it didn't have a scent, so she touched her finger to her tongue and then screwed up her mouth in distaste. Not because the powder tasted bad, because it didn't. Not really. It was sort of salty, but not like salt. More . . . flat. Kind of chemical-y.

She spit so she wouldn't swallow whatever it was.

She'd take this to the police. They'd be able to analyze it.

In the meantime, she was late for her appointment with her sister, so she stuffed the bag into her purse, coughing when it sent up a cloud of smoky powder as she crammed it in with all her other stuff. Then she ran up the stairs leading to the main entrance of the high school, on her way to meet Trish.

It was worse than she had thought.

Trish tried not to stare at the white powder marking her sister's blouse. Was it cocaine? As a high school guidance counselor, she should probably be more familiar with what drugs like cocaine actually looked like, but she wasn't. She typically saw the effects of the drug abuse—the behavior problems, the sudden attitude shifts, the falling grades—but not the actual drugs themselves.

She had no way of saying for sure whether the white powder on Lainie's left shoulder was coke, but she had more than just a sneaking suspicion that it was.

"So what did you want to talk to me about?" Lainie asked as she eased into one of the stuffed chairs across from Trish's desk.

Trish had just gotten off the phone with a friend in Tampa who had more experience dealing with drug problems than Trish had. Her friend cautioned Trish about not sounding too accusatory or judgmental when confronting her sister about her addiction. It was best, her friend had said, to let the addict know you were there to support her in her recovery efforts, but also to let her know that you were aware of the problem and weren't going to let her just sweep it under the rug.

She got up and walked around her desk. This conversation would probably go better if she presented it like two friends talking rather than an adult lecturing an errant student.

Trish sat down next to her sister, turning the chair so that their knees were nearly touching. "It seems like we've barely had a chance to talk since you've been home," she said.

"That's all right. I know you're busy with your family."

"*You're* my family, too," Trish said, laying a hand on her sister's arm.

"Of course. I didn't mean to make it sound like you were neglecting me."

"Do you feel neglected?" Was that the problem? Had Lainie turned to drugs because she was lonely?

"Not at all. I'm . . . Well, I was going to say that I'm perfectly happy, but then no one really is, are they?" Lainie gave a little laugh that sounded hollow to Trish's ears.

"So." Trish leaned forward. "You're unhappy. Would you like to talk about it?"

Lainie shot her an odd look that Trish couldn't decipher. "Not really. Look, what is this conversation about? I feel like I'm missing something here."

"Do you often feel that way? Like you're somehow inadequate?" Her poor baby sister. Sad. Lonely. Her self-esteem in the toilet. No wonder she tried to find comfort in chemicals.

"Well, doesn't everyone feel like that sometimes?" Lainie asked.

"Certainly. And there are healthy ways to manage those feelings. Exercise. Positive self-talk. Getting involved in things you care about. Surrounding yourself with people you love."

"Sure. Or I can just keep doing what I've been doing since I was sixteen and end up in an early grave."

Lainie chuckled, but Trish didn't share in her sister's gallows humor. *Do what she'd been doing since she was sixteen?* Was that how long Lainie's drug problem had been going on? If so, it was going to take more than one conversation to get her sister on the road to recovery. Lainie needed professional help.

This wasn't something Trish could handle on her own. It was time to call in the experts.

{ twenty-seven }

What a weird meeting.

Lainie shook her head in consternation. She had no idea why Trish had wanted to see her or what their conversation had really been about. Or why it had ended so abruptly.

All she'd done was make a joke about working herself into an early grave and Trish's face had gone green.

Maybe her sister was sick? Or . . . Wait a second. Could Trish be pregnant? Was she asking all those odd questions about Lainie's mental health because she was afraid Lainie might be jealous that her big sister was having baby number three while Lainie couldn't even find a date for her high school reunion?

That was probably it.

Lainie rolled her eyes as she stopped in front of the office. Of course she wasn't jealous. She loved the idea of having another little niece or nephew to cuddle with. This time it would be even

more fun because she was living in Naples and could actually spend
more than a week or two every year with her newest relative.

Geez. If Trish had just told her the news, Lainie could have put
her sister's mind to rest. She'd have to call her later and—

"Oh, good, you're back. I need you to go undercover with me
on a case tomorrow night. I'll pick you up at seven-thirty. Wear
something nice," Jack added.

Lainie blinked owlishly as she let the office door swing shut behind her.

Huh?

"A case? We have another case?"

"Yes. A client came in while you were away," Jack lied. There
was no client. No case. No undercover work that needed to be done
tomorrow night. This was just the best thing he could come up with
to get Lainie to go out with him before her date with the diet doc
on Wednesday. He knew her well enough by now to be certain that
she'd never say no to anything work-related.

She wasn't a workaholic.

Just . . . dedicated.

And maybe a little desperate. Like she didn't have anything else
in her life, so work *had* to be important. If not, she'd have nothing.

"Did you fill out the paperwork? I forgot to tell you this earlier,
but I tried calling that number you entered for Lisa Sprick and you
must have typed it in wrong. I got a towing company and the guy
who answered wasn't happy about the wrong number."

Jack coughed to cover a grin. He'd bet he wasn't.

Which reminded him, he still needed to figure out something
to do to punish his sister for coming up with that stupid joke. It
was bad enough that the case itself wasn't real—

"Oh, and I also think you should see this. I caught Mr. Sprick selling it on the high school campus. Well, maybe not selling it exactly.

But he took money from a student and this was hidden in his car. I think we've got a drug dealer on our hands."

Lainie slapped a brick of white powder on his desk, and Jack stared, openmouthed, as a puff of the substance rose into the air in front of his face.

No way.

What were the odds? He'd picked some random guy out of the crowd at the country club that night to play the part of Lisa's cheating husband. And Lainie, with no investigative skills whatsoever, had managed to not just find the guy again, but catch him in a drug deal?

Jack rubbed his pounding forehead.

He knew what his mother would have said. She'd tell him that this is what he got for lying, even if it had been for a good cause.

Now he'd landed Lainie smack dab in the middle of a drug ring.

Then he brightened. "This is great, but if we have no way to contact Mrs. Sprick, all we've got is another dead end."

"That would be true. If I didn't have this," Lainie announced, slapping a piece of paper with a license plate number down on his desk next to the brick of powder.

Lovely.

"Well. Um. Good work. We'll just hand this over to the police."

"Hey, what's that?" Duncan asked, coming out of the lunchroom and pointing to the white stuff on Jack's desk.

"Cocaine. At least, that's what I think it is," Lainie said before Jack could answer.

Duncan's eyes widened. "No way. We can't have that here. It's illegal."

"I know that. I wasn't born yesterday."

"That's true. I had lunch with her yesterday. If she'd have been born, I'd have noticed," Jack said.

Lainie snorted. "Good one, but it's not true. Yesterday was Sunday. I had lunch with my sister and her family, not you."

"Well, then, I'm sure *they* would have noticed," Jack amended.

"No fair. You guys are taking all the best lines, and the whole *Moonlighting* thing was my idea," Duncan grumbled.

"Sorry," they said in unison.

"I can't believe Lainie busted a drug dealer her first case out. I've been doing this for four years, and all I've got to show for it are a couple of X-rated photos."

"Well, let me remind you, Duncan, that one case does not a detective make," Jack said.

"Well, let me remind you Jack, that I HATE IT WHEN YOU TALK BACKWARDS."

"There. Do you feel better now?" Jack asked.

"Yes. Thank you," Duncan answered with a satisfied grin.

"Can we get back to the case now?"

"Absolutely. Sleuth away."

"So, I'll take this block of whatever-it-is down to the police station and leave it in their custody," Jack said.

"What about the license plate number? Don't we have a way to trace it?" Lainie asked, obviously disappointed to be handing over her case to the police. "I mean, how are we going to prove to them that Bob is a drug dealer without proof? How will they even know that this cocaine was his?"

"We don't even know if it's cocaine," Jack said.

"Yeah, did you taste it?" Duncan asked.

"I did, but how am I supposed to know what cocaine tastes like?"

Jack rolled his eyes. "Both of you watch too much TV. You should never put something in your mouth if you don't know what it is. This could be poison for all you know."

Duncan and Lainie both narrowed their eyes at the white brick.

"Why would a drug dealer be carrying around poison?" Duncan asked.

"We don't know that this guy is a drug dealer," Jack answered.

"Right. That's why I think we should find out who his car is registered to and tail him. I'm beginning to suspect that his name isn't Bob Sprick at all. And maybe the woman who came in here last week wasn't his wife. Maybe she was some poor kid that Bob or whatever-his-name-really-is got hooked on drugs. Maybe she wanted us to figure out that he's a drug dealer and get him off the streets. You know, to spare others the pain she's gone through," Lainie said.

Jack turned to Duncan. "She's got some imagination."

"I'll say."

Jack turned back to Lainie. "Maybe you should think about becoming a writer."

"Naw. You ever see writers getting Emmy Awards?" she asked, then answered her own question. "No, because they get theirs the week before the telecast in some offsite ceremony with the key grips and sound mixers. It's the actors who get all the glory."

"True." Jack and Duncan both nodded. Then Jack cleared his throat and brought them all back to the point. "Be that as it may, we're not equipped to go after drug dealers. Or *potential* drug dealers," he added when it looked as though Lainie might protest. "This is a case for the police. I'm going to turn it over to them."

"All right," Lainie grumbled.

"Yeah, I guess that makes sense. We don't even have guns," Duncan said morosely.

"And the world is safer for it," Jack muttered under his breath. Duncan with a gun. He shuddered. Just the thought gave him the chills. "Do you guys want to get a beer after I get back? I think we deserve something for all our hard work today."

"Do math majors multiply?" Duncan said.

"Do eggs get laid?" Lainie added.

"If you guys don't cut it out, we're going to have to start paying residuals," Jack said.

"Okay. Yes," Lainie said, then frowned. "But that's so boring."

"We need to write our own script," Jack heard Duncan say to Lainie as he headed out the door. Great. That's just what he needed. More snappy comebacks from the support staff.

"Oh, hey, Jack. Sorry, I didn't see you."

Jack instinctively held out his arms to steady Madison Case, the receptionist from Rules of Engagement, who had barreled out the door of Suite A without looking. "That's all right," he said. No harm done.

"I'm in a bit of a rush. Could you give this to Lainie?" Maddie asked.

Jack took the plastic bag she handed him and looked inside. It was a spray can of air freshener. The kind with flowers printed all over it. He hated that stuff. It didn't mask unpleasant odors. Instead, you just ended up with gardenia-scented wet dog or jasmine-smelling three-day-old fish.

Yuck.

"What's it for?" he asked and was surprised to see Maddie blush.

"She'll know," Maddie answered.

Jack shrugged. "Sure. Actually, I'll just throw it in her car right now so I don't forget." Her silver convertible was parked—top open but doors locked—a few feet away. As Maddie hurried away, Jack took the can out of the grocery bag and tossed it onto the passenger-side floor so no one walking by could easily grab it. Then he put the cocaine/poison/whatever into the bag along with the license plate number that Lainie had written down.

Without giving the air freshener another thought, Jack headed to the police station to turn over their evidence.

And as he walked back, he couldn't help but smile. Not only had he removed them from a potentially dangerous case, but he'd managed to get Lainie to agree to go out with him both tonight and tomorrow night.

So much for Lillian Bryson's forty-eight-hour rule.

So much for dating rules at all. It was a good thing that Jack didn't believe in that nonsense. Instead, he believed that if people were meant to be together, they'd find each other. No matter where. No matter what.

All he had to do now was to prove to Lainie how right they were for each other.

That, he thought, his grin widening as he swung open the office door, might even be fun.

{twenty-eight}

Trish waited until she saw her sister turn the corner at the end of the street before leaving her own house the next morning. She'd cleared her schedule that morning so she could have a chance to talk to her father alone.

This wasn't going to be easy for either of them, but they had to do what was best for Lainie.

She gripped the folder containing the Department of Justice's information on huffing as well as a list of local treatment facilities and the name and number of the therapist she'd called yesterday afternoon. Once she shared this information with Dad, they'd talk about the next steps.

Poor Lainie. The next few weeks were going to be tough on her.

Trish walked past her sister's car, glad that Lainie wasn't huffing and driving. The chemicals she was inhaling could impair her ability to—

What was that?

Trish squinted at the colorful can lying on the floor of Lainie's car. Air freshener.

She sighed and flipped open her file. There it was. Near the bottom of the second page.

Nitrites are used mainly to enhance sexual experience rather than to achieve a euphoric effect. Cyclohexyl nitrite is found in . . .

Room deodorizers.

Lainie had come home later than usual last night. She must have been out, getting high and then—

No. Trish wasn't going to think about that. She didn't want to imagine the things her sister's low self-esteem was causing her to do. Her feelings of worthlessness would make it impossible for her to set personal boundaries. If someone suggested she do something she was uncomfortable doing, she'd simply go along with it, feeling that her opinion didn't matter.

Trish saw it all the time.

She just couldn't believe she'd missed the signs in her own sister.

With a heavy heart she trudged to her father's door and rang the bell. She hadn't wanted to leave a message on his phone in case Lainie accessed their voice mail. She hated waking him up, but . . . well, he *was* Lainie's father. Part of his responsibility was to care for his daughter's well-being.

"Trish. Why aren't you at work? Is something the matter?" Carl Ames asked as he opened the front door and peered sleepily outside.

"Yes, Dad, it is. I'm sorry to wake you, but we need to talk. I consulted a therapist yesterday about Lainie's problem and we both agreed . . ."

"Agreed what?" Carl asked, stepping aside to let his daughter in.

Trish took a deep breath as she held out the folder, stepped over the threshold, and said, "It's time to stage an intervention."

For the first time in months, Lainie felt that everything in her life was heading in the right direction. Now that she was living in Naples, her relationship with her half sister was becoming stronger. She was even starting to feel a little more comfortable around her dad. Her job was going pretty well, though she wished she were busier, but that would come soon enough. Just this morning, Jack had approved her marketing plan—a plan she predicted would bring in at least twenty-five new clients within a month.

And speaking of Jack . . .

Lainie rested her chin in her hand as she snuck a glance at her boss.

God, he was cute.

She closed her eyes and tried to wipe that thought from her mind. It was supposed to be their professional relationship that she valued. That was all they had now and it was all they would ever have.

So he'd thrown a few heated glances and flirtatious comments her way.

So what?

He had never actually come right out and told her that he wanted her to be anything but his employee. Which was good. The last thing she needed was to have to turn him down and then worry about the repercussions.

Work was work, and dating was dating, and it was better for everyone if the two remained separate.

And, hoo boy, wasn't she putting carts before horses this morning?

Yeah, Jack might want to boink her (and, okay, let's be honest, she wouldn't exactly mind that), but that didn't mean he'd want to *date* her. Dating was different. Dating was meet-the-family, hang-out-with-my-friends, really-get-to-know-each-other. She wasn't the type of woman Jack would want to do any of those things with.

Which was just as well, since she had her sights set on another man anyway.

Blaine Harper.

Lainie waited for a dreamy sigh, but it never materialized.

She frowned at the bouquet still sitting on the corner of her desk. What was wrong with her? She had a date with Blaine Harper—*Doctor* Blaine Harper—tomorrow night. This was what she'd wanted since high school. He was her potential ticket to Cool-town.

So why wasn't she more excited?

"You shouldn't frown like that. You'll end up having to spend a fortune on Botox to fix it," Jack said mildly from behind his computer.

Lainie scowled and looked behind her. How did he know she was frowning?

"Duncan IM'ed me," Jack answered her unspoken question.

She peered out from around her bouquet to find Duncan grinning sheepishly at her. "Well, knock it off. And wipe that stupid grin off your face."

"This is the smartest grin I know," Duncan said.

"Yeah, well. Didn't anybody ever tell you that it's rude to stare?"

"I can't help it. I just look over there and there you are."

"Of course I'm here. Where else would I be?"

"I don't have a clue," Duncan said.

Lainie looked at Jack. Jack looked back at Lainie. "We've known that for a while," they said.

"Like shooting fish in a barrel," Lainie said.

"Yeah, you made that one too easy," Jack added. "I like it better when I have to work for it."

"According to Lillian Bryson, that makes you a typical man," Lainie murmured.

"What—" Jack began, but before he could form a coherent question, their door burst open and Shay Monroe wafted in on three-inch heels and a cloud of expensive perfume.

Lainie could almost hear the villain music playing in her head.

"Hi, Jack," Shay trilled and then nodded in the general direction of Duncan and Lainie. "And other office people."

Lainie and Duncan exchanged incredulous glances. *Other office people?* Didn't Shay realize that they were fully credited members of the cast?

After being insulted in such a manner, Lainie felt no remorse about eavesdropping on Shay's conversation with Jack. She didn't even bother trying to pretend she was working.

"I got your message. You've completed your investigation of Blaine Harper?" Shay asked, taking a seat across from Jack without waiting for an invitation. She crossed her long, slender, silk-pantyhose clad legs in a smooth motion that Lainie had never managed to master.

Let's face it. Some women just had *it*, and Lainie, she wasn't one of them. Hell, she couldn't even paint her own fingernails without making a huge mess of it. She washed her underwear in the washing machine. And dried it in the dryer. There were no frilly feminine panties hanging from her shower rod. She didn't know how to twist her hair up, either. Other women, they just *whish, whoosh, whished,* and—voilà!—they had a gorgeous French twist held in place with one of those butterfly clips.

But not Lainie.

It wasn't like she was a tomboy, either. Nope. She had zero athletic ability.

Zip. Zilch. Nada.

It was so not fair. She didn't fit in with the girly girls or the sporty girls. She didn't know where that left her exactly, other than feeling like she kind of wished somebody would just slap a label on her so she'd know where she fit in. . . .

"Yes. I know all I need to know about *Doctor* Blaine Harper," Jack said, interrupting her thoughts.

Lainie leaned forward to hear better. She was just as interested in finding out what Jack had uncovered about the once and future prom king as Shay was.

"First of all, he *is* a doctor. His degree is from some medical school in the Caribbean, so I'm not sure I'd want him taking out my spleen, but he did have to prove some proficiency in biology in order to graduate, so at least he's legit."

"Wonderful," Shay cooed.

Lainie scowled and stuck her finger down her throat in the international "gag me" gesture.

"Botox, Lainie," Jack said, shooting her a half-smile.

Lainie turned to glare at Duncan. Damn him and his Instant Messaging.

Shay ignored everything that didn't have to do with her. "What about his finances?" she asked.

"He's solid," Jack answered. "He owns a house here in Naples on the Intracoastal Waterway and a condo in Colorado. His credit rating is one of the highest I've ever seen. His company, Doctor Diet Inc., is publicly owned, so I didn't have any trouble getting an annual statement. I'm no accountant, but it appears to be a pretty healthy company. There's a copy attached to my report." Jack handed Shay a binder-clipped sheaf of papers.

"This is great. Your timing couldn't be better. Our high school reunion committee is meeting in a couple of hours, and Dr. Harper has agreed to attend. Instead of waiting until Saturday night to make my move, I'm going to get started tonight."

Shay giggled and it was all Lainie could do not to gag herself again.

Jack's findings were both good news and bad news. The good news was, the thought of walking into their high school reunion on Blaine's arm now that she knew he was wildly successful—not to mention financially solvent—was even more attractive to Lainie. Unfortunately, it meant the same thing to Shay.

And whereas Shay had a previous flame to fan with the good doctor, Lainie had nothing but her current charming self.

No way was that going to be enough.

She needed help.

Professional help.

And she knew just where to go to get it.

She grabbed her purse from her drawer and draped it over her shoulder. "I'll be back in about an hour," she announced, then hurried out. She didn't have the money to pay Lillian Bryson, but she was desperate enough to try the truth. She'd just tell Lillian she was broke and beg to pay for her services next week, after she'd gotten her first paycheck. The Mercedes people would just have to wait for their payment.

This was more important.

The convertible was just a car. This was her entire future.

Lainie ducked into Rules of Engagement, startling Maddie when she announced, "I'm here to see Lillian. Is she free?" Even if she wasn't, Lainie wasn't going to take no for an answer. She needed help, and she needed it now.

"Sure, Lainie. Go on back," the receptionist said.

Lainie nodded once, then headed down the hallway toward Lillian's office. She caught her in mid-bite of what appeared to be a turkey sandwich.

"Sorry to barge in like this. I need some advice," she said, stepping into Lillian's office and shutting the door behind her.

"This isn't as much of a surprise as you might think. So . . . What can I do for you?" Lillian asked once she'd rinsed down her sandwich with a sip of water.

"There's this guy I really want to impress, but there's another woman in the picture, and I'm not sure what I should do to shove her out, if you know what I mean."

Lillian rewrapped her sandwich in the plastic wrap it had come in. "Uh-huh," she said, drawing out the words so they lasted a good thirty seconds. "So, does this man know how you feel?"

Lainie scratched her head. "I'm not sure. I mean, I'm sort of attracted to him. And . . . Well, I think he's attracted back." God, she sounded like such an idiot.

"You have actually *talked* to this man, haven't you?" Lillian asked with a little frown creasing her forehead.

"Of course I have."

"That's good." She sounded relieved.

"I mean, we haven't been on a date or anything. Not officially." Lainie closed her eyes and rubbed her temples. No wonder she sounded like an idiot. She *was* an idiot. She was acting just like David Addison in *Moonlighting*, dancing around her feelings for Blaine without being certain of what she really wanted. No wonder Shay was going to win. She wasn't hanging back, secretly pining for a man that she could never have.

"Uh—" Lillian began.

Lainie held up her hand to stop her. "Right. I see the problem. I've got to go after what I want, show him what a great catch I am. Charm him. Woo him with my feminine wiles until he's been spoiled for all other women for all of eternity."

"Lainie—"

"I'm just kidding." Lainie sighed. "But the other woman's going to try to play her hand tonight. I've got to get to him before then, so mine will be the face he sees when he goes to sleep tonight. Unfortunately, I know about your forty-eight-hour rule, and I'm not supposed to be seeing him until tomorrow night."

"You know about that?"

"Uh-huh."

"How?"

Lainie pointed to the hallway. "Thin doors," she answered.

"Ah."

"So what can I do? If I show up tonight, he'll think I'm easy."

"Lie," Lillian said.

"Lie?" Lainie blinked. Had Lillian just said what she thought she had said? Sweet Lillian Bryson?

Lillian got up and walked around her desk, where she leaned against the top and speared Lainie with her motherly gaze. "Yes. Lie. Cheat. Don't steal, but do whatever you have to do to make an impression on this man before he goes out with this other woman. Otherwise, she'll be the one to set the standard. If this man is that important to you, you'll think of a way to get his attention before then."

"Okay," Lainie said, somewhat bemused by Lillian's take-no-prisoners approach to the dating game.

"Okay."

"Good."

"Good." Lillian grinned. "I told you how to make him love you, now get out."

{ twenty-nine }

It was time for Lainie to take fate into her own hands. If Shay Monroe got to Blaine first, the game would be all over for her.

But what could she do?

Technically, she could attend the reunion committee meeting. It was *her* reunion, too. But since no one seemed to remember her—and since Lainie preferred it that way—that option was out.

Her only other plan was to hang out at the high school and try to intercept Blaine before he went in for the meeting. Even if she couldn't get him to cancel, at least she'd have the opportunity to cement a favorable impression in his brain before being confronted by blond-bombshell-and-former-love-of-his-life Shay Monroe.

It wasn't exactly the most brilliant plan, but it was the only one Lainie could come up with on such short notice.

So, one hour after her visit to Lillian Bryson, Lainie told Jack that she had an important errand to run and that, since it was so close to five o'clock, she was going to call it a day. He gave her an odd look, but didn't protest—only reminded her that he'd pick her up at seven for their surveillance that night.

"Oh. Right. I'd forgotten about that. Our new case," Lainie said as she shouldered her handbag and nonchalantly scooped up the tiny digital camera that Jack had left on the corner of Duncan's desk.

"Yes. And I think we're going to have a real breakthrough tonight," Jack answered.

"All right. I'll be there."

"See you at seven, then," Jack said.

"Uh-huh," Lainie answered absently, her mind busy trying to figure out what, exactly, she was going to do to turn Blaine's head. First, she was going to have to come up with a plausible excuse for why she was hanging around the high school. That shouldn't be too difficult. She could say that it was something about a case she was working on. It wasn't like he'd have any reason to call her bluff.

As she left the office and headed toward the school, she practiced looking startled and saying, "Why, Blaine Harper! What are you doing here?" with just the right amount of surprise. She hadn't decided yet whether it was easier to practice lying or to just wing it. She seemed to have become quite proficient at either method these days.

She smiled wryly as she walked into the high school parking lot. There were only a few cars dotted about at this time of day— those of teachers working after hours and students whose extracurricular activities hadn't yet ended. Lainie looked around for a hiding spot where she could see the front entrance of the school but where she herself would be relatively difficult to spot. She decided on a leggy hibiscus bush with dark yellow flowers that was growing near the side of the main building. When she saw Blaine pull into the parking lot, she could step out from behind the bush, and it would appear as if she'd just come out of one of the side exits of the school.

Perfect.

Now all she had to do was wait.

Lainie shifted a little to the left to get a particularly poky branch out of the small of her back. The air was still today and the humidity higher than it had been since she'd returned to Naples. It wouldn't be long before the full heat of summer descended upon them. The temperatures almost never made it past the mid-90s, but the humidity made the heat oppressive. Lainie could almost feel her hair curling now as she stood in the bushes, waiting for Blaine to appear. One more month and she'd be dripping with sweat after being outside for half an hour.

But at least Floridians didn't try to fool people like the folks in the Southwest who always tried to make light of their surface-of-the-sun-like climate by saying, "Oh, but it's a dry heat." Hey—115 degrees was hot. Freaking hot. Wet or dry, anything over about 85 was more warmth than any human body should have to bear.

Lainie wondered why that was. If our body temperatures are 98.6, why wouldn't we be perfectly comfortable at just under 100 degrees?

She had to shelve this perplexing question when she heard voices coming from around the corner. She hunkered down in the bushes, wincing when that blasted branch jabbed her in the back again.

She held herself still, willing whoever it was to walk by without glancing over at her.

Surprisingly, she got her wish. More surprisingly, she recognized one of the people who passed her on the sidewalk. It was Bob. And he was with a younger man who looked to be no more than seventeen or eighteen, but who had an impressive array of body art, including a barbed wire tattoo around his neck and three bloody daggers inked on his right bicep.

She was guessing this wasn't the student body president.

Lainie held her breath as the men walked by.

She couldn't make out what they were saying, and she made a mental note to ask Jack about purchasing an audio booster like the models she'd seen in Duncan's *Spy/P.I. Weekly*. That would come in handy if they were going to be increasing their surveillance work. Having audio on their subjects would make it a lot easier to know what they were up to.

But since she wasn't equipped with any listening devices aside from her own two ears, Lainie crept forward in an effort to see what Bob and his tattooed cohort were up to.

Bob followed the other guy to a white, unmarked van parked near the front of the lot.

Lainie crouched down and peered at them through the thin smattering of leaves near the bottom of the hibiscus bush. She clapped a hand over her mouth to stifle a gasp when she saw Bob hand the young man a wad of cash. Omigod! It was another drug deal in the making.

She fumbled with the clasp of her purse and hurriedly pulled out the small digital camera.

"Please, let me catch this on film," she whispered as she pressed the shutter over and over again.

This was it. The evidence the police would need to put Bob away for a long, long time.

The tattooed man didn't count the bills before stuffing them into the front pocket of his torn, baggy jeans. He and Bob had obviously done business before if the guy trusted Bob enough to not double-check his math.

Bob reached out and grabbed the chrome handle of the van's back door. It *whooshed* open, and Bob leaned over to peer inside, appearing as if he were inspecting the merchandise. He nodded as he straightened up. Then he stepped back and the younger man bent forward and grabbed two plain cardboard boxes from out of the back of the van. Bob shut the door after him and Lainie froze as they headed back toward her.

They cut through the grass this time, passing so close that Lainie could count the drops of blood dripping from the daggers on the younger man's arm. There were ten of them. What did that mean? Had he killed ten people? Wasn't that some sort of gang thing?

Then they rounded a corner, and Lainie lost sight of them.

She chewed on the inside of her bottom lip. What should she do now? Yes, she was here to get Blaine's attention, but wasn't stopping a drug dealer more important?

Easy question to answer.

Of course it was.

Lainie disentangled herself from the hedge. She had to follow Bob and his partner in crime and see where they were taking their stash. If she didn't, the police might never find it.

Cautiously she left her hiding spot and followed the men's trail. When she got to where they had disappeared, she peered around the corner of the building and saw a door swing shut.

They must have gone inside.

Lainie shivered with a mixture of fright and anticipation. Ready or not, she was being thrown into some real detective work. She felt woefully unprepared. If they caught her, all she had to defend herself were a few safety pins and a ballpoint pen—not exactly serious crime-fighting weapons.

But she couldn't just let them go, so she took a deep breath, squared her shoulders, and headed in after them.

Hinges squeaked as Lainie slowly pulled the door open and peeked inside. The hallway was clammy and dark compared to the warm sunshine outside. Lainie blinked several times to get her eyes to adjust to the gloom, then pressed herself back against the wall when she heard footsteps on the tile floor.

She was standing next to a glass cabinet filled with trophies and other memorabilia—the kind that every school had stashed somewhere—and Lainie found herself wondering what percent of kids ever got the chance to see their names in there. Less than 1 percent, she guessed, as she heard footsteps retreat and chanced a glance down the hall to see Bob and his box-toting friend disappear through another doorway.

After taking another deep breath for courage, she un-suctioned her back from the wall and tiptoed down the hall.

As she approached the doorway, she could hear the murmur of voices getting louder, but her pounding heartbeat threatened to drown the words out. She put a hand to her chest and inched closer until she could just see inside the room. It appeared to be some sort of large closet with a door in the hall and another one leading to a room on the other side.

"Let's stash those boxes in here. They should be safe. I'm one of the few people who has keys," Lainie overheard Bob say.

She clamped her lips shut as the implication hit her. He had keys. That must mean he worked here at the school.

This was worse than she had thought. He had access to these kids every day. Who better to set up a drug ring here than someone on the inside?

She had one more surprise in store for her when Bob clapped the younger man on the back and said, "Great. Now that that's done, are you ready to meet with the reunion committee? I've already talked to Shay Monroe privately, and she's very interested in your services. Who knows, you may be able to build an entire empire with the people you meet tonight."

Lainie blinked.

What? Shay Monroe was in cahoots with these guys?

If so . . . No, it couldn't be.

She squeezed her eyes closed, trying to shut out the hope welling up in her chest. If Shay was involved in this and Lainie could somehow expose her, she'd come off looking like a hero in front of everyone—including Blaine Harper.

And maybe, after all these years, she'd finally be a star, after all.

{ thirty }

Jack waited approximately two and a half minutes after Lainie left before turning to Duncan and asking, "Do you think we should follow her?"

"Do I? Do . . . cats . . . um." Duncan frowned. "I'm out of material."

Jack sighed. "A simple yes or no would suffice."

"Yeah, but it's not nearly as entertaining."

"Well, I don't have time to sit around and wait for you to come up with something cute. I'm going after Lainie."

Jack grabbed his car keys from the top desk drawer and headed out the door. He slid into the driver's seat of his car and wasn't surprised when Duncan joined him. He glanced over to make sure his passenger was belted in, then did a double-take when he saw that his brother had pulled a blond wig over his short brown hair.

"What are you doing?" he asked.

Duncan shoved on a pair of oversize sunglasses. "Well, we don't want her to know it's us, do we?"

"And you think that disguise will fool her?"

"You never know. There are a lot of clueless people out there."

"There are a lot of clueless people in here," Jack muttered, but Duncan just shrugged.

With one last eye roll at his brother's ridiculous costume, Jack pulled away from the curb. He could see Lainie walking on the sidewalk, half a dozen blocks up. Fortunately, he was in Florida, so following her at a snail's pace, ten miles under the speed limit, was perfectly acceptable. No one honked at him or flipped him off; they just seemed a bit surprised when they passed him and discovered that he wasn't in the over-eighty set.

He followed Lainie to Golden Gulf High, cruising slowly past the chain-link fence as she turned into the parking lot and headed toward the school.

Jack had no idea what sort of errand she was supposedly running here. Frankly, he didn't believe she was running an errand at all. She'd pegged his bullshit meter with that excuse.

And—because he was curious and—yeah, okay—because he wanted to make sure she stayed away from Blaine Harper until after Jack could take her out and spoil her for all other men tonight—he had no intention of letting her lie to him anymore without making some attempt to discover the truth.

"All right, Sparky, let's go," he said to Duncan after circling the block and finding a parking spot at the rear of the school.

"Right-o, Boss." Duncan jerked the wig down to make sure it was firmly attached to his head, then stepped out onto the pavement. And as they jogged toward the main building, he added, "I've thought up a couple more. Do cells divide? Do lions lie? Does—"

In order to preserve what was left of his sanity, Jack stopped listening and focused on the sound of his own breathing as he headed back to the school.

Lainie slipped into the vestibule moments after Bob and his supplier left. She had her camera out, taking photos of the men leaving and of the boxes, though she wasn't certain how they'd turn out in the dim light.

As Lainie approached the boxes, she heard voices and laughter from the other side of the door. A strange sort of flashing light glowed from around the gaps in the doorframe, sudden bursts of light followed by darkness and then light again. Lainie pressed her ear to the door to see if she could hear what was going on in the other room. She heard snippets of conversation—Bob's voice, then laughter, then Shay, and then the unmistakable rumble of Blaine Harper answering her.

Lainie leaned back against the door and took a deep breath. This was it. Her chance to redeem herself after all these years.

She eyed the top box on the stack, planning her next move. She wanted it to be big. Dramatic. Something no one would ever forget.

Then, because she didn't want to look like a fool, she decided to check out what was in the boxes first. She fumbled in her purse for a safety pin, which she used to slit the packing tape holding the box closed.

She reached in and held a cellophane-wrapped package of a squishy, dry white substance up to her eyes. Yes. It was drugs all right.

With a satisfied nod, Lainie picked up the box, which was surprisingly lightweight. Then, quietly, she opened the connecting door and stepped through.

What she saw made her heart stop for a moment and then frantically start beating again.

She was in the auditorium. Bleachers lined the room, pulled out only part of the way, leaving a large, empty area at the center of the room. Near the front was a stage, the heavy red curtains pulled off to either side, revealing a giant screen. The alternating dark and light was coming from the screen, where a montage of photos flashed on and off.

This was perfect. She could hook her digital camera up to the computer controlling the slideshow and show everyone what a crook Bob was.

Lainie gripped the box tighter as she skirted around the darkened edges of the room. No one had noticed her yet and she prayed that they'd remain oblivious until she was all set.

Miraculously she made it onto the stage without anyone spotting her. They appeared to be engrossed in a discussion about what song the band should play during the coronation of the reunion's king and queen. Blaine suggested "We Are the Champions" by Queen, but someone else on the committee rightly protested that this song had been released in 1977, and wouldn't it be better to find a song from the year that they'd graduated instead?

Lainie didn't pay much attention to the argument, though a vision of her and Blaine standing onstage wearing crowns while the band played "Smells Like Teen Spirit" and the crowd cheered made her knees feel wobbly. She was so close to having that vision become reality. For once, she wouldn't be the comic relief, but a real leading lady—the one who solved the crime and got the guy and looked great doing it. What a nice change that would be from her past, where all she'd seemed to do was fail . . . and look ridiculous doing it.

She pushed the box onto the stage and slithered up after it, quickly hiding behind the curtain at stage left, gripping the heavy drape and trying to calm her pounding heart as she waited for one of her previous classmates to sound the alarm.

When the discussion about coronation songs continued unabated, Lainie let out a relieved breath.

She crouched down next to the laptop that was connected to a projector at center stage. While the montage flashed onscreen, she hooked up her camera and, with a few keystrokes, inserted her pictures into the array.

There were definitely benefits to being a former computer geek.

Now, with the stage set, it was time for Lainie's big finish.

{ thirty-one }

What in the hell is she doing?" Jack muttered as he peered into the darkened auditorium and watched Lainie scurry onstage and disappear.

"I have no idea," Duncan answered from behind him.

"That's okay. I got lots of 'em. I'll loan you one," Jack said. "But, first, I have a feeling that Lainie is about to do something really stupid. We have to stop her."

"How're we gonna do that?"

Jack grabbed his younger brother by the scruff of his neck, yanked open the door, and shoved him inside. "Create a distraction," he ordered. Then he hit the lights.

Twenty pairs of eyes blinked in the sudden brightness of the room.

"Hey! You can't just barge in here like that," a man wearing a sweater vest over a white T-shirt and jeans protested.

"Oh, yeah? Tell that to the author," Duncan mumbled.

Meanwhile, Jack had found the main entrance to the auditorium and was inching his way up to the stage while the reunion committee tried to ascertain what Duncan was doing there. He knew he had to hurry, to get to Lainie before she could do anything foolish. He didn't know why he was so certain that she was about to make a huge mistake. He just felt it deep in his bones, like the onset of the flu.

"Ladies and gentlemen, there is a criminal in your midst," Lainie announced just as Jack's foot hit the first step leading onstage.

"Lainie, don't," he said.

She looked over at him, startled. "Jack. What are you doing here?"

Jack took the steps three at a time. "Sorry for the interruption, folks," he said to the crowd that had turned their attention from Duncan and was now staring up at them.

"I've got more evidence to implicate Bob," Lainie whispered, then, before Jack could stop her, she pointed to the guy in the sweater vest. "That man sells cocaine to children. And there's at least one of you who's expressed interest in joining his drug ring. You should be ashamed." She narrowed her eyes at Shay, who appeared to be genuinely befuddled.

"Uh, Lainie, maybe this isn't the best idea." Jack grabbed her arm while the crowd started grumbling.

"Sure it is. Look," she said loudly, gesturing to the screen behind them. "I've got pictures."

Jack turned to look. Yes, she did indeed have pictures of Bob— or whatever the hell his name was—standing outside a van with a multitattooed young man. The next photo showed them bringing two boxes into the high school.

"That doesn't prove anything," he whispered out of the side of his mouth.

"Lainie? What's going on here?" Blaine Harper asked as he, too, got up onstage.

"Hey, aren't you that office person who works with Jack?" Shay said.

"My name is Lainie. Lainie Ames," Lainie answered, obviously irritated by Shay's inability to remember her name. Then she turned to Blaine and smiled. "And I do work with Jack, who owns Intrepid Investigations. We've been following this man"—she waved toward Bob—"and we . . . well, actually *I . . . I* discovered that he's been selling drugs. Not just to students here at the high school, either. We've got pictures of him doing a deal at the country club, too."

"What are you talking about?" Bob joined them onstage, barely giving the screen a second glance. Duncan followed eagerly, like a grinning lapdog who had been promised a treat.

Jack was getting a very bad feeling about this. "Lainie, maybe we should just go," he suggested.

"No. I have evidence. See?" Lainie held up a plastic-wrapped package.

"What is it?" Blaine asked.

"Drugs," Lainie answered, while Bob said at the same time, "Confetti."

Lainie shot Bob a skeptical look. "Oh, right. Confetti. Is that the street name for cocaine these days?"

Bob grabbed the package from her hand and ripped it open. White confetti flew everywhere, dusting Lainie's hair, raining down on Blaine and Shay. A flake of it got stuck on Jack's eyelashes and he plucked it off with one hand.

"Well." Lainie glanced around desperately. "Maybe the drugs are on the confetti. Didn't I see that on *CSI: Miami* once? Or was it *Law and Order?*"

Jack studied the speck of paper on the tip of his finger. It was just regular old confetti. He knew in his heart that it was.

"Hey, what's this?" Duncan asked, and everyone's heads turned his way. He had moved aside the packs of confetti in the box and found several cans stashed underneath.

"A-ha!" Lainie said triumphantly, moving to stand next to Duncan. "This must be the drugs, then. Bob was just using the confetti as a cover. Like burying them in coffee so drug-sniffing dogs can't smell them."

"Who's Bob?" the sweater-wearing man asked.

"You are," Lainie answered, momentarily distracted by his question.

"I'm not Bob."

"Yes, you are," she insisted.

"Look, if I were Bob, I would be the first to know, wouldn't I?"

"Then who are you?" Jack asked.

"I'm Mike Spencer. I teach science here at the high school. I graduated fifteen years ago and I'm part of the reunion committee."

"*You're* Mike Spencer?" Lainie asked.

Jack reached out and pushed her mouth shut. There was still a lot of confetti floating around.

"Yeah. Why?"

"We were in earth science together," Lainie blurted.

"Who are you?" he asked.

But before Lainie could answer, there was a hissing noise behind her. Lainie turned around and instinctively held up her hands to protect her eyes as she was showered with a gold mist.

"That's spray paint. For the banners we were going to make before the reunion on Saturday," Bob/Mike explained unnecessarily after Duncan lifted his finger from the nozzle and shrugged apologetically at Lainie. "I didn't want to bring it into the auditorium because . . . Well, because you know what would happen if these high-schoolers got a hold of it. They'd all end up looking like . . . Er. Looking like that." He gestured toward Lainie.

Lainie dropped her head into her hands, which didn't do much but spread more gold paint all over her face.

"Nooooo," she wailed.

"Wait a second. I think I remember you," Shay said.

"Of course you do. That's the only thing that would make this situation worse," Lainie muttered.

"You're that girl from McDonald's. The one who got food all over herself on prom night." Shay was warming to the topic. She put a hand on Blaine's arm. "Don't you remember? We went in to get sodas to mix with the vodka that Tim had brought. This girl slipped on something and grabbed the shake machine to steady herself, but ended up on the floor with stuff all over her. We laughed about that for weeks."

Ouch.

Jack looked over at Lainie, whose shoulders were slumped in defeat. She gazed back at him, her misery as clear as the gold flecks of paint on her face. He took a step forward, intending to grab her arm and get her out of there before things got even worse. He didn't know how they possibly could, but then realized that he'd underestimated the depths of human cruelty when Shay Monroe chuckled and said, "Obviously, you haven't changed much since then."

{ thirty-two }

Jack looked over at the broken woman in the passenger seat of his car and wondered if it was possible for a human being to wish herself into nonexistence. He feared that if it were, Lainie would disappear.

"Thank you for driving me home." Her voice was barely more than a whisper of sound in the quiet interior of the car.

"You're welcome." He didn't know what else to say.

"I can just imagine what I would have looked like, walking through Naples with gold spray paint all over me."

He still didn't know what to say, so he didn't say anything. Instead, he leaned over and gently unbuckled Lainie's seat belt. She seemed numb.

Broken.

And he hated seeing her like that. So she had made a mistake. Wasn't like she was the only one who'd ever done that.

"It's going to be all right, Lainie," he said, wishing that the words would reassure her, but knowing that she probably wasn't even listening. "It was an honest mistake. Baking soda does look a lot like cocaine. How were we to know that Bob, er, Mike that is, was handing out packets of the stuff for his students to use at the upcoming science fair? Or that he was collecting money for a program to help underprivileged kids go to science camp this summer? Or that he was trying to help his tattooed former student get his fledgling web-design business off the ground by introducing him to the other members of the reunion committee?"

Lainie put her head in her hands and moaned, not making any move to get out of the car, even though they'd been sitting in front of her father's green-and-white rambler for over ten minutes.

Maybe her family could help. Jack knew he wasn't doing too good a job here.

He got out of the car and walked around the hood to the passenger side.

He held open the door, but Lainie just sat there, looking miserable. If Jack thought that letting her sit there like that forever would make her feel better, he'd have gladly built a house right there around her.

But he knew that wasn't the answer. She needed people—people who cared about her—to tell her that this disaster, while momentarily embarrassing, wasn't the end of the world. He cared about her, and he'd told her that, but one voice wasn't enough. She needed to hear it from her family, too.

So Jack leaned down, slid one arm under her knees and the other around her shoulders, and lifted her out of the car.

Lainie was too numb to protest. Frankly, she hardly even noticed the hard feel of Jack's chest against her side or how good he smelled up close.

Well, okay. That was a lie. She noticed. And she snuggled closer, burying her nose in his shirt and wishing she could stay in his arms forever. It felt good here. Safe. Comfortable. At least, for her it did. She could only imagine how his arms and back were going to ache tomorrow after lugging her weight around.

"You can put me down. I can walk," she said.

Jack stopped and smiled down at her. "Humor me. I'm enjoying this."

And she could have insisted . . . if only she had the willpower. But she didn't, so she let him carry her to the door of her father's house, glad to know that Dad would be at work and that no one else would bear witness to the humiliation she had suffered today.

She was about to tell Jack to let her down so she could get the key out of her purse when the front door was opened from inside.

"Lainie, what's wrong?" Trish asked, obviously surprised to find her sister on the doorstep in a man's arms.

Before Lainie or Jack could answer, Trish started crying. "I knew this would happen. I should have done something sooner, but I . . . I didn't want to interfere. I swear, I didn't know her problem was this bad. Did she pass out? Oh, I'm so glad someone found her and brought her home. Don't worry, Lainie. We're going to get you help."

Lainie's feet slid to the floor as Jack set her upright.

They exchanged a confused look. Lainie shrugged. She had no idea what was going on here, either.

She turned to her sister, whose sobs had gotten louder. And wetter.

"Trish? What are you talking about?"

Lainie blinked when her sister threw her arms around her neck and hugged her tightly.

"Your drug problem. We know all about the huffing. The gasoline, the butane, the nitrous oxide, the nitrites in that room deodorizer. And now this. Spray paint. The DOJ website said that gold paint is particularly popular among inhalant abusers. I should have expected this."

Jack put a comforting arm across Lainie's shoulders as they stepped into her father's house. She was tempted to tell him to leave, but she feared that she might collapse if he took his arm away.

"Lainie, we love you. We're going to help you get better," her father said.

Her mouth dropped open as Trish stepped back into the living room, where her entire family was gathered.

"We love you, Aunt Lainie," Lucas said.

"We don't want you to be sick anymore," Heather added.

"This is Dr. Korbel. She specializes in cases like yours," Trish said as a woman wearing embroidered jeans and a cute pink top held out her hand.

"It's nice to meet you, Lainie. You're very fortunate. Your family cares a great deal about you. We've staged this meeting so that you can see how many people love you and are concerned for your well-being. I know that this may be difficult for you, but you have my word that things will only get better for you once you stop abusing drugs."

Had she stepped into an alternate universe?

Lainie put a hand to her forehead. "Shouldn't you be at work?" she asked her dad, because she really couldn't think of anything else to say.

"I took the night off. My daughter's health is more important than a few lousy hours at the restaurant," he answered, reaching out to squeeze her hand.

Lainie stared down at his dark hand on hers. Dad was not a toucher. He never hugged her. Never told her he loved her. Hell, he barely even acknowledged her existence.

She shook her head. She must be right about the alternate universe thing. It was like that episode of *Moonlighting* where Maddie meets her guardian angel and finds out what would have happened to Agnes and Herbert and David if she'd closed down the Blue Moon Detective Agency.

Only, this wasn't a TV show. This was her life.

And none of this was making sense.

"We really appreciate you bringing Lainie home safely," Trish was saying to Jack, who hadn't moved since this latest freak show began. "You're obviously a very caring man. Most strangers would have just left her wherever it was that she passed out. Or, worse, called the cops."

"Um—" Jack began.

Lainie could feel the rumble in his chest as he started to speak. Suddenly this was all more than she could bear.

"Stop," she said, pulling away from Jack's warm, steady embrace. "I don't understand."

"What don't you understand?" Trish asked.

Lainie waved her hands around the room. At her dad. At her niece and nephew. At her brother-in-law. At the doctor. "Any of it. What the hell is going on here?"

Her father stepped forward. Took both of her hands in his. "Lainie, honey, I'm sorry. We can't let you go on like this."

Trish moved in and put a hand on Lainie's shoulder. Then, to Lainie's horror, she announced, "We're staging an intervention to help get you off of drugs."

{ thirty-three }

She was a complete failure.

When she had received the first notice about her upcoming high school reunion, Lainie couldn't wait to return to Naples.

What a difference six months had made.

She sat on the edge of the twin bed in her old bedroom and stared down at the tattered invitation in her hands.

They'd asked for pictures, for a summary of what everyone was doing now, and Lainie had rushed out that day to get an appointment with a professional photographer. She'd spent hours polishing her answers, so that everyone reading the memory book would know what a success chubby, geeky, Elaine Ames had turned out to be.

But she was no success.

Just look at her.

She'd scrubbed at the gold spray paint for over an hour, but flecks of it still clung to her face and hands. Everything she owned could fit in the trunk of her car. After the disaster she'd made of her first case, she was certain Jack would fire her. Which left her with no job. No money. Nothing.

Worse, her family thought she was a down-and-out drug abuser.

After begging Jack to leave—how much more of her humiliation could he be forced to witness?—she'd explained everything.

Which meant she finally had to tell the truth about what had happened back in Seattle. She'd confessed it all. The bloodbath at work. Ted's gambling. The mountain of debt. The foreclosure on her house.

She'd even told them about the Garage Sale from Hell.

The worst part was, even after she'd come clean, they had looked at her as if they didn't quite believe her.

"Maybe because after all that, who *wouldn't* turn to drugs?" she muttered, then looked up from the tattered invitation to her high school reunion when someone knocked on the bedroom door.

"Yes?" she said on a sigh, wishing they'd just leave her to deal with this alone.

Her father poked his head into the room. "Can I come in?"

"It's your house." Lainie shrugged.

"Yes, but it's *your* room," Carl countered.

Lainie glanced around at the bare walls, at the empty dresser, at the nondescript bedspread, at the room that bore no stamp of hers at all. "Uh-huh."

Her father took that as an invitation to enter. He stood in front of her awkwardly for a long moment and then gestured toward the bed. "Mind if I sit down?"

Lainie scooted toward the headboard. "Go ahead."

He sat and fidgeted with his fingers until Lainie could no longer stand the silence. She cleared her throat. "How come you never remodeled this room?" she asked after fishing around for something to say.

Carl frowned at her. "Well, because it's *your* room. I wouldn't have wanted to do something you didn't like."

"*My* room?"

It was her dad's turn to shrug. "Sure. I mean, as long as I live here, it's yours."

"But I'm only here a few days a year," she protested.

"I know, but I always wanted you to feel welcome. Like you had a place to come home to. I know you didn't really have that growing up."

No. She didn't. But she was shocked that Dad recognized that. Even more shocked that he had tried to do something about it, even if she hadn't realized that was his intention. She'd thought . . . Well, truthfully, she'd thought he hadn't wanted to waste the money making this room nice when she was the only one who used it.

Lainie pulled her bottom lip into her mouth and blinked back tears.

"Well, um. I appreciate that," she said, then added, "Especially now."

"Yeah." Carl started fidgeting with his fingers again, looking around the room at everything but Lainie. "Uh, about that. I'm sorry that we misinterpreted what was going on. If we'd known how bad things were . . ."

"I know," Lainie said.

"What I'm trying to say is, I hope you know that you can always come to me if you need help. I may not be the best dad in the world—matter of fact, I know I'm not—but I love you, and there's almost nothing I wouldn't do for you. You know that, right?"

When her dad turned toward her and engulfed her in a hug, Lainie burst out in tears.

No, she wanted to say. *How am I supposed to know you love me if you never tell me?*

But she was finally starting to realize that part of the problem was inside her. She felt inadequate, so she was searching outside herself for the reassurance she needed—the reassurance that she was worthwhile, that she was lovable. That she mattered.

She wasn't a kid anymore. She was going to have to stop looking for validation in all the wrong places and find it in her own heart, instead.

Too bad that wasn't as easy as it sounded.

Lainie sniffled and wiped her eyes as Trish knocked on the door and peered inside.

"I'm sorry to interrupt," she said. "But someone's at the door for Lainie."

Lainie drew in a shuddering breath. Who could it possibly be?

She scrubbed her face with the back of her hand. Her date with Blaine was for tomorrow night and there was no way after what he'd witnessed earlier today that she was foolish enough to think that he'd want to go through with it anyway.

And it couldn't be Jack. Yes, they were supposed to work to-night, but surely he wouldn't want—

"Hey, Lainie. Are you ready?" Jack asked, when Lainie came to the door.

He looked as gorgeous as always, while Lainie knew that she closely resembled a limp dishrag. She hadn't blow-dried her hair after her lengthy shower and curls were sticking up all over the place. She also hadn't put on any makeup, settling for moisturizer and nothing else.

She'd changed into a pair of white shorts and a blue T-shirt, and her feet were bare. The only thing she was ready for was bed.

Jack, on the other hand, was wearing dark gray slacks, black loafers, and a silk shirt that made Lainie's fingers itch to touch it.

"I can't believe you want anything to do with me after all of this, but I'm afraid I'm not up to working tonight. Could you get Duncan to help you on this job?" Lainie asked, smoothing a hand over her hair. She knew it was useless. She was a mess. Nothing short of a complete overhaul was going to help.

"There's no job," Jack announced.

Lainie blinked. "What do you mean?"

"I mean, there's no job. That was just my ruse to get you to go out with me," Jack said cheerfully.

Lainie sank down on her father's sofa. If it hadn't been there, she'd have fallen to the floor.

"A ruse?"

"Yes. *Ruse*. Noun. Meaning 'a ploy. A trick.'"

"I know what it means, Jack."

He sat down next to her and shot her a mischievous grin before reaching out to tuck a lock of hair behind her ears. "Great. Then you're probably really good at Scrabble. Do you like playing games?"

"Games?"

"Yes. *Games*. Plural. Another noun. Meaning—"

"I get it. I, uh, I'm not really sure. It's been a long time since I threw the dice."

"Yeah. Me, too," Jack admitted.

Lainie was starting to get a very warm sensation at the side of her neck where Jack had laid his hand and was now making slow, lazy circles on the skin just below her ear. "You? I would have thought you were an expert game-player. The kind of guy who always won at everything."

Jack's fingers stopped making their magic. "You're kidding, right?" he asked.

"No," she snorted inelegantly. "You've got everything going for you. You're rich, you're handsome. You were probably . . . I don't know . . . captain of the tennis team back in high school. Voted Most Likely to Succeed. And crowned prom king. You're so damn perfect. The only thing I don't understand is what in the world you're doing here with me."

Damn. Why had she said that? It wasn't like Jack couldn't see how different they were. Why hadn't she just let him keep touching her, keep flirting with her? Yeah, so there was no way they were cut out for a lifelong commitment, but that didn't mean she couldn't enjoy a few hours of fun. Right?

But maybe . . . Maybe this was just self-preservation.

Jack was the kind of guy Lainie could fall really hard for. He was cute. Funny. Nice.

Rich.

What more could a girl ask for?

That was it, though. He was too perfect. She had nothing to offer him. Hell, she barely had anything to offer herself.

"Come with me."

It wasn't a request.

Jack grabbed her hand and hauled her up off the couch. Lainie felt like a doll being dragged along after him as he walked to the front door and told a startled-looking Trish that they'd be back later. Lainie was so surprised at Jack's caveman behavior that she didn't think to tell him that she didn't have any shoes on.

She wasn't sure he would have stopped even if she had.

"Get in." Jack continued bossing her around, pushing her none too gently into the passenger seat of his car.

"I'm already buckled up," she told him before he could issue another order as he got into the driver's seat and turned the key in the ignition.

Jack just grunted. Then he backed out of the driveway and headed toward town.

"Do you mind telling me where we're going?" she asked.

"Back to high school," he answered cryptically.

"No, thanks. Once was enough for me," Lainie muttered, and was surprised when Jack said, "Yeah. Me, too."

They arrived at Golden Gulf High in less than ten minutes. Jack pulled into the deserted parking lot and turned off the engine, then sat staring at the stucco building as if measuring up an opponent.

"What are we doing here?" Lainie asked after a while.

"Setting the record straight."

Jack slowly stepped out of the car. After a slight hesitation, Lainie did the same.

She didn't want to go back in there. After what had happened there today her memories of school were even more embarrassing than they'd been before.

Lainie was surprised when Jack reached out and took her hand in his. His fingers were strong, warm. Unyielding.

He tugged when Lainie would have just stayed there, pulling her with him as they approached the building.

"What if it's locked?" Lainie asked.

"I'll find a way in," he answered.

She believed him.

But they didn't have to resort to breaking and entering. The second door they tried was unlocked and Jack ushered her inside.

It was even more dimly lit than it had been earlier, the few bulbs that were on emitting an eerie glow in the gray light of dusk. Their footsteps echoed in the empty hall, Lainie's bare feet slapping the tile while Jack's shoes gave off a sharper sound.

About halfway down the hall, near the trophy case, Jack stopped.

"I graduated four years before you," he announced abruptly.

"You did?"

"Um-hmm."

"But you didn't go here. All the rich kids went to private schools."

"I attended Golden Gulf my first year of high school," Jack said. "After that I moved to Gulfside Prep."

Lainie frowned. Why in the world wouldn't his parents have sent him to private school all along?

"It's a long story," Jack said, as though reading her mind. He looked over at the trophy case and then took Lainie's hand again and led her into the now-deserted auditorium.

"Back to the scene of the crime," Lainie murmured, but Jack just ignored her so she took a seat on the bleachers and wondered what the heck this was all about.

"I grew up poor," Jack announced baldly.

"Right. Who do you think you're kidding?" Lainie tried to stand up, but Jack's dark look made her sit back down.

"My dad is a Class A asshole. He lied to my mother about . . . well, about everything."

Jack began to pace. Five steps to the left. Turn around. Five steps to the right. Repeat. "Mom was working as a waitress in some coffee shop in town when she met my dad. Good ol' J.D." He shoved a hand through his hair, making the shorter pieces stand on end.

Lainie didn't like seeing him this way. He was usually so . . . so not tormented.

"It's the same old sad story. He told her he loved her, got her pregnant, then made up some lie about how he couldn't marry her, about how he'd just been down in Naples with some buddies for the summer and now he had to get back to school in Iowa." Jack laughed an ugly laugh. "He told her he had six brothers and sisters relying on him to get a good job once he graduated, that they were all living with some ancient relative on a farm in the Midwest, and that if J.D. didn't do well, they were all going to end up on the street. It was all lies, of course, but Mom didn't know that. She was young. In love. And, yeah, a little stupid where my dad was concerned."

"You don't have to tell me this," Lainie said softly, not because she wasn't interested, but because she hated seeing him in pain.

Jack sat down on the bleachers next to her and rested his elbows on his knees. "Are you attracted to me?" he asked.

Lainie nearly fell out of her seat. "God, yes," she blurted without thinking.

"But you think we're worlds apart, right?"

Wow. He was good at this guessing game. "Well, I think you'd have to admit that we don't travel in the same social circles. Wouldn't you agree?"

"No, I don't agree. That's why I have to tell you this. You see this facade, this . . . image . . . and you think you know who I am. That's the way you're wired, Lainie. That's why you swiped my credit card that first night, isn't it? Because you didn't want to tell your sister you didn't have any money. You wanted her to think of you as a certain type of person and thought that you could achieve that by acting like you've never had to face adversity."

"I'm really sorry about that. I always intended to pay you back," Lainie said sheepishly.

Jack snorted. "That's not the point."

Lainie was quiet for a moment and so was he. Finally she turned to him and laid a hand on his arm. "You're right. About . . . why I took your card. About me not wanting my family—not wanting anyone—to know that I had failed."

"How did you fail, Lainie? Your company went bankrupt. Your ex-husband ran up debts you didn't know about and then skipped town. How does that mean that *you* failed?"

Lainie's hand shook as she pulled it back, feeling as if she'd been burned. "You know about all that?" she whispered.

Jack rolled his eyes. "I may not be the best private investigator on the planet, but I'm not completely incompetent. A couple of phone calls and a credit check told me that much."

"Why didn't you tell me?"

"What? That I knew about what had happened? Why would I say anything? It didn't matter to me. You were doing a great job. I liked you. Duncan liked you," he added with a quirk of his lips.

Lainie noticed that he was using the past tense. Did that mean he didn't like her anymore? She certainly wouldn't blame him after all she'd put him through today.

"The point is, Lainie, I don't look at those outward things—the fact that you went through a tough time and lost your house, that maybe your car's not so new anymore, that it's sometimes a struggle to pay the bills—and think that you're less of a person because of it. Just because I lucked into a lot of money, that doesn't make me any better than you or anyone else. Although, I'm having a hell of a time trying to get that through to my sister Amy . . ."

Lainie clasped her hands together in front of her and thought about what Jack had said. It was true that she had been the same person when she had money as she was without. Well, except that she hadn't had to lie back then. Or steal. Or . . . Well, she understood what he meant.

"So back to my dad. The short story is that he ran out on my mom when she was three months pregnant. He probably figured, what the hell, she'd fly somewhere and have an illegal abortion, and it wasn't like they ran in the same social circles, so even if she never left town, what were the chances that they'd ever run into each other? That is, if he even thought about it at all. But Mom didn't have an abortion. She had me and waited faithfully for J.D. to write to her, to send for her when he graduated from college. As the years went on she realized she'd been duped, but she was never one to get bitter, so she raised me here in Naples on her meager salary and we did okay. That is, until she was diagnosed with ovarian cancer when I was fourteen."

Lainie winced. She knew what was coming.

"Mom didn't have any family, and no way was she going to roll the dice and let the state take care of me. J.D. might have lied to her, but he was my father. He was her last resort. Only she didn't know how to find him after all those years. Fortunately, a friend of mine had a father who owned a private investigations firm. He gave Mom a deal on his rate"—Jack later learned that he'd actually done the work for free, which was one of the reasons Jack had bought Intrepid Investigations seven years ago for ten times what the business was worth—"and they were both shocked to discover that my dad had lived in Naples all that time. Not only that, but he was rich. Filthy, stinking rich.

"Or, rather, his parents were. And they were none too pleased when they learned that they had a grandchild that their only child hadn't told them about. They'd later learn that I wasn't the only one," Jack added wryly. "I went to live with Mimi and Papa the year my mom died. That's when I moved schools. Up until then, I was a student right here at Golden Gulf High."

Lainie shook her head, thinking of everything he didn't say. She knew what it was like to lose a mother. To feel alone in the world. To not know your brothers and sisters. To grow up without ever having enough money. To change schools in the middle of a tough year. To—

Oh. My. God.

She and Jack weren't so different after all.

The bleachers creaked when Jack stood up, offering her his hand. "Come on," he said. "There's something I'd like you to see."

{ thirty-four }

Jackson Danforth III was a geek. A dweeb. A nerd. A whatever-word-they-used-to-use for someone who was not one of the anointed few who were considered cool.

Normal, maybe?

Just a normal kid with pimples and a bad haircut who hadn't yet grown into his gangly body or oversize head.

"Yeah," he said as they stared into the trophy case in the darkened hallway of the high school. "I was on the chess team the year we won the state championships. I lost my first match, but the rest of the team did well." He released the button on the keychain of his BMW and the light shining on the faded photograph propped up in the back corner of the lowest shelf went out.

Straightening up, Lainie looped her arm through his and leaned into him. "I can't believe you played chess."

Jack shrugged and shot her a half-smile. "It was the only extracurricular activity my mom could afford. Not to mention that I sucked at everything else."

"I never did anything like that. I just worked," Lainie said. "I think that's why work is so important to me now. It's the only thing I ever did that boosted my self-esteem."

"Yeah, but I learned from my mom that even the best job doesn't love you back. She worked at that damn coffee shop for nearly fifteen years, and when she got sick, they just let her go."

"That's awful," Lainie said, squeezing Jack's arm.

"They aren't in business anymore." Jack's voice had a hard edge to it that Lainie had never heard before—a hard edge that made her think that maybe he'd had something to do with his mother's former employer going out of business.

Good. Maybe there was some justice in the world.

Jack put his arm around her shoulders and pulled her close. Lainie felt his lips against her hair as he kissed the top of her head. Then she giggled when he pushed her back against the cool concrete wall.

"Jack, what are you doing?" she asked.

"It just occurred to me that I never kissed a girl in high school."

Lainie found that hard to believe, especially when Jack's lips met hers. That electricity that always seemed to be hovering between them flared as Lainie opened herself to him. Jack pushed her knees apart with his muscled thigh and nestled himself against her, and Lainie felt the unmistakable evidence of his desire pressing into her gut.

With a softly uttered moan, she wound her arms around his neck, threading her fingers through his hair as their tongues met. Jack's hips pulsed against hers and Lainie felt a jolt of desire pass through her, pooling at the juncture of her thighs.

"Jack, we can't do this," she protested weakly when Jack finally raised his head from hers, even though the last thing she wanted was for him to stop.

"Why not?" he asked, sliding his hands down her sides and making her shiver at the want she saw in his eyes. "Don't worry, I won't spread it around the locker room that you go all the way."

Lainie laughed. "You know, I always *did* want to know what it would feel like to be a bad girl."

"Believe me," Jack said, his hands slipping down to cup her rear end, "you feel great."

She was certain that she was breaking one of Lillian Bryson's dating rules—Rule #1, as a matter of fact, "Never sleep with a guy on the first date"—but all of Lillian's rules fled from Lainie's mind at Jack's touch.

Wanting to make him as eager for her as she was for him, Lainie moved her hands between them and slowly unzipped his pants. Jack groaned when she stroked him, her thumb sliding around the tip of his penis.

He pulled back for a moment, grabbing a foil-wrapped packet out of the rear pocket of his pants before they slid to the floor. Then he trailed a line of heated kisses down her neck while his hands were busy slipping her shorts off.

Jack touched her then, running his fingers lightly over the sensitive skin at the juncture of her thighs. Lainie's eyes closed as he slipped a finger inside her and then moved out again, his thumb teasing her until she was writhing against him, wanting more.

Lainie grabbed the condom from Jack's hand and ripped open the packet, nearly desperate to feel him inside her.

Now.

Jack chuckled as he leaned down to gently bite her earlobe. "I think you would have made a very good bad girl back in high school, Lainie Ames."

But all thoughts of mirth fled his mind when she grinned slyly up at him and then inched the condom on so slowly that he was nearly ready to come when she finally finished torturing him. Yeah. She would definitely have made a very good bad girl back then.

But she was an even better one now.

Slipping his fingers out of her slick wetness, Jack pressed himself into her, tightly holding onto his control as Lainie's breath came in panting moans that tickled his ear. God, she felt good.

He wasn't going to be able to hold on much—

Lainie tightened her legs around his waist. She spasmed against him, her shoulders thrown back against the floor, and Jack lost it. The wave of his own orgasm crashed into him, all thoughts disappearing in its wake. Lainie stiffened against him, their groans echoing off the empty walls.

Then it was over, and as they collapsed into a post-fantastic-sex boneless heap, Jack wrapped his arms around Lainie and said, "We both deserve an A-plus for that."

{ thirty-five }

That does it."

Lainie took the handheld mirror her big sister was holding out to her and held it up to her face. "Oh, Trish. It's beautiful," she breathed.

Unlike Lainie, Trish *was* one of those girls who knew how to do hair. She had pinned Lainie's up with a dozen crystal clips shaped like butterflies and curled the loose ends into soft corkscrews.

"I look like a movie star," she said, her grin so wide that she was afraid her face might crack.

"You do. You look amazing," Trish said, standing back to admire the total package.

Lainie had on the red dress that her father had saved from all those years ago. Thanks to her depression diet—and the fact that she'd been chubby until some miracle occurred at nineteen when she lost all her baby fat—she actually fit into it. She stretched out her feet and admired the red polish Trish had painted on her toes. Her sandals were gorgeous red Stuart Weitzmans that Trish had borrowed from a friend of hers who wore the same size as Lainie.

"Are you sure you don't want me to go with you?" Trish asked, a concerned frown making little wrinkles in her brow.

Lainie considered the question for a moment.

Her fifteen-year reunion and she was going.

Alone.

Was she nervous? Hell, yeah.

She was still broke. Still divorced. Still the victim of a cruel lay-off who was back living with her dad.

But if those were the things that mattered to her former class-mates, then so what? She'd spend a few hours drinking and dancing and then she'd come home. And if she reconnected with some old friends—friends who cared about who she was on the inside and not the amount of money in her bank account—so much the better.

She didn't need anyone's help to get through the evening be-cause her life did not hinge on whatever happened tonight. She was going to be okay, no matter what.

Which didn't mean she wasn't disappointed that Jack had disap-peared after their little trip back to night school . . . She had wanted so badly to invite him to come with her tonight, but when Duncan told her the next morning that his brother had to go to Miami to handle some emergency, Lainie lost her nerve. She hadn't seen him since that night and she was too much of a chicken to call him on his cell.

Besides, wasn't *he* supposed to call her? Wasn't that one of Lil-lian Bryson's rules—Rule #6: Never call him?

So she hadn't.

And she was okay with going to her reunion alone. It would be fun. If not, she'd just leave.

"I'm sure, but thank you for the offer. Thank you for everything. The hair, the nails, the shoes. I really appreciate it," Lainie said to her sister.

"You're welcome. Now, you'd better get going. You don't want to miss it when they choose the king and queen."

Lainie chuckled as she rose from the chair in the dining room where Trish had performed her miracle with Lainie's hair. "Right."

She pulled her keys from the small cocktail purse Trish had loaned her and headed out to her car. She'd already put the top up—one minute in this humidity and all of Trish's hard work would be for naught. With a full tank of gas—thanks to the paycheck Duncan handed her on Friday—Lainie arrived at the high school with no trouble.

Tonight the parking lot was filled with a familiar mix of expensive sedans and SUVs along with regular old minivans and pickup trucks. Lainie sat out in the lot for a minute, gathering her courage. When a movement to the right caught her eye, Lainie turned to see another woman sitting alone in her car, staring at the well-lit building in front of them. At that moment the woman turned.

Lainie guessed that the same look of trepidation was mirrored on her face.

She smiled, and the woman smiled back.

Lainie reached for the door handle and let herself out into the warm night.

"Hi," she said as the woman from the other car did the same.

"Hello. I'm Janice Early. Used to be Janice Isaac, but I'm recently divorced."

"Me, too. Lainie Ames. Elaine Ames, that is," she said, holding out her right hand.

By the time they reached the auditorium, Lainie and Janice discovered that they had shared a torturous fourth-period gym glass one semester, that they both did admin work, and had both recently moved back to Naples.

As they clipped on their nametags, Janice told her to give her a call if she ever wanted to go to lunch.

It was, Lainie discovered, as easy as that.

No one asked to see a bank statement. No one asked what kind of car she drove. No one even asked how much her borrowed sandals cost.

Lainie smiled as she took a cup of punch and retreated toward the bleachers. The reunion committee had done a fabulous job. A giant disco ball lazily spun overhead as the montage of photos from their high school years reflected in the thousands of panes of mirrored glass. As Bob/Mike-the-science-teacher had said, they'd used red and gold spray paint to make up dozens of banners welcoming everyone back.

The band was lame—what did you expect?—but they were at least playing songs that Lainie recognized from when she—

"You stood me up."

She swirled around, the beads of her dress clicking together as she thanked the Punch Gods for not spilling punch all down her front.

"Blaine," she said, somewhat stupidly. He probably knew his own name.

"Lainie," he acknowledged with a mocking smile and a dip of his square chin.

"I'm sorry. I just assumed . . . After, er, what happened the night of the reunion committee meeting, I figured you'd be glad you'd seen the last of me," Lainie said.

"Why?"

"Um. Well, I embarrassed myself in front of all your friends."

"Those weren't my friends. I've hardly spoken to any of them in years." Blaine lifted one foot up and rested it on the lowest step of the wooden bleachers. Lainie was surprised to notice that he looked good in his black tux with a deep blue bowtie—not surprised that he looked good, but surprised that she didn't feel even the slightest bit attracted to him, nor sad that she hadn't arrived at the reunion on the former prom king's arm.

"I thought for sure that once you saw Shay again you and she would get back together."

Blaine snorted out a laugh. "You're kidding, right?"

"No." Lainie took a sip of her punch, her gaze seeking out the gorgeous blonde in the midnight-blue, floor-length dress who was surrounded by men in the middle of the room. "She's beautiful, successful—"

"Narcissistic to the point of bordering on the psychopathic?"

Lainie grinned. "I was getting there."

"I learned fifteen years ago that your value as a person is not dependent on who's wearing your letterman's jacket."

"I must be a slow learner. I just figured that out, myself," Lainie murmured into her punch.

"In any event, it was you I asked out. Not Shay. And I was disappointed when you didn't show."

Lainie reached out and touched Blaine's hand. "I'm really sorry. I truly did think that our date was off after I made such a fool of myself."

Blaine turned his hand over and laced Lainie's fingers in his own. They stood there for a moment, Lainie looking up at him, for the first time seeing not Blaine Harper, Captain of the Football Team, or Blaine Harper, Guy Elected Prom King, or Blaine Harper, Wealthy Diet Doctor, but Blaine Harper. The real Blaine Harper.

And the thing was, with all that stripped away, she realized how shallow she had been. She hadn't wanted him for who he was, but for what him choosing her would tell the world about Lainie Ames.

But she didn't need his reflected image shining on her to make her somebody special.

She was already somebody special.

Herself.

Just as she was.

"That's all right," Blaine said with a sigh as he let go of her hand. "I can see now that your heart belongs to someone else."

Lainie swallowed the lump in her throat and finished off her cup of punch, setting the empty glass down next to Blaine's foot on the bleachers. "Really?" she asked. "Who?"

"From the murderous look in his eyes, I'd say the guy bearing down on us right now."

Lainie turned, and for that moment time stopped. It was Jack. His black tux gleamed in the dim light reflecting off the disco ball and the red tie at his neck was askew, as if he'd been in a rush to tie it.

And, yes, he had a murderous look in his dark brown eyes, but Lainie could also see the fear beneath the surface.

"I was supposed to arrive first but I got waylaid by yet another family crisis," he said, nearly shoving Blaine out of the way as he reached Lainie's side.

She smiled. "That's okay. I'm just glad you made it at all."

They stared at each other wordlessly, like two awkward teenagers who liked each other immensely but didn't know what to say when they were in the same room. Then Jack reached out and tenderly brushed a curl away from her face. "I'll always be here for you, Lainie. But if you've gotten what you need to from this reunion and are ready to go, there's someplace I'd like to take you."

* * *

The black sedan drove slowly from the high school to the recently renovated fast-food restaurant near her old neighborhood. Well-dressed children playing in the fenced playground didn't stop to gape as her long, slim legs swung out of the car. Four-inch-high red stilettos hit the sidewalk. The driver reached out and offered his hand to the lone occupant. The light overhead highlighted her French-manicured nails. The crystal butterflies in her hair glistened in the moonlight as Lainie stepped out of Jack's car.

He offered her his arm and smiled down at her as they walked toward the familiar golden arches.

A wave of things assaulted her senses as he pulled open the front door. Memories, good ones this time of the friends she had made and the laughter they'd shared as they worked long shifts side-by-side; the smells of freshly made French fries and hamburgers on the grill; the noise of children shrieking from the playground; the familiar yet nearly forgotten beeps and clicks and buzzes that Lainie used to know all too well; the easy listening music that ran on a never-ending loop day after day.

Jack held out his hand.

"May I have this dance, Ms. Ames?" he asked.

Lainie put her hand in his and smiled. "I'd be delighted, Mr. Danforth."

And as the restaurant patrons clapped and the employees cheered, Lainie noticed one sad girl hiding out next to the shake machine. She wanted to stop, to tell the girl that everything would be all right.

But this girl, she had her own lessons to learn, her own journey to make, so Lainie grabbed on to her own destiny, inhaling Jack's scent as he whirled her around and around, finally happy because she had realized that in the game of life, there were no winners or losers. There were only players, doing the best they could with the hands they'd been dealt.